POSSESSION

JAIMIE ROBERTS

POSSESSION
Copyright © 2017 Jaimie Roberts
All rights reserved.

FUTURE TENSE

I can taste and smell the bourbon on his breath as he lazily spreads kisses to my lips, along my jawline, and down towards my neck. I can feel the slight buzz of my own alcohol coursing through my veins as I lie here with him on top of me, digging something alien and never before felt between my legs. I feel lightheaded. I'm not drunk; I just feel the nice, tipsy effects of the two shots I had at the bar tonight.

With a heady moan coming from above me, I try to blank out all sounds and feelings. I don't want to be here with this stranger, but circumstances have forced me here.

***He** forced me here.*

My virtue and free will have both been promised to one man. I don't even want to think about this man, but I can't stop myself from reaching out to him whenever he beckons. I have known him for six years, and for the last couple of those, my woman parts have responded to the idea of entertaining his sick, twisted desire for me.

I shouldn't be here with this stranger.

*I don't **want** to be here with this stranger.*

Even so, my stubborn mind has brought me here to this seedy hotel with its fluorescent lights, outdated bed sheets, and creaky bed. My heart wants to tell this man to stop, but my mind urges me to defy the man who put me here. If I can do this, then I'll hate him even more. It's his fault I ran away. It's his fault I went to a bar. And it's his fault I'm currently lying here, letting a strange man feel his way up my legs.

"Your legs feel so smooth and silky soft. I can't wait to find out what your pussy feels like."

Panic resonates inside of me. I don't want to lose my virginity like this. Furthermore, I know it will hurt. This man—Ben or Brandon or whatever the hell his name is—doesn't know I'm a virgin. I deliberately left that part out. I must admit ... when he kissed me at the bar, some sparks did fly, but now that I'm here, all I want to do is run. Run as far away as possible from my parents and from this whole situation.

From **him**.

"Are you ready for me, baby?" he whispers in my ear as he kisses his way up to my lips.

I nod shakily as words get stuck in my head. My heart is screaming, "No!" but my mind is freezing me—locking me in place. "Just get this over and done with!" it bellows.

The stranger shifts off of me momentarily to reach for a condom in his jeans pocket. I still have my summer dress on, but it's now rising up around my hips. Sheer panic spikes again when he starts to pull my panties slowly down my legs. He's doing it for effect, and it is certainly having an impact on me. It's just not having the effect he's aiming for.

As he discards my panties, he hovers over me with a smile before looking down between my legs. I see the gleam in his eyes as

4

he licks his lips. "Such a beautiful pussy," he purrs as he starts to unbutton his jeans.

Panic is escalating to sheer terror. Seeing him undoing his jeans has my fear level creeping up exponentially. My mind is now in tune with my heart. I don't want this.

I don't want this.

And yet, I'm frozen. I can't move. Time seems to be standing still. As he undoes one button, the next one follows with agonising slowness.

I don't want this.

My heart thumps against my chest as tears start to well in my eyes. The stranger looks at me, cocking his head with a frown. He has noticed my distress and is about to say something when ...

BAM!

The door is busted open, and in comes my saviour and personal predator—combined into one fucked up package.

Drake.

He pauses momentarily, taking in the sight of me on the bed—almost in tears—with this man in between my legs. His face scowls into nothing but evil. Nothing but hate. His dark eyes are scanning the scene in front of him, but then they widen as he finds my panties discarded on the floor next to the bed. His broad, muscular chest expands before he rushes towards the stranger on top of me.

"What the fuck?!" the stranger shouts. As soon as the words come out, he's off me like a shot and being thrown up against the wall.

Drake ignores the man and turns to me. "Did he rape you?"

I wince at his words, but find the courage in my voice. "No! I wanted it!" I scream, finally defying this man in the worst way possible.

"Then, why were you fucking crying?"

I don't answer him. Instead, I turn my head away from him in defiance. It's only when I hear the stranger's strangled cry that I turn back to him. "Stop, Drake! You're going to kill him!"

With gritted teeth, he motions to his men. In no time at all, two of them grab me by the arms and hold me in place. "Drake, what are you doing?!"

He ignores me. All of his attention at the moment is focused on this stranger, who Drake's currently holding by the neck. "One question," he barks into his face. The stranger's eyes dart around in fear as his face starts to turn blue from the pressure on his neck. "Did you fuck her?"

The man's eyes grow wider still as he tries to speak, but can't get the words out. Instead, he shakes his head vehemently as if trying to appease Drake.

Drake looks deep into his eyes like he's trying to sense whether or not he's telling the truth. Once he gets what he's after, he reaches into the waistband of his trousers, pulls his gun out, and shoots him in the head.

I scream, but my cries are soon restricted by the big, beefy hand covering my mouth. Tears pool in my eyes as I try to make sense of the scene in front of me. This stranger—this random, innocent stranger—is dead because of me.

I scream into the man's hand. A mixture of anger and remorse is eating away at my insides. Drake snaps his head back to me, and there's fire in his eyes. "Do you see what you fucking did? Why do you defy me, Evelyn? Why?!" Suddenly, he storms towards me, grabbing my neck and squeezing a little. My eyes widen in response as a different type of fear creeps up my spine. "I'm going to teach you a lesson you will never forget. Don't ever think you can get away with this without there being some sort of repercussion. I was going to take it slow, but your actions tonight have forced me to decide on a different course. Just remember something, Evelyn. **You** did this. Not me. You."

What does that mean?

I have no time to dwell on this as he pushes himself off of me with a huff and angrily orders two of his men in the room to take care of the stranger. I watch in horror as they drag his lifeless body away. Drake watches it too before turning his attention back to me.

Our eyes lock, and that same spell he is so adept at casting on me comes bursting through me like a tidal wave. I don't want it to come, but he forces his way through me with a crash.

Disappointment.

That's all I can see in his eyes as he stares at me. For a moment, my eyes drift down at his reaction. I feel... What is this feeling? Regret?

My eyes meet his again, showing him the remorse I feel. Again, my heart wants to give in to him, but my head is trying to outwit my heart. This time, my heart is winning.

Gritting his teeth, he shakes his head from side to side, but doesn't utter the words that are so painfully itching to get through. Instead, he just stands there—all six-foot-seven of him with his impressive chest showing through a tight navy v-necked t-shirt. He wears his jeans low at the hips with a bulky belt strapped around them. He's still surveying me. Still staring at me with those light caramel eyes of his. They seem to be burning their way into my soul—deeper than ever. I don't want him to affect me, but he does.

He coaches it out of me. In fact, he commands it.

And just like that, he finally breaks his spell, motioning to the men to move me. They immediately comply with his commands, hoisting me up from the bed and pushing me out of the hotel room. As I step out, I look around to see if anyone has come out of their rooms to watch the commotion, but there's not a soul to be seen. This doesn't surprise me. Drake is well known around these parts, and people wisely leave him alone to do whatever the hell he pleases. Even the police know not to be anywhere near wherever the great Drake Salvatore conducts his business. Everyone knows whatever he deals in isn't legal, but everyone also chooses to look the other way.

No one wants to save me.

I can't be saved.

As the men pin my wrists behind my back, I'm carefully pushed down the stairs and into a waiting limousine. I frown, wondering why his chosen method of transport tonight is this one.

In no time at all, I find out why.

As I push myself towards the other end of the seat—as far away from where he will sit as possible—Drake joins me, and his door is quickly shut behind him. He's still wearing that same look of anger and disappointment on his face as he clocks me cowering in the far corner.

"Up," he commands to his driver. "Drive home, but don't fucking disturb us until I tell you to."

"Yes, sir," the driver says before putting up the visor.

I feel when the car starts to move and can see Drake studying me again. He inhales sharp breaths. It's almost as if he's trying to calm himself.

Then, he notices it. "Where's your ring?"

I don't say anything, but my eyes betray me. They land on my bag that was thrown in before me. Drake's eyes travel to where I'm looking, and I watch as he opens my bag and combs through it a few seconds before pulling the ring out.

He motions to my hand. "Give me your fucking hand, and don't make me ask you again."

He's so mad that I immediately bend to his will. With a shaky hand, I guide it towards his where he shoves the ring back on my finger. "I don't ever want to see that off of your hand again." He glares back up at me before inhaling sharply. "Was he telling the truth?"

I try pulling my legs up in front of me, but my dress rises up too high. I notice Drake looking, so I purposefully place my legs down and try to straighten my dress.

In an instant, Drake yanks my legs down, pulling them apart so he can get in between them. Feeling my stubbornness creep back up again, I hiss and buck underneath him, trying to get him off me. It's no use. He's too strong. Instead, he pins my arms above my head and catches my eyes again.

"I asked you a fucking question."

Feeling angry, I blurt out, "No. He was lying. He had already fucked me. We were just about to get to round two when you so rudely interrupted us."

Feeling his grip tighten, he growls down at me. "Is that so?"

"Yes!" I seethe. He can tell I'm lying, but doesn't call me out on it.

"I will have to find out for myself then, won't I?"

My eyes widen. I'm about to ask what that means when it

becomes *painfully obvious as he starts unbuttoning his jeans. Shaking my head violently, my voice trembles. "I didn't mean it. I was lying. I'm sorry. Please don't do this."*

Like a bolt of lightning, he hitches up my dress, and I feel when he positions his cock at my entrance. "Why do you disobey me at every turn? I have been waiting a millennium to get in between these silky thighs of yours, but you constantly want to fight me. Don't you ever defy me again, Evelyn. And don't ever deny me what is rightfully **mine.***"*

With a growl, he pushes forward and the sting burns like a motherfucker. "No!" I cry as he pushes in even more. Bit by agonising bit, he gets deeper and deeper inside of me. Taking my innocence in the most fucked up, unromantic way possible. I want to scream at him. I want to fight him. But the only thing I can concentrate on is how much this fucking hurts. How on earth can anyone get enjoyment out of this? It kills.

Opening my mouth to sob, Drake captures it with his mouth. He darts his tongue in, coaxing me to open up to him. Slowly, as if knowing this is hurting, he starts moving in and out of me with unhurried thrusts.

He moans on top of me, letting me hear how much he's enjoying this. I don't want to be pleased by this, but somehow that sensation washes over me. The pain subsides, but doesn't fully go away. It dials down to an acceptable throb—one which I welcome.

Breaking our kiss, Drake looks me in the eye with a brand new expression. His eyes are hooded, telling me how much he's enjoying being inside of me. I don't want the pleasure to come, but somehow, it does. The pain is still there, but he's coaxing me to enjoy it.

Now, he's commanding me.

"I didn't want it to be like this," he said with a strained voice. "Just remember, you did this, Evelyn. You did this. You made me do this." And with a laboured moan in his voice, his movements become faster ... more uncontrollable. "Fuck, Evelyn, you feel better than I ever imagined. I'm never letting you go."

With that last sentence swimming in my head, he pushes faster, grunting and nibbling at the side of my neck. I lie there, trying not to feel the pain and also trying not to feel the pleasure. It's no use. Both come crashing down on me, urging me to feel every single bit of him.

"Oh, Jesus! Evelyn, I'm going to come!" He screams as he groans out one more time before I feel something shooting inside of me.

It's over.

I'm no longer a virgin.

I lost it to this tyrant of a man—one who has been waiting for me for six years. One who I have defied for the last four.

But, it was all my fault. Drake has made sure of that. I could have complied, but I went behind his back. Now, I have paid in the worst way possible. My punishment is now complete.

As I feel Drake's breathing calming, he pulls his head up to look into my eyes again, and all I can think about are the words that stuck to me when I was thirteen. "Just remember one thing for me, Evelyn. No matter what I do, I am not a monster."

He lied. Of course he's a monster. I may have known this day would come, but he never gave me a chance to be ready for it. He just took it instead.

He swipes my hair back gently with this fingers and gazes longingly inside my eyes. "Who do you belong to?" When I don't answer straight away, he tugs at my hair, making me yelp. "Who do you belong to?"

"You," I answer with a quivering voice. "You, Drake."

He smiles at my answer, but then, as quickly as it comes, it vanishes. "It's going to take a while for me to get over your betrayal tonight. I'm not going to trust you for a while. I'm going to need to keep a very close eye on you. Do you hear me?" He tugs at my hair again, so I obediently nod my head. "Good. Now, isn't there something you want to say to me?"

I know exactly what he wants to hear, so I robotically reply, "I'm so sorry. I promise not to do it again."

Having gotten what he's after, Drake nods his head and lifts his weight off of me. He slowly pulls his cock out of me, making me wince as he does. "Sorry," he offers. "You will be sore for a little while, but it will pass. The next time will be much better. I promise."

Slight fear from knowing this creeps up my spine. But also mixed with it is a sick, twisted expectation of the next time. I don't want him anywhere near me after that, but he also seems to command that I do.

Staring down, a big smile lights up his face as he strokes his finger along his shaft. I can see the traces of blood all over him as he pulls his finger up for me to see. "Look at this. This is what I've been dreaming of. You're all mine now, Evelyn."

My name dances on the tip of his tongue as he places his finger inside of his mouth and tastes my blood. "Hmm," he moans, closing his eyes. "The taste of your innocence is the sweetest fucking taste on earth." He crawls towards me, and I try to crawl back, but I have nowhere to go. "Do you know how much it turns me on to know that your pure blood is coating my dick? Best. Fucking. Feeling. Ever."

He grabs my hair again, pulling my head back. As soon as he's done this, his tongue is forcing its way into my mouth. Once he breaks free, he stares at me again with those hooded eyes. I don't want them to turn me on, but they force their way through me.

"You're mine now—all mine." Without warning, he enters me again, and my mind is awash with so many feelings and emotions. Desire, hatred, longing, anger, bliss, pain, yearning, and rage. I don't want them to come, but they do.

I try shutting down—pushing my emotions to one side, so I don't have to feel anything anymore. I try singing a song in my head. Sentence by sentence, verse by verse, I sing it over and over again until my head hurts.

Happy Birthday to me.
Happy Birthday to me.
Happy Birthday ...

CHAPTER ONE

Age Seventeen – Present Day

At the age of nine, I learnt to ride a bike. I was a little unsteady at first, but being the stubborn fool that I am, I persevered for seven hours straight until I perfected it.

At the age of ten, I was given my first pair of dancing shoes, and I spent many an hour twirling in front of my bedroom window.

At the age of eleven, I received my first kiss from my very first crush, Peter. For a while, we were encased in a world of laughter, innocent play, and stolen kisses.

At the age of twelve, I met Drake Salvatore, owner of an empire and one of the most powerful men on earth. He scared the shit out of me, but at the same time, his presence made me feel safer than my mum and dad ever did.

At the age of thirteen, the roof I lived under was plagued by arguments and the constant rejection of my parents. Drake was always there to save me, though. My life was more bearable with him in it.

At the age of fourteen, my parents almost became bankrupt. Drake Salvatore saved the day. I was sold to him—to become his on the day of my eighteenth birthday.

At the age of fifteen, I became a priceless trophy. Something to dress up and admire, but never to touch.

At the age of sixteen, Drake's obsession with me became the source of my obsession with him.

At the age of seventeen, I became defiant. I met a few boys and proceeded to risk those precious stolen kisses I once shared with Peter. Those encounters never lasted long. I imagine Drake must have found out about them because the boys inevitably and "inexplicably" lost interest, and I never saw them again.

When I turn eighteen, payment number two will be made, and I will become Drake's.

I'm seventeen, and I only have four months left.

Time is running out.

CHAPTER TWO

Age Twelve

"Evelyn, sit up straight. We have a very important guest coming over for dinner, and we can't let him see you sitting there slouching." My mother turns her head towards my father and scowls her disgust of me.

"Yes, Mother. I'm sorry, Mother." Robotic responses roll off my tongue. I'm used to this. Used to the constant critical analysis of the way I dress, the way I do my hair, and the way I conduct myself.

As if in time to save the day, the sound of our doorbell ringing stops my parents from speaking of my slouching any further.

"Ooh, he's here!" Light dances in my mother's eyes. I've never seen her look so animated before. What's so special about this man? Is he a king or something?

"William, go and answer the door, please. I need to straighten the table up a little."

With an excitable walk I've never seen him use before, my father dutifully steps out of the dining room and into the hallway. My mother does start straightening something, but it's not the dining table. Instead, it's her hair. I frown, studying her as she *carefully scrutinises her face. Her blonde hair is up in a tight bun, and her face is painted with so much makeup, that she almost looks like a china doll.*

Pouting her lips, she flutters her eyelashes and puckers her cheeks before noticing my stare. "What are you looking at?"

Immediately, I look away. That's when the door opens, and I hear the sound of a very masculine voice. I can't hear what he says, but I clearly hear my father afterwards. "I'm so glad you accepted our invitation for dinner. I have been eager for you to meet the family."

My father soon emerges, and ever so quickly, my mother appears, standing behind me with a hand on my shoulder.

Are we posing for a family portrait?

Momentarily, I frown, but then, I see the look on my father's face. His look says everything. I simply **must** *behave.*

"Drake, you've already met my wife, Charlotte, but I want you to meet my lovely daughter, Evelyn." My eyes widen a little at his "lovely daughter" comment, but I have no time to dwell on this as Drake suddenly appears from the doorway.

My first impression is that he's big. In fact, he's bigger than any man I have ever seen. Not only is he big in height, but he's extremely muscular too. My eyes widen again, but for a different reason this time. I have never met a man so imposing or so ... huge. The second thing I notice about him is his eyes. They look sinister—maybe even a little evil. I know this should scare me, and there is a little fear, but then he smiles at me, and all my fears wash away.

"Evelyn," he whispers, light sparkling in his eyes. "What a beautiful name for a beautiful girl." My parents laugh, but I don't look at them. This man seems to have a power that holds my

attention. I can't look away. I couldn't even if I'd wanted to.

I suck in my breath as Drake stalks towards me, and like the dutiful daughter I am, I offer him my hand. My mother shoves me a little, so I stand and wait for Drake to take my hand. He does so, and soon after, I notice how soft he feels to the touch. He obviously looks after his hands very well.

Pretty soon, I feel his gentle lips, and for some reason, my cheeks flame red at the feel of his mouth on my skin. He notices my blush, lets go of my hand, and gives me a cheeky grin.

"You should be very proud of her," he says, addressing my parents.

My heart drums as the force of his words hit hard. I don't know why he says this so vehemently, but I'm surprised when my father speaks up.

"We are, aren't we, Charlotte?"

"Oh, yes," my mother quickly answers. "She's the apple of our eyes."

I frown again—not knowing where this is coming from—but when I look back at Drake's smile, my own suddenly lights up. He may be scary and a bit intimidating, but I like him. He doesn't even know me, but he apparently felt compelled to force my parents to express their approval of me—something they don't even do privately. Could it be that he knows about the way they treat me and was somehow sticking up for me? I can't figure it out, but I do know that I like it. In fact, I like it a lot.

"Come, have a seat, Mr Salvatore. I'll fetch you a drink. What would you like? I have a fifty-year-old Macallan just for you."

I remember going shopping today with my mother. She was looking everywhere for the most expensive whiskey simply because

I watch as he smiles with a nod, and my mother—in a fluster—walks out of the room to fetch him a glass of this very expensive drink. I know it's expensive as I remember my mother ringing my father to ask if it would be okay to spend over twenty thousand pounds on a bottle of drink. This drink must be pretty special if it's worth that much.

"So," my father begins as my mother leaves the room, "how is business treating you?" Drake rolls his eyes in my direction, and I can't help the giggle that escapes my lips.

"Is something funny, Evelyn?" my father snaps.

Seeing my eyes widening in fear, Drake speaks before I can even muster the courage to do so myself. "It's my fault. I pulled a funny face to make her laugh. Luckily for me, it worked."

I breathe a huge sigh of relief—grateful to this man for saving the day. It works because my father laughs, earning him a smile from Drake. My father seems to like this. For some reason, this man's acceptance means a great deal to him.

"Business is going really well. In fact, I'm expanding to the Middle East. That's why I wanted to get your opinion. I hear you're quite knowledgeable with regards to the laws of the land out there."

My father clears his throat with a smile and pulls his chair in a bit more. He places his hands together on the table like he's getting himself ready. "Sure. What is it you want to know?"

Drake looks across at me for a moment, and I don't know why, but my heart starts fluttering. "Maybe we shouldn't talk about business tonight. I'm sure Evelyn here doesn't want us boring her with trade deals and logistics." He gives a little chuckle, and it makes me smile. This complete stranger is making more of a fuss over me in one night than my parents have in about two years.

Don't get me wrong; things used to be good around here. At one time, my parents did seem to care about me. Then, one day, things changed. My parents seem to have this terrible habit of spending more than they can afford. I've often heard them arguing over money. I'm going to a private school, and they often argue over that too. Over time, they started to resent me. I cost money and lots of it apparently.

My father looks at me like I'm a burden, but smiles in Drake's direction and nods his head "Of course. Maybe you can pop by my office on Monday. How does that sound?"

Drake smiles. "Sounds perfect."

CHAPTER THREE

Age Seventeen – Present Day

"Is he officially your boyfriend now?" Mandy asks as I lick my ice cream. We've just finished shopping where I purchased myself some sexy lingerie. Drake likes to lavish money and gifts on me. Normally, I don't accept it—which pisses him off—but today I decided to spend a little. The only reason is so I can wear them for someone else. What better way to stick it to the great Drake Salvatore than to buy lingerie which I have no intention of wearing for him?

"Who?" I ask ... even though I know exactly to whom she's referring. Everybody knows about the great and infamous Drake around here, and most people also know that I am not to be messed with. Every boy at school gives me the widest birth possible because they know me as Drake's girl. I'm not Drake's girl. I'm not anything to Drake.

"You know... Mr Salvatore. He's always around you and hangs around your family a lot. I've seen the way you two look at each other."

I stop licking my ice cream and frown at her. "What do you mean by 'the way you two look at each other?' How do we look at each other?"

She rolls her eyes. "Oh, come on. Don't tell me you can't see it? I guess you bought the lingerie for him, huh?" She nudges me with a wink.

"No, I have not. He's not my boyfriend."

"Then, what is he? Because the times when I have seen you two together you both look at each other like you want to rip each other's clothes off."

I gasp. "No, I do not!" I protest.

"Evelyn, please. You can't fool me. Besides, I can't blame you. Every woman within a hundred mile radius wants a piece of that man. Hell, even I wouldn't say no. But for some reason he only seems to have eyes for you, my friend. Lucky bitch!"

She snorts, but I don't find any of this funny. Yes, part of what she says is true. He is that way around me, but only because he's waiting for me. Only because in four months time I will turn eighteen and be his forever. Mandy doesn't know or realise this. It would be too embarrassing to tell her that my parents sold me when I was just fourteen. She would also pity me. I don't want her pity.

"Well, I don't want him. So ..."

"Really?" she huffs. "Next time I see you both together, I'll shoot you a nice video to watch later." I shake my head at her, but I can tell she's not going to stop anytime soon. "How would you feel if I made a move on him?"

My gut twists. What is that? Jealousy? It can't be. I hate the man with a vengeance. I shouldn't care if he fucks Mandy or anybody else for that matter, but for some reason, the ache still comes.

Mandy—the ever observant one—notices my shift in mood and smirks at me. "I thought as much."

"It doesn't mean anything," I snap. "Sleep with him for all I care."

"Okay then. I will."

"Fine," I answer through gritted teeth.

What the hell is wrong with me? I'm acting like a child rather than a nearly eighteen-year-old girl.

Luckily, all goes quiet after that, and I think she's finally stopped when she suddenly speaks again. "I heard he's killed people."

Rising up out of my seat, I start walking to the trash to throw the rest of my ice cream in. "For fuck's sake, Mandy," I hiss. "Will you give it a rest?"

"I'm just saying." She frowns, looking at the rubbish bin. "Hey, I could have finished that."

She looks like a child who didn't get her toy. It's so comical that I start to laugh. When I start, so does she. "Come on," I say, gathering my bags and wrapping my arm around her. "Let's go watch a movie or something."

Turning around, we're about to head out of the mall when we almost collide with a very solid chest. We step back in a daze, and that's when I notice he's standing there. "Ladies," he says as he greets us with that stupid handsome smile of his. It doesn't help matters that he's wearing a very expensive-looking black Armani suit, a crisp white shirt, and a black tie. His jet black hair is gelled back slightly with spikes at the front. He looks like he hasn't shaved for a couple of days, and I hate to admit it, but it really suits him.

A little too well.

Standing here with my blonde hair back in a messy ponytail, a pair of tatty jeans, and a t-shirt which reads, "No means no," I look positively scruffy next to him. I don't know what he sees in me.

Drake notices the t-shirt, and of course, it makes him smirk. He knows I wore it just for him.

"Wow. I mean … hi, Mr Salvatore. How are you? We were just talking about you actually." I nudge Mandy to shut up. I really don't want to encourage him.

He looks smug at the thought. "Really? And what things were you saying? All nice I hope."

I nudge Mandy again, silently telling her to shut up, but of course she doesn't. "In a nutshell, I was just telling Evelyn how nice you two look together." I roll my eyes and notice Drake's smile growing wider.

Nice one, Mandy. Nice one.

I decide to get her back. "She also said she'd heard that you killed people."

She gasps. "No, I did not!"

I shrug my shoulders. "Whatever." I turn my attention back to Drake, who's staring at me. He's always staring at me. For some annoying reason, it never seems to be in a creepy way, though. As much as I hate to admit it, I like it when he stares at me.

"What are you doing here?" I try to sound more bored than anything, but it's hard when I have Mr Distracting standing in front of me with that handsome face, gorgeous body, and delectable smell. I don't know what aftershave he's got on, but man he smells good.

"I was thinking of buying some new shoes, so thought I'd stop in here for some."

"Well, don't let me keep you." I try pulling Mandy away, but she's stuck in place, staring up at Drake as she flutters her eyelashes at him.

"I see you two have been shopping." He obviously chooses to

ignore my remark and instead gazes down at our shopping bags. "Pick up anything nice?"

"Oh, yes," Mandy gushes. "Evelyn got some beautiful lingerie."

Snapping his head to me, Drake smiles widely. "Did you now? I'll look forward to seeing it on you once you move in with me. In fact," he suddenly snaps his fingers and a couple of his men come over, "why don't I just take your lingerie for you? That way, it will be there waiting for you once you do move in."

His two henchmen come over, retrieving not just my lingerie bag, but all of my bags. I'm too pissed and Mandy's too shocked to say anything about this.

"You're moving in with him?!" she shouts.

Taking a deep breath, I close my eyes. "No, I'm not."

Drake starts laughing, but nods his head in Mandy's direction. "Yes, she is."

"So you *are* boyfriend and girlfriend?"

Drake smirks. "I would say we're a little more than that. Next year, Evelyn will become my wife."

With my mouth open wide, I glare at Drake. Did he just say what I thought he said?

I feel a slap on my arm and it makes me jump. "Why did you hide this from me? You said you weren't serious." She starts giggling. "In fact, I was just telling Evelyn how handsome I thought you were." She giggles annoyingly again. "I was hoping to ask you out, but now ..."

Drake offers Mandy a heart-warming smile. "As lovely as you are, Mandy, I'm promised to another. I only have eyes for Evelyn here."

"Aww, that's so romantic." She nudges me again. "Don't you

think that's romantic?"

No, I do not. I also didn't find it romantic when he got his henchmen to steal our bags from us. "Do you think we can have our bags back now?"

"Evelyn," Mandy scorns. She leans in and whispers, "Stop being so rude."

Ugh. If only she knew what was being forced upon me against my will. I'm not an object, but yet I'm being made to feel like one. I barely have my freedom now. What's it going to be like once I turn that magic age?

"It's almost lunch time. Do you ladies fancy some lunch?"

"Actually, we were just about to—"

"We'd love to," Mandy interrupts.

I snap my head to her. "I thought we were going to the cinema?"

"What were you going to see? I could take you there too if you'd like. I can be at your disposal."

I suddenly want to escape. I can't go to lunch with this man, and I certainly cannot—without a doubt—sit in a darkened room next to him. His body already does things to me that I don't want it to. Not to mention that the smell of him is hitting me right between the legs.

God, I hate this man!

"We would love to," Mandy says, tugging at my arm. "Why don't we get your shoes, and I'll have a look at what time the films starts?"

Drake smiles widely. It seems that no matter what I feel, this is their plan. "That sounds good to me." He motions to one of his men. "Reese, go take the ladies' bags down to the car. We'll be in Berluti when you're done."

Reese gives Drake a sharp nod. "Yes, sir."

"Shall we?" Drake motions for us to start walking, so I

begrudgingly start to move.

I guess there's no way of getting out of this now.

We walk to the shop where Drake ends up spending over two thousand pounds. The shopkeeper gave Drake a heavy discount, so lord knows what the price would have been. I guess everyone here knows him, and everyone wants to be in his good books. Everyone, but me of course.

As if that wasn't enough, Drake then insisted on taking me and Mandy to Prada where he bought us each a handbag. I said that he shouldn't, but Mandy nearly punched me. We both ended up with matching, new to the range, black Prada bags—much to my chagrin.

"Aren't these so pretty?" Mandy gushes.

"So, what time is the film on, Mandy?" Drake asks.

Mandy reluctantly takes her eyes from her bag and gazes at her watch. "There's one showing in twenty minutes, and there's another one in three hours."

"Which one do you want to see?" Drake questions, looking in my direction. "We can either eat now or after the film."

I rub my tummy. "I'm actually not that hungry."

I'm about to tell him I feel sick and want to go home when Drake speaks. "Okay then. How about we try and make the first one?"

"Okay," Mandy says excitedly.

I inwardly groan, but move when everyone else does. I'm actually rather pissed at Drake. He has no interest in Mandy whatsoever, but he's acting like he does just so he can spend time with me. I hate it!

"Mandy, how about you sit at the front with Reese? I'm sure he could do with some company on the short ride there."

He motions to the front passenger door of the huge Bentley and

Mandy's eyes pop out. Of course she won't object to spending time with a big, bulky man like Reese. "Of course," she beams. "I'll give you two some alone time in the back." She winks at Drake, and I roll my eyes. This is just going from bad to worse.

Shutting Mandy's door, Drake then opens the back and motions for me to get in. "After you." I stand for a moment and deliberately sigh my displeasure. All this does is make Drake's smile widen. I think he sometimes finds me a challenge. "You have two choices, Evelyn. You can either get in yourself, or I can quite happily pick you up and throw you in there myself. Your choice."

Knowing he will go through with his threat, I wisely move and get inside the car. "See, that wasn't so hard, was it?"

I ignore his remark and instead scoot up as far as I can towards the other door. I don't want to be too close to this man. Not when every part of me starts to tingle when I am lately.

Once he shuts the door, he scoots over towards me, leans forward, and reaches his hand up over the back of my shoulder. I get a whiff of his aftershave and my insides burn. Purposefully, he leans in close to my lips and smiles when my breath hitches. "I have to make sure my baby's safe." He pulls my seatbelt down over me and clicks it into place. I'm practically trembling. Everything inside me has come alive. My heart beats rapidly, and I feel the strain of my nipples against the fabric of my t-shirt.

"Comfortable?" he asks, finally pulling away.

At last, I can breathe!

"Yes, thank you."

Nodding his head to me with a knowing smirk, he barks orders to Reese to get going and pretty soon, I can hear Mandy chewing Reese's ear off.

"Give me your hand."

I look at Drake and shake my head. "I'm okay as I am, thank—"

"It's not a request."

Reluctantly, I move my hand towards his, and I feel when his soft, yet strong hand envelopes my tiny one. "So, tell me ... How have you been? Are your parents treating you well?"

In front of him, they treat me like an angel, but when he's not there, I either get horribly snide comments, or I'm treated like a leper. Thankfully, the majority of the time, they leave me alone. I'm untouchable thanks to Drake. And they know it.

Ignoring his question, I in turn ask him one. "Why did you tell Mandy that we are getting married next year?"

I await his answer eagerly, but I know I'm not going to like it. "Because we are."

"And I suppose I don't get a say in the matter?"

"You made me promise, remember?" he asks with a stupid smirk.

"Yes, but I was barely fourteen—just a stupid little kid. I didn't know what I was saying back then. Back then, you were sweet and kind to me, and you ... made my head dizzy."

He looks affronted. "But, I'm sweet and kind to you now."

"Sometimes, but not all of the time. You can also be a menace."

He raises an eyebrow. "A menace, huh?"

I nod. "Yes, that's right. How can I marry a menace?"

His hand squeezes mine slightly. "I will ask, and you will say yes."

I frown and he notices. "But, I won't."

"Yes," he says, squeezing a little harder, "you will. That's the end of that discussion. Now, I want you to answer my question."

Sighing, I close my eyes. "Yes, everything's fine at home."

"Good." Leaning forward, he strokes the side of my face with his fingers. "I am the only one who knows how to look after you."

Without my willing it, my breathing hitches again. I hate when he's so domineering, but I equally hate it when he's sweet to me. I don't know which one is worse.

"Were you following me earlier?"

He sucks in an angry breath and pulls his fingers away. "I needed new shoes."

"That's not what I asked."

With his hand still clamped on my own, he answers, "That's all you need to know."

"What else do I need to know?"

Frowning, he looks at me. "What are you talking about?"

"What else do I need to know about you?" He laughs like my question amuses him. I'm deadly serious.

"We've known each other for six years. I think we both know enough about each other by now. I certainly know everything about you. I know that you're favourite colour is peach, your favourite food is steak, and your favourite film is *An Affair to Remember*. I saw how much you cried when you watched it."

"I did not," I protest. I'm also a little annoyed at the fact that he got all of my favourite things spot on.

Placing his fingers on my chin, Drake turns my head to meet his dazzling brown eyes. "You were vulnerable and let me hold you then. Do you remember that? I like it when you're vulnerable. I wish I could tell you how much, but I have to hold my tongue for now." He leans closer rewarding me with the softest of kisses to my lips. "Four months. Four months, Evelyn, and you'll be mine."

With a quick turn of his head, Drake stares out of the window like what he just did was nothing. Meanwhile, I'm still sitting here with the tingling feeling of that soft kiss he just placed on my lips. I don't even have time to be angry about what he said. All I can think of is how much I want him to kiss me like that again.

Feeling flustered, we make the rest of the drive in silence. Well, Drake and I stay silent. Mandy is still talking away with Reese, but I drown out the noise and stare directly out of my window. I need to calm down.

Once we arrive at the cinema, my nerves are awash with excitement and fear. I know Drake's going to sit next to me, and I know I won't be able to concentrate on the film because of him.

Drake still keeps a very possessive hand on mine as we queue up to get the tickets. It seems we are all going in, including Reese and this other guy who's just joined us. In fact, whoever he is looks kind of cute. He must be new because I've never seen him before.

Once our tickets are in hand, Drake turns to the others. "Why don't you get the drinks? Evelyn and I will meet you in the theatre."

The two men nod, and Mandy smirks knowingly at me. She probably thinks we're going to make out. Despite the kind of man he is, Drake has only ever touched my hand, face, and hair. He's never gone further than that. Well, not until today that is when he brushed his lips with mine. A fire like no other ignited within me when I felt his mouth graze my own. I wanted more. And I hate the fact that I feel this way.

"We're right at the back," he says, motioning for me to go up the stairs.

I notice people stare as we walk up. I also notice a couple of people obviously talking about us. I can hazard a guess as to what they're saying. I wonder if people realise that I'm practically a prisoner—someone who is being held against her will. Even if they did, they would never dare say anything. Mandy was right about one thing. He *has* killed people. I haven't seen it with my own eyes luckily, but I'm not stupid. Someone like Drake is not feared unless he's done something worthy of that fear. I've heard the rumours too. I just choose not to gossip about it.

Once we reach the top, Drake points to the chair in the far corner.

Great. Nowhere to hide and nowhere to run. I'm going to be virtually trapped here.

Against my better judgment, I walk over to my seat and sit down. Drake takes his place next to me without taking his hand away from mine. It's like he fears I'll run if he does.

"This is nice," he says, stroking his thumb across my hand. As much as I don't want to like it, I do. As if things can't get any worse, the lights dim, and Drake looks across at me with an expression I've never seen before. He looks like he wants to kiss me, and for some reason, I want him to.

As if sensing the change in my mood, Drake leans over to whisper, "Why are you looking at me like that?"

My breath hitches, and without meaning to, my eyes travel down to his lips and back up again. I'm not sure, as the sound of a trailer is rather loud in the background, but I could swear I heard him growl. This just makes my cheeks flame. Suddenly, I feel like I'm on fire.

"Like what?" I manage to answer, trying to swallow.

Why is my mouth dry all of a sudden?

Looking down at my lips again and back up, he purposefully moves in closer. "Like you want me to kiss you."

POSSESSION

I can't say anything. My mouth parts, but no words come out. My breath does, though. I can feel my heart thundering against my chest, and it's leaving me practically gasping for breath.

His eyes slowly dance over my face, and I lick my lips in anticipation of what he's about to do next. "You want me to kiss you, don't you, *Evelyn*?"

Oh, my! The way he said my name... It was like it was a sweet melody dancing on his tongue.

I try to shake my head—to speak—but nothing seems to happen. It's like I'm frozen. Held inside by a spell only Drake can cast on me.

Bit by bit, he inches closer, and instead of pulling away, I find myself being pushed towards him. I swallow hard as he comes closer, and I feel when his lips touch mine. Ever so gently, he brushes them with my mouth, and an incoherent sound leaves my lips.

"Evelyn," he whispers.

I think I'm going to pass out. He doesn't seem to move. It's like he wants me to be the one to give into him. I try to resist the temptation to move my mouth, but my body is having other ideas.

Without another thought, I press my lips to his and feel when his breathing hitches along with mine. Grabbing me by the waist, he pulls me towards him and darts his tongue into my mouth. I moan, grabbing his hair and squeezing him to me.

My word, what has gotten into me? I'm usually trying everything to get away from this man, but now I'm practically cradling his lap and raping that delectable mouth of his.

I find myself in this never-been-in-before zone with Drake. He's normally my kryptonite, but now I can't seem to get enough of him. I hate to admit it, but I often fantasised about what it would be like to kiss this man, and now that I've felt him, I know it will be harder

33

and harder to resist.

Bit by bit, he pulls me to him, and bit by bit, I lose a part of myself to this monster. He once told me he wasn't a monster, but I see it inside of him. I see that part of him simmering near the surface.

With his hands touching everywhere but where I actually want him to touch, I do something I would never normally do. I pull at his hand to try and get him to feel my breast. "Evelyn, stop," he urges against my mouth. "I'm barely hanging on to restraint as it is. Fuck, you taste incredible."

He attacks my mouth again, and my mind is awash with something new. Is this lust? This feeling that I will burst soon if he doesn't do something to relieve this throbbing ache in my stomach and between my legs? I feel desperate. Desperate for him to act, desperate for him to push this further, and desperate for him to claim me as he so constantly tells me he will.

My mind doesn't want to give into this man, but right now, the feel of him, the smell of him, and the taste of him is intoxicating me beyond rational thought. As if in tune with one another, our tongues dance, coaxing each other to open up. For some reason, I can't break away.

But, just as we're losing ourselves within each other, the sound of someone clearing her throat alerts me to the fact that we're in a cinema, and we're not alone.

Snapping back from Drake, I hear his growl of discontent as I stare like a deer caught in the headlights at Mandy, who is standing in the row below us with her phone pointing in our direction. She smirks, noticing my flushed cheeks and messed up hair. Straightening myself up, I pull my hair out of my ponytail and try to compose myself.

"What was that about not wanting to rip his clothes off?" She raises one eyebrow at me before smiling and saying, "I'll send you the video later."

I scowl at Mandy's smug grin, but notice her smirk has disappeared the moment she looks at Drake. She immediately turns, sitting down with Reese and the other guy. My attention turns straight to Drake. He looks both flustered and pissed off at the same time. As he straightens his suit jacket, he catches me staring and leans over to speak to me. "In a way, I'm kind of glad Mandy interrupted us, but I'm pissed at her at the same time. That's the first time you've opened up to me. If I had known that all it would have taken was a kiss from me to make that happen, I would have done it ages ago." Suddenly, he shakes his head. "Four months is a fucking long time."

Grabbing my hand again, he says no more, and soon afterwards the film starts. But no matter how much I wanted to concentrate on the film, I just couldn't get my mind off of Drake's smell, Drake's touch, and Drake's lingering kiss. New feelings I don't want come crashing over me like a wave. I don't want to give in to them, but he makes me want to.

For the first time ever, I feel like fighting him is going to be a losing battle.

CHAPTER FOUR

Age Thirteen

My parents are entertaining those men again. I don't know who they are, and normally I'm told to stay up in my bedroom and not come out. One night when they were here, my curiosity got the better of me, and I came downstairs to take a look at what was so secretive that I had to go to my room and keep my door shut. When I spotted one man, I could see why. If ever there was a man who was evil personified, this guy was definitely him. His eyes held something so poisonous that the urge to run away was instinctive. He also had a scar on his face which ran from his eye down to his lips. It looked ghastly.

Since then, whenever I know he's here, I stay in my room and lock my door. I didn't get to see whoever else was there, and by the looks of what I saw in him, I didn't want to.

Tonight is no exception. In fact, I would do anything to not be here right now. Clutching my phone, I contemplate texting Drake. He bought me this phone a few months ago and told me to use it whenever I wanted. He's been quite the constant in my life now, and every time I know he's visiting, butterflies swarm my stomach. I like it when he visits as my parents behave themselves. They're actually nice to me, which is an unusual occurrence.

As I stare down at my phone, a sound coming from behind my door makes me jump. I can hear footsteps, then creaking. Sucking in my breath, I stay still, staring at the handle on my door. My heart thumps against my chest as the sound of something even worse comes.

The sound of silence.

Clutching the phone to my chest, I try hard not to breathe too loudly, but the more I try not to, the more my breaths seem to want to leak out in bursts. The sound of nothing continues, and it seems to go on forever. I continue to stare at the door as if it will somehow move. It can't move because I made sure I locked it when they arrived.

I did lock it, didn't I?

I jump again and nearly gasp out loud when a knock sounds on my door. I don't say anything. I daren't say anything. My heart jumps into my throat when I see the door handle push down.

Please say I locked the door. Please say I locked the door.

I breathe out a sigh of relief when I see that whoever is behind the door is meeting with resistance when they try to push. I wait again, wondering what this person will do next. It seems like an eternity of silence, but when I hear the sound of footsteps retreating from my door, I breathe out a sigh of relief.

Not wanting to be here anymore, I shakily pull my phone away from my chest, scramble towards my bathroom door, and very carefully and quietly close it behind me. I dial Drake's number, and I'm surprised when he answers after only a couple of rings.

"Evelyn, is that you?"

"I'm scared," I whisper into the phone.

"Where are you?" His soft voice turns angry and urgent.

"I'm in my bathroom, and I don't want to come out. Some scary men are here, and I think one of them tried to get into my bedroom." My voice sounds shaky, and I have this overwhelming urge to cry.

"Okay. Don't move. Keep your bedroom door locked and stay in your bathroom. Lock that too. I'm coming to get you."

"How long will you be? I'm scared."

"Nothing's going to happen to you, sweetheart. I promise you. Okay?"

"Okay," I say, my voice breaking.

"You're safe with me. I swear it. Just hang in there. I'll be ten minutes at the most." At first, I don't say anything. I feel the lump forming in my throat, and for a moment, I can't speak. "Tell me you understand, Evelyn."

"I do," I manage. "Please hurry."

"I'll be there before you know it."

He hangs up, and I shakily check my watch. It's ten-thirty-seven now. He said ten minutes.

I pace the bathroom floor, waiting for every second and then every minute to pass by. Every sound makes me feel like someone's in my room, and it takes everything in me not to scream out. My home should feel safe, but I feel anything but right now. My heart is racing, my body's shaking, and my mind is filling itself with ideas of the bogeyman, knives, evil faces, and picked locks.

I check my watch again and see that only four minutes have gone by. The bathroom starts to close in on me, and the urge to run is great. I do as I'm told, though, and stay put in my bathroom.

It's another four minutes that go by before I hear the sound of voices outside my bathroom door. "What have I told you about bringing in that scum?" He's here! Thank God.

"He's my client. I just like to entertain my clients."

"Not when your thirteen-year-old daughter is in the fucking house."

I breathe out a sigh of relief and hear when a quiet knock sounds. "Evelyn, it's me. Open up."

With a monstrous feeling of relief, I open my door and crash-land into the waiting arms of Drake. "Thank you," I say, finally letting some tears fall.

I feel his arms squeeze me tightly before kissing my head. "You don't have to thank me, sweetheart."

I look up to him and see his smiling face. "I don't want to be here," I whisper.

"You can't take her away. You have no right," my father snaps.

Too quickly, the hold Drake had on me is gone, and my father is pushed up against the wall by the scruff of his neck. "Don't ever question me. And don't you ever answer back to me like that again. Do you hear me? I'm taking Evelyn with me. She's staying at my house, and there isn't a damn thing you can do to stop me."

My father's eyes widen in fear. "But Isaac will see her. I know that's not what you want."

With a frustrated growl, Drake digs into his pocket and pulls out a wad of notes. "This is for keeping Evelyn away from him. I'm taking her now, and I want you and your wife to make sure they don't come out of that dining room. Capisce?"

Once my father's nod registers, Drake turns to me. "Do you have a jacket?" I nod my head. "Go and get it now. Be quick, Evelyn."

I don't hesitate. Within an instant, I'm in my wardrobe, and Drake is right behind me. I feel him reach over me and pull my hooded jacket on. I don't normally wear it as it's miles too big for me, but, for the moment at least, Drake seems to want me to wear it.

One arm after the other, Drake helps me into my jacket, zips me up, and gently raises the hood up, over my head. "I want you to promise me something." I nod. "Whatever happens, don't look up. Do you hear me?" I nod again, and Drake rewards me with a big smile. "Good. Now, come with me." He takes me under his arm and turns to my father. "I would suggest you go downstairs and make sure your guests don't leave your dining room. Do you hear me?"

"Yes," he answers shakily.

My father hastily retreats, but as he starts to disappear, Drake says one more thing: "You haven't heard the last of this, William."

A cold shiver runs down my spine at his words. I guess my father felt it as well, since he, too, looks ashen. Once he disappears from sight, Drake squeezes me a little to make me look up at him. "Remember what I said. No looking up, okay?" I nod my head again. "Let's get going."

Letting Drake lead the way, I keep my head down, and we silently creep down the stairs. I can hear voices. I can also hear a man asking where my father has been, but he quickly responds by saying he had an urgent call. I then hear my father ask if anyone wants something else to drink, but I don't hear the answer. Drake has me outside and in a waiting car before I can even blink. Once inside, he buckles up my seatbelt and then kisses my head. "Are you okay?"

Once I nod, he breaks away and turns to the driver. "Lock this door behind me, and whatever you do, don't let anyone but me back in. You got me? Any hint that someone else is trying to get into this car, and you drive off. Do you hear me?"

"Yes, sir."

The front passenger gets out, and Drake is about to go too, but I grab him. "Don't leave me."

Turning, he offers me a bright smile and kisses my hand. "I will only be a few minutes. I promise. I just need to do something first. You're safe, Evelyn. With me, you're always safe. Remember that."

I nod my head again before he leaves and the door is quickly locked behind him. I notice another car, and four other men get out of that one and join him. One by one, they cock their guns and place them behind their backs as they enter the house. For a moment, I fear for my parents' safety, but something tells me that the guns have nothing to do with my parents and everything to do with the nasty men, who are eating and drinking inside my house right now.

I stare at the house for what seems like hours, but must have only been mere minutes. "Is he okay? What's taking them so long?" I ask the big, beefy driver sitting silently at the front.

"Don't you worry, Miss Montgomery. Mr Salvatore will be fine. He shouldn't be too long now. Just sit tight, and it'll be over soon."

I see him staring at me through the visor, so I nod my head and turn my attention back to the house. I feel safer than I did earlier, but I won't feel totally safe until I see Drake come out of the house and get back into this car.

A few more minutes pass before I finally see Drake leaving the house with his men in tow, walking back to the cars. The moment Drake is by the car, I hear the lock pop open, and Drake makes his way in. He sits next to me in brooding silence as the car pulls away. I'm desperate to ask him what happened in there, but the look on his face halts me. He looks wired like he wants to kill someone.

Knowing I shouldn't stare, I glance away and instead concentrate on staring at all the houses and trees that eventually pass us by. I feel a great deal safer than I did, but I still can't help but feel something niggling me in the pit of my stomach. I don't know what it is, so instead of harnessing it, I try to think of something else.

In my musing, I think of Drake's house. I have known him for almost a year now, and never once have I been round to see his house before. In a way, I'm quite looking forward to it. I know it will be big, and I know it will be lavish. I guess I will see for myself soon enough.

After a couple more minutes of staring, I feel something graze my hand. Snapping my head to Drake, I jump. "Don't pull away from me. There's no need to." He takes my hand gently, but forcefully. "Better?" he asks with a smile. He still looks angry, but a softer edge is now seeping through.

"I am now. Thank you." I take a deep breath. "Did I make a mistake tonight ... calling you and making you come to get me?"

He tugs at my hand. "No. You did the correct thing. And I want you to promise me that if this shit ever happens again, you'll immediately give me a call, okay?" He grits his teeth, so I nod my head again.

"I promise."

Drake lets out a deep breath before looking out of the window. I can tell he's angry again, so I leave him to it.

About ten minutes later, we enter a driveway, and in front of us are some big, black wrought iron gates. They immediately open and we drive in and eventually come to a stop at this massively *impressive square house. It looks more palatial than I'd imagined.*

In front of the house is a water feature that we drive around to get to the bottom of the stairs. "Wow," I say without meaning to voice my thoughts.

"Do you like it?"

I turn my head to Drake. "I love it."

"Good because—one day—you'll be seeing a lot more of this."

I frown, but have no time to dwell on what he's just said as he opens his door and then mine quickly after. I notice a man standing by my door, and I smile as I get out. Drake is soon there, helping me, and for the first time in my life, I don't feel like a child. I feel like a lady.

"Welcome to my home." Drake takes my hand, his eyes light up, and he seems to lose all the anger he had from earlier. "Let me show you inside."

I can't help the huge grin on my face. I don't feel scared any longer. For once, I feel safe. I have seen the rage inside of this man, but, for now—in this moment—all I can see is his kindness.

We take the stairs which lead to a big, wooden brown door. Inside is a huge round hallway, and an equally huge grand staircase. The lighting is bright, making me look up to its source. Hanging from the ceiling is the most impressive chandelier I have ever seen. That alone must be worth more money than what my house costs.

"What do you think?"

Biting my lip, I try hard to suppress a smile. "I love it, Drake. You have a beautiful home."

This seems to please him as he walks me in farther. "I will show you it all tomorrow morning. For now, we must find you some bedclothes and get you to bed. You've had a long night."

I frown. I don't want to go to bed yet. I'm too wired to. "I can stay up a little—"

"No more discussions, Evelyn. You need your beauty sleep. I can show you to your room, and I'll have Henry bring you some hot chocolate."

"Who's Henry?"

"My cook," he answers. "Don't worry. You can trust him. No one here will hurt you. I promise you that."

Smiling, I nod my head and he leads me up the big staircase. Once on the landing, we travel a short distance down the hallway where he points to a door. "This is my room. If you need anything during the night, this is where I will be. But, please, only come inside if it's urgent, okay?"

The way he asked me was as if he was pleading. I have never heard Drake plead before. Why is it that I can't go and visit him during the night? Does he think I'm hideous or something?

I quickly scrap that thought when I think of all the trouble he's gone to tonight to make me safe. I don't know why the thought of me needing him during the night displeases him, but it's one I note down just in case.

"You're room is right next door." He pulls me farther down the hall and opens up a big, white door. Inside is the biggest bed I have ever seen. Without hesitation, I walk in, noting the plush cream carpet, massive red velvet drapes, white chaise longue, and soft tan walls. "Wow," I say again, walking up to the huge windows that seem to dominate the room. "You have a pool!" I squeal.

Drake laughs behind me, but soon joins me by my side as we stare out into his garden. The pool is big and currently glistening in the moonlight. It looks so inviting. I would give anything to jump in there right now.

As if sensing my thoughts, Drake turns me to face him. "All in good time, Evelyn."

"Sir," a voice sounds behind him. I snap my head towards the voice and see a young-looking maid with dark hair placing some items on the bed. "This is for Miss Montgomery."

"Thank you, Louisa," Drake answers before she quickly retreats. She didn't even look at us.

"You must get some rest, and I must get some work done."

He goes to move, but I grab him. "Aren't you going to stay with me for a little while?" I see something pass over him, but I'm not quite sure what it is. Could it be frustration?

"No, Evelyn. You must go to bed."

Hearing the harshness in his words, I feel it wise to nod my head. Drake sighs and is about to leave the room when he suddenly turns and stalks towards me.

Placing my face in his hands, he commands my attention. I look up into his deep brown eyes and for the first time, I sense a hint of something different inside Drake.

"Just remember one thing for me, Evelyn. No matter what I do, I am not a monster. Okay?" He holds my stare, awaiting my answer. When I nod my head, Drake exhales, kisses my head, and walks out the door, leaving me as confused as ever.

CHAPTER FIVE

Age Seventeen – Present Day

I don't see Drake again for another two weeks after that day out at the cinema and subsequent dinner. Later that night, he dropped Mandy home, and the whole journey back, I was itching to feel his lips on mine again. It never happened. He knew I wanted it, but felt compelled to hold back. He said, "If I kiss you again, I will take you home now and never let you go." A part of me was disappointed, and another part of me was relieved.

Now, the biggest part of me feels resentment towards him. I don't know what it is about that man, but he brings out the worst mixed emotions in me. A portion of me thinks it may be teenage hormones, but another portion thinks it's because of his uncanny knack of being sweet one minute and damn right domineering the next. I may not be *his*—as he calls it—yet, but I know that's not really the case. I'm already this man's prisoner ... in every conceivable way. Things were always a mix of good and bad between us, but lately, I feel something shifting. It's as if a sudden change of tide is coming. I see the way he looks at me now. I notice the expectation and flurry of excitement shining through. He wants me. I *know* he wants me.

It's funny really because I have been of a legal age for almost two years now, and yet he still insists on keeping me at arm's length until I turn eighteen. A part of me wants him. Oh God, does it want him— especially since that kiss at the cinema. I find myself thinking of nothing else ever since.

And that's why I hate him even more.

It's not enough that he's invading me in every other way possible? He also has to invade my thoughts?

That is definitely one area I consider to be my own, but in true Drake fashion, he has managed to seep in there too. Also, if I'm honest, a part of me hates the fact I haven't heard a word from him in two weeks. There have been days when we've lost contact, but never this long. It burdens me that I'm thinking this way. I want nothing to do with him, and yet I find myself unable to help feel that pull I have towards him.

And that's why tonight—for the first time ever—I chose to really defy the man who seems to have this hold on me. I deliberately drove more than thirty miles out of our little town of Cobham, Surrey to a little, tiny village south of High Wycombe. I wanted to escape, but I also wanted anonymity. Unfortunately, too many people knew who I was where I lived, and it was starting to get on top of me.

Sighing, I order my second drink of the evening, not caring if I get drunk. I'll sleep in the car if I have to. My phone rings for the thirtieth time since I set out, and I do what I did with the other twenty-nine times—ignore it.

"Someone's eager to reach you," a voice sounds at the end of the bar.

I look up and find a young guy, who must be in his twenties, smiling at me. He looks nice enough with his well-pressed shirt and trousers, cropped blond hair, and nice smile. But, I know nice smiles mean nothing. I get them often enough with Drake, but I still know something sinister lives within him—no matter how much he tells me otherwise.

Looking down at my phone, I silence it. "I'm sorry if it's disturbing you."

"It's not. I was just trying to think of an excuse to talk to you." He chuckles a little, making me smile, and he sees this as his cue to get a little closer. Once sitting next to me, he holds out his hand. "Chris."

I take his hand and shake it. "Evelyn."

He smiles brightly with a drunk gaze in his eyes. "Can I offer you a drink, Evelyn?"

Shaking my head, I point to my drink. "No, thank you. I just got one."

He nods his head, and I can tell he's just itching to ask me something. I don't have to wait long to find out what that is. "So, did you have an argument with your boyfriend or something?"

I frown, my heart rate picking up a little. "Excuse me?"

He points to my phone on the bar. "The person trying to reach you. Whoever it is seems persistent. I'm just assuming it's your boyfriend."

I breathe a sigh of relief. I don't know why I'm so immediately afraid of strangers. Maybe being with Drake for so long has had a lasting impact. I shake my head. "No... Well, it *is* a man, but ... it's complicated," I sigh.

Chris chuckles. "Isn't it always?"

I smile, warming to him a little. "I guess."

"Do you mind telling me what he's done to make you run out on your own to a strange bar in the middle of nowhere?"

"Who says this is a strange bar? I might come here all the time."

He laughs a little. "I say that because this is my regular, and believe me, I would have noticed you drinking in here before." He lets out a silent laugh and I smile. "You seem wary of me, and I don't want you to feel that way. Not all men are bad ... and we're not all like the man you're obviously running away from."

"You make a lot of assumptions."

"Well, am I right or wrong?" I stare at him a moment, but can't help the smile that rises on my face again. "I knew it!" he blurts, making me laugh. "See, that's much better. Whoever he is doesn't deserve you."

I take a sip of my drink before replying. "What makes you say that? I may have run away, but what if it's because I did something terrible to him?"

"Did you?"

"No," I chuckle.

"Well then. You really don't make this easy, do you?"

"I didn't ask you to sit next to me." I don't mean it in a rude way, and luckily he doesn't take offence to it. Instead, he just nods.

"So, are you going to tell me why you ran? I may be able to offer you some great advice. I've been known to help out many a friend before."

"But I've only just met you."

"Try me."

Sighing, I wonder whether to tell this random stranger all the things I have never dared to tell anyone. Only Drake, my parents, and I know about this stupid deal that was made behind my back at the tender age of fourteen.

"There's a man I've known for a number of years—"

"Boyfriend?" he interrupts.

"As I said, it's complicated."

He nods. "Sorry. Go ahead."

"He wants me to be his. I like him and all, but he's too much. It's like being without him isn't even an option for me."

Chris frowns, a scowl forming on his face. "Sounds dangerous. I would leave him if I were you. Do you know how many women fall victim to domestic violence from controlling men like that? He may seem only controlling at first, but this could just be the beginning."

Frowning, I shake my head. "I don't know. He hasn't hit me in all the years I've known him so far."

He hisses in a breath. "Yes, but how long will that last?"

I sit there, blinking a few times. Could Drake hit me? Yes, of course he could. I've seen the anger inside of him. But would he actually take it out on me?

I'm so engrossed in thinking about it all that I fail to feel fingers on my hand at first. It is only when he speaks that it registers that he's stroking me, and not only that, but he seems a little too close for comfort. "You should be cherished. Not treated like an object."

For some reason, I don't feel all too comfortable with this guy anymore. I move my hand away and offer him half a smile. "Sorry. Was that too much?"

I nod my head. "I don't even know you."

"But you could get to know me," he urges with a bright smile. "I'd promise to treat you better than that fucknugget."

A rush of anger rushes through me. I don't know why I feel compelled to stick up for Drake, but the feeling comes nonetheless. "You don't know anything about our situation."

Chris is about to speak, but something he sees out of the corner of his eye stops him. He moves away, and at first, I'm grateful for the distance. But then, I notice him squaring his shoulders like he's getting ready for a fight.

"Evelyn, get your arse up now and get in the car. Don't make me tell you again." The hairs rise on the back of my neck at the sound of his voice. He is monumentally pissed.

"Ah. So, you're the fucknugget."

Closing my eyes, I shake my head. Chris obviously doesn't know who Drake is and has just made his worst mistake ever.

"Evelyn," Drake urges again, "get the fuck out of this bar before I drag you out." I don't hesitate. I pick up my phone and bag from the bar and start moving.

"Hey! You don't have to go anywhere," Chris shouts. "Sit down, Evelyn."

I hastily shake my head and watch as Drake pokes Chris' chest. "Outside. Now."

Chris smirks. "With pleasure. After I beat your arse, I'm taking your woman home with me. How would you like that?"

Shit, I wish he would stop talking. He's obviously more drunk than I thought if he thinks he can take on Drake. I can see the rise and fall of Drake's shoulders and chest. He's madder than hell.

As we step outside, Drake points to the back passenger seat of his Bentley. "In," he demands.

"But what about my car?"

With gritted teeth, he comes close to my face. "Am I speaking a different fucking language?"

I rear back and hastily get in the car. As I turn, I see Chris shaking his head. "Can't face me head on, huh? You have to get your minions to come and help you fight me." He then waves at me in the car. "Don't worry, darling. This will all be over in a—"

He doesn't have time to finish his sentence. With one bone cracking punch from Drake, Chris goes down. When Drake is satisfied that he won't come back up again, he moves over to the other passenger side. "You three take her car and follow us," I hear him shout.

Nodding their heads, they get in my car, and Drake joins me in his. "Drive," he orders without another word.

The driver obliges, and we are quickly on our way home. Drake doesn't say anything for a while. I can tell he's pissed as hell and trying to rein himself in. I know that monster inside of him is just itching to get out.

After an agonising few minutes, Drake decides to speak. "Why?"

I sigh before replying. "I wanted to get away for a while. Somewhere where nobody knows me and knows I belong to you. I wanted some space."

Finally, he turns his head to me. I can see the fire in his eyes. It should scare me, but it doesn't. "And that involved going to a bar and having some arsehole drool all over you and call me fucking *names*?!" He shouts the last word and it makes me jump.

"I didn't invite him to talk to me. He just appeared and started asking me questions. I didn't want him there. I just wanted some space."

Sliding over to me, Drake grabs my chin and pulls my head to him. "When is it going to get into that head of yours that you belong to me, and what I fucking say goes?"

I should feel fear, but all I feel is anger. Hot, red anger. "Why is it so necessary to own me? Why not some other girl? Why me? I can't do anything without your say so."

He squeezes harder and gets closer to my face. "Damn fucking right too. In less than four months, you will be in my home, doing everything that I fucking say."

I try shaking my head, but he holds it still. I can feel the tears brimming at his words. I know what he says is true. I know I can't escape him. But I can't help wanting to fight him at every turn. "You were wrong about not being a monster. You *are* a monster."

I see when those words hit home. He doesn't like that I've said this. "You may think I'm a monster, but I'm your monster. Can't you get that through your head?"

"No. I hate you. You're a vile, despicable monster, and I hate you," I seethe. I'm rattling his cage, and yet I can't seem to help myself. I'm so pent up with frustration, rage, and pity. Yes, pity—for myself and this shitty position I've been borne into.

"You want to see how much of a monster I can be? Do you?" In one quick yank of my legs he has me beneath him and crushes his lips to mine. "Do you want to push me, Evelyn? Do you want to see just how fucking monstrous I can be?"

He starts sliding my skirt up and yanking at my panties. "No!" I scream. "No, Drake. Stop. Please stop!" He doesn't listen. With his other free hand, he places it over my mouth and tries to pull my panties down. Flailing my arms and legs about, I try hard to get free, but he's too strong. In my fight, I somehow manage to grab his hand and bite down hard on him. I hear when he screams, and finally, he's off me.

"Stop the fucking car!" he orders.

The driver doesn't hesitate. With a screech of his tyres, he comes to an abrupt halt at the side of a deserted road. No one is around. All

I can see are trees around us and black ... nothing but black.

Maybe if I run inside, the black would surround me and take me away from him.

With a violent tug on the door handle, Drake gets out, punches the car, and roars his frustration. He starts pacing as he threads his hands through his hair.

"Is everything okay?" I hear a voice coming through a walkie talkie. It's obviously one of the guys in the other car.

The driver picks it up and says, "Everything's okay. Just give him a few minutes."

"Understood." I hear the click and look out at Drake again. I've never seen him so mad.

"Are you okay?"

Snapping my head to the driver, I feel a tear run down my face. I only just now notice that he's the cute guy from the cinema the other day. I nod my head. "I'm fine." He hands me a tissue. "Thank you."

"Don't mention it."

"What's your name?"

"Kane, ma'am."

I dab my eyes with the tissue he gave me. "I noticed you at the cinema the other day. You're new."

I see him smile in through the visor. It's a nice smile. "That was my first day on the job."

Nodding my head, I turn my attention back to Drake outside. He's leaning on the boot, smoking a cigarette. He must be really stressed as I hardly ever see him smoke ... if at all.

Seeing him standing there—looking so angry—should make me angry too. He just attacked me in the back of the car in front of his new driver. But why is it that I feel I want to go to him? Why is it that

I feel I need *his* forgiveness? I should need him to ask for mine instead, but I don't. None of my emotions make sense. I should want to run, but all I feel is this overwhelming desire to get out of the car and go to him.

And that's what I do. Slowly, I creep out of the car and walk over to where he's leaning on the boot. He acknowledges I'm there, but doesn't say anything. I walk forward, placing my arm through his, needing him to hold me. He stands as still as a statue at first, just smoking his cigarette. It's not enough. I need him to hold me. I need him to wrap his arms around me and give me his acceptance. Yes, he is a monster, and yes I should be running. The only thing that's stopping me from really fleeing from him is the fact that he's the only man who has ever really taken care of me. He's the only man who has shown me any love. I need to know he still feels it. I need to know he still has it in him to love me.

So, I grip tighter to him and snuggle my head into his chest. It works because, pretty soon, he discards his cigarette and wraps his arms around me in a warm embrace. I know when I think of what he's done later on, I will hate myself. But for now, I just want to feel his tenderness.

"You drive me fucking crazy," he finally says, kissing the top of my head.

"Did I hurt your hand?"

"Yes."

I can't help the impish smile that forms. "Good."

Pulling me away, he holds my head in his hands. "Don't ever do that to me again. You got me to stop just then, but I can't guarantee what will happen if you push me like that again."

I search his dark eyes and nod. "I understand."

"Do you?" he urges. "I don't think you do ... and it's probably just as well."

I frown. "What is that supposed to mean?"

He shakes his head. "Nothing. Just don't fucking run from me like that again. I won't be held responsible." Placing his forehead on mine, he sighs. "Fourteen weeks. Fourteen fucking weeks." Pulling my head closer, he kisses me again, but this time it's not out of anger or frustration. This kiss is the kiss I have yearned for ever since that day in the cinema two weeks ago. It's the kiss I've been dreaming about getting every day since he swept me away. I can taste the cigarette on his breath, but instead of being repelled by it, I yearn for more.

"I can't lose control around you," he says, pulling away. "You make it so fucking hard." He shakes his head. "I'm trying to keep away, but the closer it gets, the less control I have."

Throwing my arms around his, I stand on tiptoe and kiss his neck. "Can I stay with you tonight?"

He grabs my arms and pulls me away from him. "I just told you I'm losing control, and *now* you want to stay with me?" He shakes his head again.

"I just thought that—"

"No," he warns. "As much as I don't fucking like it, I'm taking you back to your parents' house." He then pushes himself off the boot of the car and motions for me to get in.

This time, I willingly oblige without a murmur.

CHAPTER SIX

Age Fourteen

"Have you seen those men at your house since?"

I lick my ice cream, staring across at Drake. He looks handsome today with a casual pair of jeans and a t-shirt. Others have noticed it too. I see women looking at him, and for some reason, I don't like it.

"No," I answer. In fact, it's been nice and quiet since that incident a few months ago. "Do you know who they are?"

Slouching back in his seat, he sighs. "Unfortunately, yes."

"Who are they?"

"That doesn't matter. You shouldn't want to know who they are. Now, finish your ice cream. That's all you should be concerned about."

I suddenly get angry. "I'm not a child."

"Oh, yes, you are. Despite the fact that you look older than you are, your age doesn't lie. Believe me, I remind myself of your age every day."

I frown. "What's that supposed to mean?"

"Nothing. Just eat. I have a surprise for you once you're done."

My eyes light up, making him smile. "Really? What is it?"

"Finish your ice cream and I'll take you."

I bite my lip, trying to suppress my smile. It makes Drake laugh. I like making him laugh. "Okay," I answer, relishing my ice cream. I'm suddenly raring to get going.

Once done, he leads me to his waiting car and we both get in the back seats together. It's on the journey that I start thinking about Drake. He's been a constant in my life for almost two years now, and for some reason, he likes spending time and money on me. It makes me wonder.

"Drake?"

"Yes," he responds, giving me his undivided attention.

"Do you like spending time with me?"

He laughs again. "Of course. I wouldn't be here if I didn't. What's brought this on?"

I shrug my shoulders. "I don't know. It's just... I would have thought you would be more interested in spending time with my mum and dad, but it feels like you spend more time with me."

I see a little bit of panic in his eyes. "Do you not want to spend time with me?"

Jumping up straighter, I shake my head. "Oh, no, no... That's not what I meant. I love spending time with you. In fact, I think I would be really sad if you stopped coming to visit me."

"Really?" he asks. "So, you wouldn't like it if I left?"

Now it's my turn to panic. "You're not leaving, are you?"

He laughs. "Never. Wild horses couldn't keep me away from you if that's what you wanted."

"So, you'll promise me you'll never leave me? You promise I will always be close to you?"

Taking my hand, he squeezes it a little. "Of course I promise. Anything for you, Evelyn."

"So, you like me then?"

Shaking his head, he frowns. "You're full of questions today, aren't you? Why do you ask?"

I look away, embarrassed. "Because I'm so young. I worry you'll get bored of me."

Grabbing my chin, he gently pulls me to look at him. "You could never bore me. Besides, you won't be this young forever."

"So, you'll marry me when I turn eighteen?" He starts laughing—a full belly laugh that turns my insides out. It hurts me that he finds this so amusing. "I'm glad you find this so funny." I turn my head away in both embarrassment and anger. Why did I have to say something so stupid? It just slipped right out.

"Evelyn, I didn't mean—" I turn away more and hear him laugh again.

"Evelyn, look at me." When I don't turn, he unbuckles my seat belt and pulls me into his lap. He cuddles me, and I hate to say it, but he feels warm and nice. He also smells incredible too. "Okay, I'll make you a deal. If you promise me that you'll call me day or night if those men come over again, then I'll marry you when you're eighteen. Deal?"

With a bright smile he can't see, I nod my head. "Deal."

He squeezes me one last time and then places me back on the seat. "Good," he says, strapping me back in. "We're almost there."

I feel a certain rejection when he pushes me away from him so suddenly, but when he mentions that we'll be there soon and I will see my surprise, all my fears melt away. I seem to want acceptance from this man all the time, and I don't know why. I guess it's because *he's the only person I have who cares for me.*

"Ah. We're here now."

I see the gates to his house open. "The surprise is in your house?"

He turns with a gleam in his eyes. "Well, not exactly in my house, but close to it."

I frown, wondering what he means, but I find out soon enough once I'm out the car and being led to the back of his house. I see in the distance that something new has been built. "You have stables?" I ask excitedly.

Drake nods his head. "Yes, but that's not the best part." He motions for me to take his hand, and we go running across towards the stables. I can't help giggling as we run.

Once we reach the stables, he takes me round to the booths where two horses are being kept. One is dark brown and huge, and the other is not as big but is white with a brown patch on its nose. "They look beautiful."

He motions towards the dark brown one. "This one's Max. He's my horse." He strokes Max's nose, and Max seems to like it. He sniffs around his hand and nibbles a little on his palm. It makes me giggle.

"And this," he says, walking in front of the white horse, "is a three-year-old female who hasn't gotten a name yet."

Smiling, I stroke her, loving the way she feels when I do. "Why not?" I ask, running my hand across her neck.

"Because the person who owns her should name her." When he doesn't say anything more, I look at him. "So, what are you going to call her?"

I shriek, making him laugh. "You bought me a horse?" He nods his head, and I go running into his arms. He starts laughing as I wrap my legs around him and spray kisses all over his face.

"I take that to mean you like my present?"

I keep my arms locked around his neck. "Like it?! I love it. Thank you." Caught up in the moment, I bend down and kiss him on the lips. Immediately, he drops me to the floor, the moment lost.

"You're welcome." He completely pulls away, and I wonder for a moment if I've done something wrong, but I have no time to dwell on this. "Do you want to go for a ride with me?"

My smile returns. "Do I ever?!" I scream.

He starts laughing again. "Okay, come on. Let's get you and your horse ready. Do you know what you're going to call her?"

Walking up to her, I stroke around her brown patch and notice how much it looks like the map of Ireland. "I think I'll call her Ireland."

"Ireland?" he asks with a frown.

"Yeah. Look," I urge, trailing my finger around her patch.

He squints, getting a closer look before it dawns on him. "Oh, yeah." He strokes my hair, making me blush. "Ireland it is, then. I think it's perfect."

CHAPTER SEVEN

Age Seventeen – Present Day

I gallop through the fields with the wind in my hair. Today is a warm spring day which brings with it the aroma of blossoming flowers. There's no one here but me and Ireland as I ride her into the forest and circle back round towards the house. Before taking a trot back, I take in the immense size of the house. Unless something drastic happens, I will be living there very soon. I sigh knowing that a lot of women would give their right arms to live in a house like that.

As I near the stables, I notice Drake is standing by his horse like he's waiting for me. It's been another three weeks since that incident at the bar and the subsequent outburst from him.

I hadn't seen him since.

We'd exchanged text messages, and I could tell his men were following me. Like this morning when I went out for a walk, Kane was snooping, but wasn't doing a very good job of it. I caught him and we got to talking.

"Kane told me you were here."

He looks good again today, and I hate the fact that he does. I was happy staying mad at him for three weeks. Happy that—for a little while—I was able to breathe without this constant pull I get from him weighing me down. Now that he's here, looking every bit the strong, brooding male I have come to love and hate in equal measure, however, I find myself drawn to him like a moth to a flame.

"I caught him following me, so I asked him to bring me here so I could see Ireland. It's been a while."

"How is she?"

Leaning over, I lovingly stroke her neck. "She's doing great."

"Ride with me?"

Biting my lip, I want to say no, but my body calls out to him. "I want to, but I'm a little tired. Can I ride with you on Max?"

He looks taken aback by my request, but nods his head. "Come on. I'll help you with Ireland, and then you can help me with Max." He offers me his hand, and I take it. Pretty soon, he has me off the horse and in his arms.

Our eyes lock as I slide down, and for a moment, we can't move or breathe. He searches my face with those luscious brown eyes of his, and it hits me right between my legs. My belly dances and my cheeks flame as he draws me in, little by little, bit by bit.

"You know it's there; you feel it. Yet, you continue to defy me."

"You've been gone again," I reply breathlessly.

"I can tell you want me to kiss you, but I can't. If I do, I won't hesitate in taking you up to my bedroom and finally making you mine. I made a promise, and so far, I've kept it, but I only have so much control. Why do you think I've been away? It's not because I want to stay away from you. It's because I can't control myself around you."

I still, shocked at the vulnerability of his words. Does he say I make him weak? "What is it about you?" I wonder out loud.

Drake silently laughs. "I'm not sure what that's supposed to mean."

"You're like Jekyll and Hyde," I observe. "You can be nice and gentle one moment, but then mean and nasty the next."

Pulling away from me, he grabs Ireland's reins and clicks his tongue for her to move. I guess that's the end of the discussion then.

In silence, we put Ireland back and proceed to get Max ready for his ride. Once Drake is on, he motions for my hand and pulls me up. I snake my legs around him, and then wrap my arms around his waist—equally hating and loving how good he feels.

He sucks in a breath. "Ready?"

Placing my chin on his right shoulder, I nod. "Ready."

"Come on, boy," Drake urges and Max suddenly flies into action. In an instant, we're galloping through the fields again, but this time I can close my eyes and relish the sensation. With one sense shut down, my other two kick into gear. I can smell the spring air, listen to the birds sing, and I can feel the warmth of Drake's body on mine. For a brief moment, I wonder what it would be like to wake up like this with him, feeling the heat from his back pressed into my breasts. But then, all too soon, I realise that it's not something I have a choice in. It's not something I have been asked. It's something that will be forced upon me whether I like it or not. And now, as with every other time, I feel the urge to run rather than to embrace. I don't want to be a prisoner. At times, like today, I wonder how he can seem so normal. He's not, though. I see what lies within him. I know it's there, waiting to get out.

It's just a matter of time.

After half an hour of riding, we eventually head back home and put Max back into his booth. As we do, a man I have never seen before approaches Drake. "Sir, Mr Stewart is on the line. Do you want to take it?" He holds out the phone, and Drake eagerly takes it from him before turning to me.

"I need to take this, but I'll be right back."

I nod my head and off he goes. I start taking the reins off Max, but notice in the corner of my eye that the guy who approached us hasn't moved. When I look at him, he's casually leaning on the wall observing me with a cocky smile on his face.

Frowning, I wonder whether to say something, but decide against it and carry on doing what I'm doing. "So, you're what all the fuss is about."

I immediately stop and stare back at him. "What is that supposed to mean?"

"You're Drake's girl."

I want to argue that I'm not, but something tells me not to. "So?" I ask, placing the reins on their hanger. I then take his saddle off and bend down to place it on the floor.

"You're even prettier than I imagined ... and that arse ... fuck me."

Snapping my posture up, I turn to the arrogant twat. "Who the hell are you?"

Pushing himself off the wall, his cocky grin disappears as he offers me his hand. "I'm Joe. The newbie."

I don't accept his offer. Instead, I stand with my hand on my hip and stare at him. This just makes that cocky grin come back again. "Okay, Joe ... the newbie, I think you need to learn some boundaries. I doubt Drake would like it if he knew you were talking to me like this."

I observe him as he shrugs his shoulders. I can't tell whether he's overly confident or just too stupid for his own good. He's young—not that much older than I am—with a good four inches in height over me, dark blond, spiky hair and blue eyes. He's attractive in a sense, but he does nothing for me in particular. In fact, his eyes tell a sinister tale which I do not want to explore.

"Maybe I like pushing boundaries. Have you ever thought about that?"

I snort. "Well, that's painfully obvious, considering you're the first guy working here who's dared to talk to me like that."

Not caring for my words, he stalks towards me until we're only a couple of feet apart. "They might not say it to your face, but believe me when I say that they all think it. They're just too chicken shit to voice it out loud."

"How old are you?"

"Twenty," he says, waggling his eyebrows. "Why? Do you dig me?"

Huffing, I move away from him and start walking out of the stables. "You're full of shit," I mutter under my breath.

I'm sure he's about to retort, but as we venture outside, Drake is stalking towards us. He notices that we've just come out of the stables together and his face turns to thunder. "Can I help you, Joe?" he asks vehemently.

"No, sir. I was just asking Miss Montgomery if she needed my help."

I feel like laughing again, but instead walk up to Drake and place my hand in his. "Are you finished, baby?" Drake frowns at my *baby* comment, but little does he know I'm doing it deliberately in front of this jerk-off who's now smirking at me.

"Yes, all done. I'll take you home now."

I don't want to go home. Lately, home is an ugly place with two equally ugly people living in it. I don't condone people hating their parents as a rule, but if they had ones like mine, I think I could make an exception.

But, not wanting to argue with Drake in front of this arsehole, I nod my head. "Okay, you can take me home now."

CHAPTER EIGHT

Age Fourteen

I heard Drake and my parents arguing a couple of days ago, and things have been tense ever since. I'm not sure what it was about, but I certainly heard my name being mentioned once or twice. I hate the fact that they may be arguing over me.

Also, lately, my parents have been acting really weird. They've been fussing about my hair, makeup, what dresses I should wear—you name it. The other times, they ignore me like I'm not even there. I don't like it when they fuss, though. That's definitely worse than being ignored. I'm not sure why, but there's something rather... disturbing about their behaviour.

Today is a good day. Today, I'm being ignored and it feels like I can have some breathing space. I'm in my bedroom, getting ready for a day out shopping with my new friend, Mandy. I'll be fifteen soon and want to get a new outfit for my birthday party round Drake's house. He's been such a good friend to me. I would even say he's fast becoming the father I never had. Although, for some reason, I don't like to think of him in that way.

Feeling thirsty, I decide to go downstairs to the kitchen to get a drink. *My mother is out at her yoga class, but my father is here, conducting business as usual.*

As I get down to the bottom of the stairs, I start to walk past his study when I hear my name being mentioned.

"Evelyn's almost fifteen. She's beautiful ... and highly popular." I frown, but then smile at my father's compliment of me. That's the first time I've heard him refer to me as beautiful.

"We can discuss finances when you get here," he says, making me frown again. "When are you next in town?" It goes silent for a moment before he speaks again. "I know there's a couple of others who are definitely interested, but I'll see what I can do. In this day and age, you have to strike whilst the iron's hot." He starts laughing, and all I can think about is what in the hell is he on about?

"Okay, I'll set it up and get her ready by then. See you Tuesday. Bye, Isaac."

Frowning, I hear the phone click and rush away before my father catches me. While I'm in the kitchen getting some water, all I can think about is that phone call, how strange it was, and who the hell Isaac is. In fact, his name sounds all too familiar.

Shivers run down my spine when I think of that evil-looking guy at my house a year or so ago. Could it be him? Drake knows him, and I remember him telling me to tell him if I saw him again. Technically, this isn't the same, but I have to ask.

Rushing back up the stairs with my bottle of water, I grab my phone off my bedside and text Drake.

Me: This guy you told me to tell you about. His name's not Isaac, is it?

My phone immediately rings. It's Drake. I'm about to say hello, but he beats me to it. "Is he there?" He sounds really angry.

"No, but I heard my father on the phone. I think they were

discussing me."

I hear a loud crash, and I'm about to ask if he's okay when he speaks. "Tell me everything, Evelyn. The whole conversation you heard."

I tell him all that I heard being discussed, and when I'm finished, Drake immediately says, "Don't go anywhere. I'll be there in ten minutes. Just stay in your room until I come for you. Okay?"

"Okay," I answer a little shakily. For some reason, his reaction is scaring me. Who is this Isaac and what does he want?

The line goes dead, and I sit, waiting and wondering what's going to happen. I'm supposed to be meeting Mandy in an hour. Getting up, I start pacing the floor, wondering what's going to happen once Drake gets here. After a few more minutes, I hear the thunderous wrapping on the door and then my father answering. The shouting gets louder as they talk, but pretty soon, it fades away. They must have moved into my father's study.

At first, I sit there, waiting for when Drake will arrive, but then curiosity seems to get the better of me. Step by step, I wander over to the door, open it a little, and creep through. Whatever argument they were having seems to have died down, but I can still hear voices. Once I reach the bottom of the stairs, I take tentative steps towards my father's study, so I can hear them better.

"I don't want to hear any more of this, William."

"Of course not, sir," my father answers. "You've made me a very happy man. I'm sure Charlotte will be thrilled when she hears the news. You've very generously brought us out of a rather messy situation."

Wondering what they're talking about, I lean in further and notice that the door isn't completely shut. It opens slightly, making me gasp. I close my eyes, thinking they'd heard me, but when I open them again, all I can see is Drake leaning over my father's desk, writing something. After a few seconds, he rips out a piece of paper—which looks like a cheque—and hands it to him. "This is first of two instalments. I want you to keep Evelyn here and away from prying eyes. Do you fucking understand me?"

"Of course." I can hear the slight tremble in my father's voice.

"Once she turns eighteen, you can have the other half, and I will be taking her into my care. I'm offering you a very generous deal here, William. She's a fucking child at the moment. Don't ever forget that."

Gripping my shirt tight to my chest, I feel like I want to hyperventilate. I want to run away, but I just can't seem to move my feet.

"I know, Mr Salvatore. We'll do our best by her, you can be assured of that."

"Now that I've paid this down payment on Evelyn, I will assure she is also kept safe and secure in my care. I will pay for anything she needs and will provide for her in any way I can. Do you understand that?"

Down payment? How is this possible? They're talking about me as if I'm an object. Something to own.

I hear my father's chair push back, and I see when he offers Drake his hand. "I do understand. It was a pleasure doing business with you. I'm sure Evelyn will be very happy with you."

Drake shakes his hand back. "On her eighteenth birthday, she's mine." His tone makes me shiver.

"That goes without saying."

I can't listen anymore. In a panic, I turn—not caring if I've made too much noise—and go running out of my house. Once outside, I see a couple of Drake's men milling around the car and they see me. At first, they're not sure what's happening, but I don't wait around long enough to find out what they do about it. Instead, I turn to the side of my house and go running for the hills. I don't care where I go. I just want to be far away from my house ... far away from my father ... far away from Drake.

All these years, I thought I really knew him. I thought he really cared when all he was interested in was what? Owning me? Possessing me like a doll bought in a toy store? For some reason, this betrayal hurts more than the fact that my own parents want to get rid of me.

Feeling sick and disgusted, I keep on running. Tears are streaming down my face, and I'm finding it hard to breathe, but I keep going.

In the distance, I hear my name being called, but I ignore that too and keep going. Yesterday if he had called me, I would have gone running to him. Now, all I want to do is run away. I want to get as far away from that sick man as possible.

"Evelyn, stop running!" he shouts, but again, I ignore him. I don't even turn to see where he is. I just keep running as fast as I can.

Once I reach the trees, I run in amongst them, hoping that they'll camouflage me somehow, but it's no use. I hear Drake calling my name again, but this time it sounds as though he's right behind me.

Again, I don't look. I keep on going for a few more seconds until I feel a hand grip my wrist and spin me around. "Will you stop when I tell you to?"

We're both breathless as I lean up against the tree for support. "How— How could you? I thought I could trust you."

He suddenly looks annoyed. "You **can** trust me."

"So what was that about with my father? You just put a down payment on me like I'm some … some hooker."

Drake smacks his hand against the tree by my head, making me jump. "Don't call yourself that."

"Well, that's how you made me feel. Did my ears deceive me? Was what I heard really true? Are you buying me once I turn eighteen?"

Still catching his breath, Drake drops his head down for a moment before looking back up to meet my eyes. "Yes."

My eyes widen and then the anger sets in. "Well, I refuse to be … to be owned like that."

Drake smiles, but it's not a nice smile. It's one I've not seen before on him. One I don't like. "You don't have any say in the matter. Once you turn eighteen, you'll be living with me."

Not being able to take in what I'm hearing, I try moving out of the way. "You can't tell me what to do."

Drake grabs my arm, pulling me back to the tree trunk. "Yes, I can. And I will."

"Why are you doing this?"

Leaning closer to me, Drake snarls, "Because I want you. Plain and simple. And when Drake Salvatore wants something, he gets it. You're just going to have to get used it, sweetheart."

A lone tear drops down my face. I don't know who this man is all of a sudden. What happened to the Drake who was sweet to me, made me laugh, and bought me a horse for crying out loud?! I thought he genuinely cared, but all he was doing was … grooming *me?*

Ugh! Suddenly, I feel sick. I feel abused and I feel betrayed. I was starting to love the man who I thought loved me in return. I was starting to open up to him in ways I thought I never would with anyone.

"I thought you were a nice man. I thought you cared about me and that you loved me, but you were just waiting ... biding your time."

"I do love and care for you."

"Well, you have a funny way of showing it!" I shout.

"Keep your fucking voice down," he snarls. Immediately, I still. This is definitely a new side to him, and I don't like it.

"This is an arrangement you're simply going to have to get used to. Wouldn't you rather it be me than someone else?"

"Is that how you justify what you just did in there? You treated my life and my future like a transaction ... like I'm property."

"You are property. **My** property."

"I hate you."

I go to move again, but he holds me in place. "Things are going to be different around here from now on. I'm going to be around whether you like it or not. You're simply going to have to shut up and start doing as you're damn well told. Do you understand me?!"

Yeah, I understand. I understand perfectly.

CHAPTER NINE

Age Sixteen

"Roman, stop it," Mandy says, giggling her drunk arse off as he tickles her and snuggles his head into her neck.

"I can't help it, baby. You smell and feel so good."

She giggles again, slapping his hand away. Eddie passes me a drink. "Thanks," I say, taking a swig of the brandy and letting the burn pierce my throat.

An hour ago, I snuck out of my room when I got a call from Mandy. She, Roman, and Eddie wanted to go hang out at the park, and because I think Eddie is cute, I said yes. I also said yes to stick the knife into Drake. I don't want him to find out what I'm doing by any means, but I certainly love knowing that I am doing what I want without his knowledge.

"Are you coming to the party on Saturday?" Eddie asks as I hand him back the drink.

I screw up my face in distaste and shake my head. "Can't. My parents are having a party that night, and I've been told I have to attend."

"Ooh! Is Drake going?" Mandy asks with a huge smile.

I huff. "What do you think? He's always the guest of honour." Lately, my parents have been having lots of these gatherings where I'm made to dress up and am paraded around like some sort of object on display. Every time, Drake is there, staring at me like he's waiting for something, and every time, I want his stares to give me the creeps. Unfortunately, they elicit another emotion—an all too unwelcome one. For a while now, I've been looking at Drake in a completely different light. It's almost as if he's coaxing it out of me day by day. When I see him, I want him, but then I remember the deal he struck with my parents two years ago, and it makes me mad all over again. And then there are the times when I don't hear from him for days and I miss him. I hate the fact that I miss him. I also hate the fact that I keep dreaming of kissing Drake while he runs his hands all over my body. I always wake up at the point where we get undressed and are about to have sex. It's frustrating as hell.

"And why wouldn't he be? He's hot as fuck!"

"Hey!" Roman wines, pulling her into him.

She laughs. "You know he doesn't hold a candle to you." She turns her head towards me and mouths, "He does."

"That's good then," Roman says as I start laughing.

Eddie wraps an arm around me and pulls me closer to him. There's a chill in the air, so his warm arms are welcome. Mandy notices, and although she's smiling, I can see the warning behind her eyes. I know what she's telling me. My relationship with Drake might be secret for now because of my age, but that doesn't mean I don't belong to him. This is partly the reason why I'm here, letting Eddie place his arms around me. I would also let Eddie kiss me if he tried. I know it's naughty, but I can't help the little imp in me that sticks it to Drake whenever I get the chance. Mandy knows this, and that's the reason why I'm getting "the look."

"Don't hog all the drink," Roman complains, holding his hand out. Eddie laughs, but hands the drink over to him.

"Fuck, I feel drunk." Mandy starts laughing and everyone follows suit. I'm feeling rather drunk myself. Not so much that I don't know what I'm doing, but certainly enough to feel slightly unsteady and woozy.

"Six more months and school will be over."

I groan. "I can't wait."

"Ugh, me neither," Mandy complains. "That new geography teacher's driving me crazy. She's worse than Mr Trimble, and that's saying something." She gasps. "Did you hear about Mrs Martin?"

"No," we all say in unison.

She smiles mischievously and leans forward. "Well, I heard from Bethany, who heard it from Lucy, that she caught her in Mr Tomkins' office kissing Mr Flaherty. And it wasn't just a peck either. It was full-blown tongues, and their hands were all over each other."

"Really?" I screech.

"Yeah. She had her skirt up and everything. I reckon they were going to fuck if they hadn't been caught. It's a pity Lucy didn't get a video of it. Can you imagine?"

Roman hands me the drink, so I take another swig. "The gossip is the only bit of fun we ever have at school."

"Don't you know it?!" Mandy agrees.

I feel Eddie tugging me. "Hey, do you fancy going to the cinema tomorrow? That new Tom Cruise film is out."

"Ooh! I love Tom Cruise," Mandy says.

I look up to Eddie's eyes and smile. I would love to say yes, but a part of me knows that Drake would know about it and straight away put a stop to it. But, in my drunk-filled haze all I can think about is rebelling against him as much as possible. Maybe if I snuck around—wore a hat or something—then I could do it.

"Okay," I find myself saying without thinking too much. "What time do you want to meet, and where?"

Eddie rewards me with a big, beaming smile. "How about I come pick you up at two?"

Biting my lip, I look across at Mandy. She glares at me, and I know the reason why. I look back to Eddie. "You can't come to the house."

He frowns. "Why not?"

"Because my parents don't like boys calling for me."

Eddie laughs a little. "But you're sixteen. You can leave home if you really wanted."

I sigh. "I know, but until I finish school, that's the way that it is." It's partly true, but only because Drake makes it that way. The only lie is about the school thing. I'm not allowed to date. Period. I should imagine even when I turn eighteen I won't be dating. Not unless Drake decides to. It makes me wonder if he would ever take me on one if I asked.

I shake my head clear of that errant thought. Why on earth am I thinking about Drake dating me? I'm trying to run away from him—not toward him.

"So, would you prefer that I meet you at the cinema then?"

I nod my head. "That would be better."

I notice Mandy's looking at me as if to ask, "How on earth are you going to pull that off?" All I do is smile at her and give her a cheeky wink. She smirks back, shaking her head. "Rather you than me," she mutters under her breath.

"What's that?" Roman asks, tugging at Mandy.

"I said … give me some of that brandy." I start laughing, but hand her the drink.

Afterwards, Eddie pulls me in and snuggles his nose in my hair. "You smell so fucking incredible." I feel him nibbling on my ear and it starts me off giggling.

"Get a room," Roman complains.

"You can talk," Eddie jibes back.

We're immediately silenced by a set of car lights moving towards us from the park's entrance. Panicked, Mandy looks at me, and I immediately pull myself away from Eddie. I don't know who it is that's coming, but I have a fair idea.

"Do you think it's the fuzz?"

I see when the tell-tale Rolls Royce grills come into view, and I know for a fact it's him. "No, that's not the fuzz. In fact, it's worse than the fuzz."

"Who is it then?" Eddie squints his eyes and leans forward to try and get a better view.

"It's Drake," Mandy answers.

Eddie looks confused. "Drake? You mean Drake Salvatore? What would he be doing here?"

I already know, but I don't have time to answer him because the car is right beside us in no time, and the big Drake Salvatore gets out. I can tell already—even in the dark—that he's unimpressed.

With a stern look, he takes in the scene. We're sitting on a park bench together. Eddie and I are on one side, and Mandy and Roman are on the other. From anyone on the outside looking in, it would look like two couples hanging out. I doubt very much Drake will think any differently either. A part of me relishes the idea that he's caught me, but another part is scared of what the consequences might be.

Two of his men get out of the car and just stand by the door, looking menacing. I'm guessing it's deliberate as Drake has to have a presence no matter what. Looking at him alone is scary enough, but I'm familiar with Drake. Roman and Eddie, on the other hand, aren't. The same as everyone else, they only hear of the whispered rumours about the great Drake Salvatore. The feared one ... the one you don't cross. Unless of course you don't value your life.

As he stares across at me, sitting comfortably beside Eddie, his eyes narrow, and I can't help but feel that heat he always manages to entice out of me. He looks positively sexy in his crisp grey suit and long dark coat. He oozes sex appeal, and I hate him for it.

"What do we have here?" he finally asks.

"We were just hanging out." I smile at him, but it's not a nice smile. It's deliberate. From the way he glares back at me, I can tell he's not impressed.

"Evelyn, Mandy, get in the car. I want to have a word with these two young lads."

My heart starts thundering as I look across at Mandy. She makes the first move, and I follow after. I just hope Eddie doesn't say too much. As I walk to the car, I look back briefly and smile at Eddie. "Bye," I simply say before getting in the car. Eddie doesn't say anything back. I think he's too confused and worried to say anything.

Once in the car, Mandy tugs my arm. "What do you think he's going to say?" She looks worried.

I scoot over to the passenger side and press the button to try and hear what Drake's saying. "I'm going to try and listen," I whisper as I practically lean my head out of the window.

It's a little muffled at first, but I hear Eddie talking. "We were just hanging out and sharing a drink."

"But you're underage, and so are the girls. They should be at home in bed, not here with you." He then slowly walks up to Eddie, deliberately pointing at him. "What interest do you have in Evelyn?"

I notice Eddie's eyes widen slightly, and it makes me swallow. I just hope he doesn't say anything stupid.

"We're just friends," he says, making me breathe a sigh of relief.

"So your only interest in her is purely a platonic one? Be honest, little boy. I can tell when someone's lying."

Oh my God, Eddie looks like he's going to pee himself. I notice his Adam's apple bobble up and down before looking across at Roman briefly. "Your friend's not going to answer for you," Drake probes.

"Erm—" Eddie starts.

"Spit it out, boy."

"I find her attractive..." he stutters.

"Yes?"

Eddie's eyes start darting to me and then back to Drake. "I–I was hoping to date her?" The way he said it was almost like a question.

"That's not going to happen." I sigh, feeling pissed off, but still a little scared for Eddie. He's done nothing wrong except for liking a girl.

Eddie's expression is a cross between confusion and a frown. "It's not?"

"No. Evelyn is off limits. Do you hear me?" he slightly raises his voice, causing both to automatically nod their heads.

"Yes, sir," Eddie answers, looking scared to death.

"Good. Now, get yourselves home to bed. I'm sure your parents would prefer you wrapped up in bed instead of out here in the dark."

"Yes, sir."

As I watch them get off the table, a part of me sags my shoulders in relief, but the other part of me is really pissed off. Now that Drake has done this, I've no doubt it will get spread around school, and people will start treating me like a pariah. Slinking back into my seat, I sigh and close my eyes.

"I'll be taking that from you," Drake says. I open my eyes and find Roman handing over the brandy to him.

"Just to be sure," Roman says.

"Yes?" Drake answers looking exasperated.

"I'm allowed to date Mandy, right?"

"Did I address you?"

"No," Roman answers.

"Well then, fuck off."

"Yes, sir." They're soon walking hastily toward the exit of the car park. Drake then gets into the front passenger seat, and with a pissed off tone, he tells the driver to get going.

Winding up my window, I look across at Mandy. She looks both shocked and bewildered by what's taken place. I am too, but I'm also quietly brooding. I always knew my life was controlled, but at least— as far as school was concerned—I was just another teenage girl. After that incident, I will now be known as Drake's girl. Someone who you can look at, but by no means touch.

The drive to Mandy's house is quiet, but I'm glad. It allows me time to sit and silently brood. The only time I speak is to say goodbye to Mandy as she gets out of the car and walks to her house.

Once she's inside, Drake gets in, replacing where Mandy was once sitting. He motions to the driver to get going, and soon we're pulling away. He doesn't say anything at first. He just sits there, jaw ticking and his fists clenched. I can tell the anger is pouring off of him.

"What makes you think you can sneak out late at night like that and I wouldn't hear about it?"

"How did you know—"

"How I know is no concern of yours. You sneak out and run to the park with boys and start drinking. Anything could have happened."

"I've known Eddie and Roman for years. They wouldn't do—"

"I don't care to know their fucking names or how safe you think you are with them. They're young boys, and their hormones make them do crazy things. Especially when drunk."

I sigh. "And you would know from experience?"

The jaw ticking starts again. "I just know how they feel at that age and how they act on those feelings."

"I'll be treated like a leper in school now because of this."

Drake picks at a bit of fluff on his shirt and then smoothes it out. "I don't care as long as anything in trousers stays the hell away from you."

"I hate you."

He sighs. "So you keep telling me." He looks out of the window before finally looking at me. "You're fine until you pull a stunt like this and then you get angry at me."

"That's because of the deal you made with my parents. Because, since then, you've been an overbearing, possessive fucking arsehole."

Leaning over, he grabs my chin and pulls me closer to his mouth. His aftershave invades my nostrils, making them flare. I hate that— although obviously angry—he can make me feel this desire that immediately crawls up my spine when he locks me with those deep brown eyes of his.

"Don't you fucking dare speak to me like that."

"Or what?" I ask breathlessly. "What are you going to do to me Drake?"

I find myself eagerly awaiting his answer. I want him to whisper dirty, vile things into my innocent ears. I may be pure. I may be a virgin. But it still doesn't stop me from thinking dirty thoughts. It still doesn't stop me from wondering what it would be like to have Drake press his body against me in this car and fuck my brains out.

"Stop trying to push me, Evelyn. I'm not someone you'd like to push. I'm reining it in because of your age, but there's only so far you can push me."

"I'm sixteen now. I'm legal for a lot of things." There's a lot of innuendo in what I'm saying, but I don't care. I can feel the heat of Drake's breath against my own. Smell the mint and aftershave aroma which hits my nostrils and travels all the way down until it reaches a certain area between my legs. I don't know if it's the alcohol, but right now I don't care.

Drake looks down towards my lips making the heat between my legs rage worse than ever. He then looks up into my eyes like he's searching for something. "You're drunk."

"Yes," I admit. Gone are any thoughts of Eddie and what Drake did. All I can think about now—being so close to the sexiest man on earth—is how much I want him to kiss me.

"Your reaction to me is always strong, but this time it's amplified."

I smirk. "I guess brandy makes me randy." I start giggling, and Drake pulls away, turning his head towards the window. He's hiding his face, but I saw the little smirk he had before he turned. He wasn't quick enough to hide that from me.

"Don't you ever think about touching me?" Unfortunately, I think about touching him all the time.

Drake snaps his head towards me. "I try extremely hard not to."

His confession makes me think of something. "Do you touch other women?" I hate that it sends a pang to my stomach just thinking about it. A part of me doesn't want to know. Despite the fact that I don't want Drake forcing his rules on me, I can't stand the thought of him with another woman. What that means, I have no idea. But the ugly green-eyed monster rears its head in a quiet, jealous rage whenever I think about it.

"Would the thought of me doing so displease you?"

He watches me with interest. I know he's eagerly awaiting my answer. Instead, I turn my head away and let the lie leave my lips. "No. It shouldn't matter to me what you get up to. It just makes me pissed to think that I can't touch other boys, and yet you get free rein."

Drake grabs a hold of my chin again, but instead gently pulls it to meet him. "Number one, don't ever mention other boys touching you again. And number two, I know for a fact that you're lying. I can see it in your eyes and the way your body reacts at the thought of it. I've known you long enough to know a lie when I see it. You can't stand the thought of me touching another woman."

"Why did you buy me from my parents?" I ask, shocking him.

He immediately lets go and sits back. "I already told you. I want you, and what I want, I get. Two more years, and you will be mine."

How quickly my yearning for him can turn to hatred. "That's also a lie and you know it. If I were free, I would be sitting in the park now with my friends instead of being dragged back home by... What are you to me, anyway?"

"I am your man."

I start laughing. "So, you're my boyfriend now? Sorry, I don't remember you taking me out on any dates before asking me the question."

Drake surprisingly smiles. "So you want me to ask you out on a date?"

I shake my head. "That's not what I said. I'm trying to explain to you that you tell me I'm free for two years on one hand, but I'm not, am I? I'm already yours before I even turn eighteen. You treat me like your property."

Drake sighs. "I don't know how many times we're going to go over this."

"I'm never going to quit fighting you, Drake. Just you know that."

Drake laughs sarcastically. "I already know how much of a stubborn little thing you are. You're going to be quite a challenge, but I will look forward to breaking you."

"What is that supposed to mean?"

"You'll find out one day."

I want to bite back. I want to scream and shout at the injustice of it all. Who does he think he is? "I should be able to choose how to live my own life."

"Your life is with me. It's as simple as that."

"And in the meantime, you get to live yours, having sex with women while I sit at home, waiting until I turn eighteen. Is that it?" Drake smirks, and I know why. He knows I'm still fishing.

He doesn't answer me. Instead, he chooses to turn his head toward the window, effectively cutting off our conversation.

Gritting my teeth, I sigh before looking out of the window myself. I hate that he winds me up so much that I bite. I hate that I always end up feeling that he wins every fight we have. He always ends up having the upper hand. He knows it, and he also knows that I know he knows it.

Another few minutes go by, and soon we're pulling into my parents drive. Drake immediately gets out and proceeds to my side before opening my door. He offers me his hand, but I ignore it getting out. He just smirks at my stubbornness.

Once we reach my door, Drake pulls me to him and plants a kiss to my forehead. I close my eyes at his touch and again berate myself for doing so.

"Make sure you drink plenty of water before bed. You'll most probably have a hangover tomorrow. I'll call in the morning to make sure you're okay."

"Why does it bother you so much whether I'll be hung-over tomorrow or not?"

Drake shakes his head. "You still don't get it, do you? I care about you. I've invested too much not to care."

I huff, getting angry. "Yeah, I must be a real disappointment to your wallet," I reply sarcastically.

Drake smiles. "I wasn't talking about money." With that, he walks away, leaving me both angry, flustered, and bewildered at the same time.

I'm about to turn and go into my house when Drake calls me. I turn, and with a big smile, he says, "Just so you know, I've not touched a single woman since I met you."

He immediately gets into the car, and I'm left standing completely dumbfounded by my door. He doesn't drive away, and it's only when the car slightly revs its engine that I realise Drake is waiting for me to get into the house before he leaves. He'll never drive off until he knows I'm safely inside my house.

So, I turn, placing the key in the lock and walk into my house. As I quietly close the door and wander up the stairs towards my bedroom, I realise something that both annoys and confuses me.

I'm smiling.

CHAPTER TEN

Two Weeks until Eighteenth Birthday – Present Day

My parents are having another party tonight. They always seem to be having parties. I know I am a burden to them, but what they fail to realise is that if it wasn't for me, they wouldn't actually have the money to host all these lavish functions. Am I resentful? Of course I am. I should be treated like their daughter, not a valuable asset. I know they've already pre-booked their world cruise because I heard them gloating to one of the guests. They leave the day of my eighteenth birthday. They couldn't even wait a day or two.

In the meantime, I'm supposed to smile, sit still, and look pretty. That's my job. I do as I'm told, and I get to hear the odd conversation. Every now and then, they stare at me like I'm an object on display. I am to be silent unless spoken to. Sit unless asked to stand. That is my duty as the daughter of the infamous Montgomery's. Apart from the odd leering from old men, the only person who acknowledges me—who *ever* acknowledges me—is Drake. It's gotten to that stage where I look forward to when he comes, so I can at least have someone to talk to. Unfortunately, he's not here yet, so I have to make do with sitting still and clamping my fingers together for support.

"Evelyn, meet Charles Bellingham. He's the CEO for Channel Six." My mother raises one tiny eyebrow at me like I should be impressed. I'm not impressed. Only my parents are impressed by this narcissistic show they like to put on every couple of weeks.

Putting on my best winning smile, I dutifully stand and hold my hand out to him. Already, he makes my skin crawl. His eyes are predatory and too big for his head. He's bald, looks to be in his late forties, and has a slight beer belly.

"Evelyn," he almost whispers, curving up one side of his mouth. I force down the urge to shudder when he takes my hand and kisses it. My hand instantly feels dirty.

"She's almost finished school and wants to be a psychologist."

"Really?" he asks, looking at me with a smirk. "Can you tell what's on my mind right now?"

I almost screw my face up in disgust, but my mother's cackling stops me. "Oh, Charles, you are such the outrageous flirt."

I try taking my hand away from him, but he grips it tightly. "Well, I did try to woo you, but unfortunately, you are married to another."

My mother blushes and cackles again. It's only now I realise how much she sounds like a witch when she does it. "You are awful." She lightly places her hand on his shoulder. "But, even though Evelyn is not married, she is promised to another."

He raises his eyebrow. "Is that so? Who is the lucky young gentleman?"

I smile as my mother is about to answer, but she's quickly thwarted by one of her tennis friends virtually screaming at her for attention. That's another thing they love to do here. It's almost like they have to talk over the other because each thinks his or her voice is more important than the other's is.

"Excuse me?" my mother says, leaving to deal with her friend.

I think Charles will leave also, but he doesn't. Instead, he still holds my hand and makes an obvious attempt at showing me just how much he admires the way I look. "How old are you?" He looks down at my breasts when he asks.

"Almost eighteen."

He licks his greasy, slobbery lips. "Hmm. Just ripe for the taking."

I pull my hand away from his grip. "Excuse me," I say, gritting my teeth. This man is disgusting.

"Hold on a moment. I haven't finished with you—"

"Charles, there you are," a woman behind him says. I see the moment his eyes look irritated by this woman's arrival. She lovingly places her small hand on his shoulder and looks at me. "Chatting up the young ladies again, I see." She laughs, extending her hand. "I'm Leyla, Charles' long-suffering wife."

"I'm Evelyn. Nice to meet you." I shake her hand, and she nods her head at me. She then turns to Charles. "Saul was hoping to have a small word with you about tomorrow. I said I'd come and find you."

Charles sighs. "Okay, where is he?" His tone is anything but eager, but I don't care. All of a sudden, the room feels claustrophobic, and I'm desperate to wash my hands.

Leyla points across the room. "He's over there." She places her hand on his back to motion him forward and turns to me. "Nice to meet you, Evangelica."

"It's Evelyn," I say, but I know it falls on death ears. They're already moving. I take my chance then and leave the room. I quickly head to the bathroom, wash my hands, and walk outside onto the patio for some fresh air. The night is warm, but not sticky. It has a fresh, summery breeze in the air making it feel more comfortable. I take in a deep breath and close my eyes, listening for the sounds of distant crickets. As I stand by the patio doors, I look up toward the stars in the sky, and immediately, I wonder how Drake is doing.

"Do you like the stars?"

I look up to the sky and nod my head. "I do. I think they're beautiful."

"If I could, I would travel the stars in the sky and pick out the biggest, most beautiful star for you."

A huge smile spreads on my face. "You would do that for me?"

I feel when his finger brushes my cheek and I like it. "I would do anything for you, Evelyn."

I smile as I think about the memory from when I was thirteen. Drake was always so sweet and charming back then. How innocent his words of affection were when I was that age. I know differently now.

"I wondered where you had gotten to. I was hoping to finish our little conversation."

Jumping, I turn to the source and find Charles standing way too close for my liking. He's behind me, blowing his hot, vulgar breath on my neck.

"What is there to finish?" I try sounding as aloof as possible when in fact my heart is racing a million miles an hour. I thought things were bad when I was standing in a room packed full of people. But here, I'm alone. Alone and vulnerable.

"When your spotty little boyfriend fucks you, does he make you come? I would put money on the fact that he doesn't. You should try a real man, sweetheart. Someone who's been around long enough to know the game."

This man is vile. How he could even think I would consider sleeping with him is beyond ridiculous.

It's at times like these that I wish I'd brought my phone with me. At least then I could call Drake for help. It pisses me off that I only have him to help me, but I know for a fact he would be pissed at this guy for daring to speak to me like this.

"If you knew who my boyfriend is, you wouldn't dare speak to me like this."

He starts laughing and pulling my hair away from my neck. "I highly doubt that for a second." He then places his mouth on my neck. When I struggle, he grips my arms. "Now, now, come on. This is the sort of thing that happens at parties. Whenever I have one, it's a free-for-all." He starts pulling me around to face him. "Now, turn around and kiss me like a good girl. The more you struggle, the more I'll like it. Just a word of warning." He growls in my ear, and it sets me off struggling more than ever.

"Get off me, you pervert."

He places a hand around my mouth, but I bite him. He starts grunting in my ear. "You fucking little vixen." His hand starts moving down towards my breast, so I struggle even harder.

"Let go of me!" I scream.

He starts to laugh again, but then I feel him being yanked off of me. Turning, I straighten myself out and look toward my saviour. It's Drake. I can't help the huge smile that spreads on my face at his presence. He's not smiling, though. He's absolutely livid as he holds Charles by the scruff of the neck.

"Meet my boyfriend," I say to Charles. I watch as his eyes widen in fear as he looks at Drake. He starts to shake his head.

"If I had known, I would never have—"

Charles has no time to finish that sentence. All too soon, Drake is dragging him out into the garden before starting to punch him over and over again. I hear Charles sob and protest his innocence, but Drake isn't listening.

"You ever go near my fucking girl again, I will not hesitate to cut your hands off. Do you hear me?"

"Yes!" he screams as Drake kicks him. "I promise I won't even look at her. I swear I didn't know. I'm sorry. So, so sorry."

He looks up to where I'm standing, but he's not looking at me. He's looking past me at something or someone. "Get this fucking scumbag off the property before I kill him." I feel someone brush past me and see it's one of Drake's men. He picks him up and starts dragging him around the side of the house. "If I ever see you within a five mile radius of this house, I won't hesitate to end you. Do you hear me?!" he shouts.

"Yes," Charles answers in an almost wail. The man looks pathetic as he hunches over, blood pouring onto his bright white shirt.

As Charles disappears, I turn my head towards Drake and admire the chest-heaving beast before me. His fists are clenched, and his jaw is tight. I can tell he's livid. I can tell he's nowhere near done. For some reason, looking at him right now has a fire raging. I want to run into his arms, straddle him, and kiss that anger out of him.

"Are you okay?" he asks me.

I nod my head, and with a breathless whisper, I answer, "Yes."

He's still standing there, and the urge to go to him is becoming unbearable. He won't move, and I can guess the reason being is because he's still so pent up with rage.

But, like always, I can't help myself when I'm around him. More often than not, I want to run from him, but tonight is having the opposite effect. Tonight, I realise that Drake—as usual—is my saviour. Whether I like it or not, he's always there for me, protecting me the only way he knows how.

So, my body does the thinking for me and moves, gliding towards him effortlessly. Once I reach him, I throw my arms around his waist. He's unmoving at first, and I can feel the anger pouring off of him in waves. But when I snuggle my head into his chest, I feel him wrap his arms around me and kiss the top of my head.

Smiling, I look up to him and see the smirk he returns to me. "To what do I owe the pleasure?"

"Thank you for rescuing me."

He silently laughs under his breath. "Baby, you don't realise this, but I'm protecting you all the time."

I frown. "What is that supposed to mean?"

"Nothing. It's just the type of people your family associates with." I watch as he looks towards the house in disgust, and for some reason, it has an effect on me that I can't comprehend.

Biting my lip, I watch him staring out towards the house. Then, I get a whiff of his scent. I close my eyes and feel when an ache pulses through me. Suddenly, everything about Drake is heightened. The feel of him against me. The touch of his hands around my waist. The smell and look of him are driving me wild. His brown eyes are orbs of fire mesmerising me. I can't seem to take much more.

Pulling his head down towards me, I capture his lips on mine. At first, he's hesitant, but when I moan and slide my tongue into his mouth, he relents. I feel his body go limp against me as our mouths explore one another. Ever since that kiss at the cinema, I have been dreaming about kissing him again and again and again. He's simply addictive.

As we carry on kissing, my desire spikes to new levels. I run my fingers through his hair and grab a fistful, pulling him into me. I hear when he moans against my lips, and something snaps inside of me.

Grabbing his hand, I pull it up towards my breast and try to wrap my leg around his waist. "Drake, please," I beg. I long to be taken. Right now, in this moment, I want him to take me.

I force his hand onto my breast, and at first, he relents, squeezing me. "Take me," I whisper against his lips. "Don't wait two weeks. Take me now."

Suddenly, he pushes me away and stands for a moment, panting. "Fuck me, woman. What's wrong with you? You're going to be the end of me."

"I don't want to be here. Take me home with you now."

He looks me in the eye—all anger gone. Instead, all I can see is the look of pain which crosses his features. "You know I can't do that."

My anger quickly surfaces. "Oh, yes … of course. The contract."

"Don't say it like that."

I frown at him. "How else can I say it? In what way could I possibly say it that makes it any less fucked up than it is? What about free will? What about the fact that since the age of sixteen, I have had the legal right to leave? Why is it that I can't?"

"You can't leave until you're eighteen. Then, you'll be one hundred percent in my care. If I take you before that date, then the contract will be null and void."

"I guess I will have to leave of my own volition then."

Drake stalks towards me and grabs my chin, forcing me to look at him. Gone are the lust, hunger, and pain I saw earlier. He's angry again, but this time, it's aimed at me. "If you do that, I will hunt you down. There is no escaping me. I keep telling you that time and time again, and you never listen. You have your last exams next week. The week after that, you need to prepare. If you even dare disobey me, there will be consequences. I mean it, Evelyn. I don't fuck about. Do I make myself clear?"

I snap my chin away from him and pull away completely. "Crystal." I hate him when he gets like this. One minute, I can't keep my hands away from him, and the next, he says or does something that reminds me of our situation, and it really pisses me off.

"Are you okay?"

Snapping my head back to him, I scowl. "What?"

"That fuckwit, Charles. Did he do anything?"

I sigh, my anger fading once again. "No. You arrived just in the nick of time."

"What did he say to you?"

I shake my head. "I don't think you really want to—"

"What did he say to you?"

"Back in the living room, my mother told him I was taken. He asked who, but my mother was interrupted. Soon after, so was he. I left the room to wash my hands and came out here for some fresh air. He must have noticed that I had left and followed me here. He told me that he bet my spotty teenager couldn't make me come. That's when he started kissing my neck."

His jaw started ticking again. "If you had told him who your boyfriend is, it would have ended then and there."

"I'm sorry, but I didn't have time tell him anything during his groping and slobbery kisses." I raise my voice to him, and he comes towards me.

"I'm sorry. I'm not blaming you. I'm just so fucking angry."

Again, my anger is completely gone, and replaced with it is this need to be near him. "You came to my rescue."

He sweeps my hair away from my eyes, causing me to look up at him. "You called me your boyfriend."

Shaking my head, I pull away, but it's no use. He pulls me closer to him. "Don't get too cocky. It was a slip of the tongue."

"You know you're more to me than that, don't you? You and me we're—"

"Fucked up."

"Hey," he says tugging me to him. "You and I have a special relationship. One that no one can take away."

"Not even me?"

Drake runs his fingers through my hair before grabbing a fistful and making me look into his eyes. "Not even you."

CHAPTER ELEVEN

Age Seventeen … but Not for Long

In two days time, I will turn eighteen, and from midnight on that day, I will belong to the great Drake Salvatore. I feel sick, and I have a desperate need to run. In fact, I have been planning my escape in my head over and over in the last couple of days.

"I think the dress looks beautiful," Mandy coos as she longingly trails her eyes down my white chiffon dress. A dress that denotes innocence and purity. A dress picked out by my parents to please my master.

"It's very long, but it is beautiful. Look how elegant it is, Evelyn. I'm so jealous."

I laugh sarcastically under my breath, but she doesn't notice. Yes, the dress is beautiful. It has sleeves with slits down the sides and is held up elegantly on the shoulders by silver and diamond jewellery. It comes in at the waist and cascades down to the floor. I will be the *belle of the ball* … as my mother calls it.

Tonight, my parents arc having a party in honour of me and Drake, and anybody who's anybody will be there. I am to conduct myself with dignity and grace, but all I want to do is escape. All I want to do is run.

When I don't say anything, Mandy turns and frowns at me. She's about to say something when there's a knock on my door. "Come in," I shout.

The door opens, and in comes Drake with a huge grin on his face. He spots Mandy hovering around the dress. "Good afternoon, Mandy."

Her cheeks instantly blush. She makes it so obvious that she likes him. "Hi, Mr Salvatore. How are you today?"

He sucks in a breath, making his chest expand. Why does he have to look so good? He's wearing a navy button-up shirt today with beige chino trousers. His hair is spiked with gel, and his eyes are sparkling with mischief. I hate to admit it, but he looks good enough to eat.

"I'm doing well today. In fact, I'm on top of the world." He purposefully looks at me when he says this.

Mandy, noticing our exchange, moves a little closer to my door. "Would you two like some privacy?"

At the same time as I say no, Drake says yes. He gives me a frustrated glare, and Mandy looks hesitant. "I don't think you'll want Mandy here for what I have to say."

Feeling defiant, I stand my ground. "Mandy is my friend, and she was here first. It's rude of you to barge in here and expect her to leave."

Drake glances across at Mandy, and she timidly shrugs her shoulders. "Very well," he says walking towards me. Once standing a few inches from me, he kneels down in front of me. "Close your eyes, and give me your hand."

"Why?"

"Just do it, please," he replies through gritted teeth.

Sighing, I close my eyes and give him my right hand. Nothing happens for a moment, but then I feel him tug at my left hand instead. Soon after, I feel him placing a ring on *that* finger. It's Mandy's gasp that makes me snap my eyes open.

I look at Drake first, and he's smiling. Mandy starts clapping. "Oh my God! Oh my God! Evelyn, it's beautiful. Look at it!" she screams. Drake chuckles, obviously glad that he has someone in his corner.

"So, what do you think?"

Bewildered, I look down at the big diamond I have on my finger. It's a single diamond with smaller diamonds surrounding it on either side.

"It's a white gold, eighteen carat diamond ring. Nothing but the best for my girl."

I hear Mandy go, "Aww," and it makes me want to hit her. Maybe making her stay here was a bad idea after all.

"And what is this for?"

Drake looks at me like I've grown two heads. "Your engagement ring of course. I meant to give it to you for your eighteenth, but plans have changed. Now you can show everyone at the party tonight."

Realisation dawns on me. "So, that's why we're having a party?"

"To announce our engagement." Drake stares at me like I'm stupid. It makes my blood boil.

"You haven't done this traditionally, Drake. You've forced this upon me. You haven't asked, and I haven't said yes."

Seeing the anger in my eyes, Drake's frustration rears itself. I see the moment his jaw ticks and he grits his teeth. "Mandy, I would appreciate the privacy now." Although it sounded like a request, it wasn't.

"Sure," she says, quickly scurrying out the door.

The minute he hears the door click, he grips my hand. "I thought we had already discussed this?"

I shake my head. "No. See, that's the thing. We haven't discussed anything. As usual, you're making plans behind my back."

"What is there to discuss? I love you, and we're getting married. It's as simple as that."

I try to get up, but Drake grabs my hips and sits me back down. "You're not going anywhere."

"I'm not wearing this tonight," I spit.

He grips my hips tighter. "Yes, you fucking well are. If you defy me, Evelyn, I *will* punish you."

"And how can you possibly punish me more than you already have?"

Without warning, Drake pulls my hips up, and I land with an undignified huff on the bed. Soon, Drake is in between my legs, and with a hand on my face, he starts stroking my cheek.

Arousal and fear creep up my spine as he tenderly trails his finger down from my cheek to my jaw before placing his hand around my neck. He doesn't squeeze, but he's certainly giving me the idea that he holds the power. As usual, he commands me like a puppet on his not-so-delicate string.

"Tonight," he whispers, pushing my head to the side before kissing my neck, "we will be having our engagement party, and one of the hosts will wear that ring with pride."

"I don't want—"

"Shh," he murmurs, placing a finger to my lips. "You've said enough. Now, it's my turn." He starts kissing me around my neck again, and I can't help the spike of arousal I feel as his warm lips touch my skin. With every glide of his mouth over my neck, the sparks fly, and a want like no other crawls into every pore of me. I don't will it, but my heart races, and with it, my breathing becomes laboured. I know Drake can feel it because he's just as affected. He, too, is breathing heavily. He wants to take this further just as much as I do.

"Two more days," he says breathlessly. "Two more days, and I'll get to see you bare, feel skin on skin. I know you want it just as much as I do, Evelyn. Stop denying what your body obviously wants. I can feel you tremble beneath me. I can feel your heart beating just as wildly as mine. You want me to take you. You want me to caress you. You want me to *fuck* you." He emphasises the word "fuck," and I can't help what that does to my insides. I don't mean to, but the sound of that word on his lips makes me moan with want. What makes it even worse is the fact that I can feel his hardness digging into me. He wants me, and knowing this makes my own arousal spike that much higher. I hate him, though. I hate what he's doing to me, and I hate what he's making me do against my will. Maybe if he was nice about it, I would love him like he wants me to. But he's not asking for my love.

He's trying to force it.

"I'm not wearing the ring." The trembling in my voice betrays me.

His fiery kisses stop as he pulls his head from my neck. With a tug of my chin, he makes me look at him. "This isn't a request. If you do not comply, then I shall have to take matters into my own hands."

"What does that mean? What could you possibly do?"

Without a beat, he sighs and with a matter-of-fact voice says, "I had guests around my house a few days ago. I showed them our stables. They were most taken with Ireland."

My eyes widen. "You wouldn't."

He frowns. "Wouldn't what? Sell her? They are offering a very good price."

"You're lying."

"Do you want to bet on that, *darling*?"

Feeling my face flush with anger, I try pushing him, but it's useless. "You're a hateful, spiteful, despicable man."

"Is that a yes then?" he asks with a smirk.

"I hate you."

"I love you. Now, if you want me to be a gentleman and ask you, then I will. But if I don't like the answer, I'm afraid I will be making a certain phone call today."

I can feel the tears prick my eyes, but force them down. He knows how much I love and care for Ireland. "Did you buy her deliberately so that you could use her against me like this?" When he doesn't answer, realisation dawns on me. "You did, didn't you?"

Ignoring me, Drake gets off, pulling me up and positioning himself between my legs. "Now," he says, grabbing my left hand. "I'm going to ask you two questions, and the answer better be yes to both."

I feel like crying, but I stop any tears from falling. I'm not going to let him see that he's winning. He has me and he knows he has me. He knows I would do anything and give anything to keep Ireland ... even if it means selling myself to him.

As he looks me in the eye, I try to take steady, even breaths. I'm so angry with him ... so pent up with rage. He wants me to agree to marry him, but all I want to do is scratch his eyes out.

"Evelyn," he finally says, holding my attention, "will you marry me?"

Through gritted teeth, I say, "Yes."

His face lights up with a breathtaking smile. For a moment, I feel lost in that smile, but it quickly fades when he asks me the next question.

"And will you wear your ring tonight to show everyone that we're engaged and that you're mine and mine alone?"

I take in another deep breath before answering him. "Yes."

"Good." He places my hand down and pulls me in for a kiss. It's not a tender kiss. It's a forceful, no holds barred kiss. With anger and resentment building in my veins, I kiss him back. But, the more I kiss him, the more intense and passionate it becomes. The anger and rage feed into passion and longing.

Without thinking, I start tugging at his shirt, pulling it out from inside his trousers. Heat pulses through me as Drake trails his hand up my leg before resting on my thigh. He squeezes gently, making me moan with desire. I feel frenzied. I feel wanton. I feel suddenly alive with fire.

"Fuck me," I demand as I try pulling his shirt over his head.

It's then I feel a douse of cold water over my head as Drake pushes me away and stands—all six-foot-seven of him and an erection so tall a male porn star would be proud of.

With hooded eyes and uneven breaths, I stare at his flustered state. He is as breathless as I am as he tries hard to compose himself. "Fuck. What are you trying to do to me?"

With a sultry smile, I cock my head. "I need you to fuck me. Isn't that what you want me to say?" I go the extra mile by placing my hands behind me on the bed and opening my legs wide for him.

Drake growls and looks at me with a heated, but angry stare.

"Evelyn, stop this right now. If you keep pushing this, then I will snap. And believe me, I won't be gentle. I've waited too fucking long for you already." When I don't move, he sucks in a breath. "I mean it."

His command snaps me out of it. I dutifully close my legs, and I notice the slight relief on Drake's face. He bends down, grabbing my face. "I'm going to ask you one question, and you'd better listen to it carefully: Do you know what happens when you rattle an animal's cage for years and then suddenly let him out?" My eyes widen a little, making him smile. "Just think about that every time you pull a stunt like this." Getting up, he straightens himself and his shirt before moving towards the door. "Just remember what I said, Evelyn. That ring stays on your finger tonight no matter what. In thirty-four hours, you will be mine."

He leaves after that, looking every bit the pissed off, controlling alpha male I've come to know these past three years. Not long after that, Mandy rushes in and sits beside me.

"Wow, you two look positively fucked. What on earth happened in here?"

What on earth did happen in here?

Mandy's words drill deeper and deeper into my brain, making the fear, anger, and anxiety crawl back up. To make matters worse, she picks my left hand up and inspects my ring. "Oh my God, it's beautiful. You're such a lucky fucking bitch. I would give anything to have Drake plaster a ring on my finger like that. I hate you."

She places my hand down, and I know I should answer her, but I can't. All I can do is stare into space and wonder how the fuck I can possibly get out of this. I guess it boils down to one thing. Tonight, I will go to this party. I will show everyone the ring and be the diligent, obedient guest. Then, in the dead of night tonight when everyone is in a drunken sleep, I will escape.

Only thirty-three hours, fifty-two minutes, and twenty-six seconds left.

CHAPTER TWELVE

Age Sixteen

It's my sixteenth birthday today, but I don't feel like celebrating. My parents have had my hair straightened, my eyebrows plucked, my face painted, and my body dressed in a delicate peach dress. It's a beautiful dress that is supposed to make me feel beautiful. I don't feel beautiful. I feel put on display for the world to see. I feel like a freak show with the number one guest being the great Drake Salvatore.

For the past year, Drake has slowly but surely shown me the monster that lives inside of him. Sure, I do get moments of his sweet nature with his great, dazzling smile to go with his equally dazzling eyes. I hate to admit it, but for the past few months, I have also been adapting to new feelings that I have for Drake. Sure, hatred is one since he paid to put a down payment on me a year ago, but there's also been something else. Something needy and heated ... primal even. To me, he's unfortunately starting to look more and more appealing. I want to violently quash these feelings. But, it seems like the more I try, the more I fail to ignore the obvious pull he has for me. Sure, he looks after me. I never want for anything. He also makes my parents treat me somewhat civilly, which I must admit I'm grateful for.

I just stumble over one word every day that makes my hatred for Drake grow.

Choice.

I should have a choice, but that option has been stripped from me. In my own mind, I'm choosing to want Drake more than I should, but in another sense, I can't help thinking he's somehow forcing me to want him. Maybe he's just a great magician.

"I saw this and thought of you." Pushing a small, wrapped gift my way, Drake smiles. I notice the light in my parents' eyes when they see it. It looks an awful lot like a small jewellery box.

"Oh my. Is this what I think it is?" My mother gushes, making my eyes widen. He hasn't … has he? I've only just turned sixteen.

"Not quite," Drake says, making me sigh with relief. "But close."

My eyes snap to Drake, and he urges me to open the gift. I do as expected of me, and when I open it up, my eyes widen again. A beautiful silver ring with diamonds encrusted in a figure-eight shape stare back at me. It's beautiful.

"It's an eternity ring. It's a symbol of my devotion and dedication to your daughter. I hope you don't mind?"

I know he's only asking to be polite. He doesn't care whether they approve of him giving me this or not.

"Of course not," my mother chimes. "I think it's so romantic. Isn't it romantic, William?"

"It is." My father nods his head with a smile, but notices my hesitation. He gives me a disapproving frown. "What do you say, Evelyn?"

I turn my head to Drake and smile. "Thank you. It's beautiful."

Taking the ring from the box, he takes my right hand. "Not as beautiful as you." He places the ring next to my right index finger. It's on the right finger, but wrong hand.

Once securely on, he smiles back up at me. "Every time you look at this, you can be sure in the knowledge that I'm here for you—no matter what. This is a symbol of what we mean to each other. Look," he says, grabbing my hand. He holds it gently in his, and with a finger, he gently glides it over the figure eight. "This is us. We're never-ending. Constantly going around and around and never stopping. That's what we are, and that's what we'll continue to be."

My mother places her hand on her heart. "That's just so beautiful." She smiles, and I know what she means is genuine, but I can tell there's a hint of something in that smile. Jealousy maybe? There's definitely something. I ignore it. I'm past caring what my parents think at this point. They obviously never loved me, so why should I care?

Squeezing my hand a little, Drake makes me look at him. "See, you and I are infinite. You're stuck with me forever now."

CHAPTER THIRTEEN

Three Days after Eighteenth Birthday – Present Day

I stare at the ring Drake got me when I was sixteen. The one that denotes our infinite love. It makes me laugh when I think about it.

I then take a look at the other ring he bought and forced me to wear five days ago, and it makes me laugh even louder. I am his now in every sense of the word. He promised that we would get married next year, but I know for a fact he's already planning our wedding. The reason I know is the because of the little visit I had yesterday from a woman who came in and measured every nook and cranny of me. When I asked what she was doing, she laughed like I was stupid and said, "It's for your wedding gown, silly."

I've been held prisoner for three days after my insubordination on my eighteenth birthday. I could have been good and let him take me, but—just like always—I fought him at every turn. Now, I'm stuck in my allocated bedroom day and night, planning my escape during the day and yearning for Drake's touch at night.

I haven't seen him since he drove me to his home three nights ago and shoved me with disdain into the room I sometimes slept in as a child.

I know he's punishing me. I know he's still most probably reeling at the fact that I ran. But, I reckon the thing he's most angry with is my betrayal with another man. I didn't want that man and it pissed me off. It also pissed me off that I wished it had been Drake.

Surely this is some sort of joke? Or is it that being with Drake so long and living with his dual personality has finally made me loopy? These mixed feelings that I have for Drake are just as strong now as they ever were, and yet I can't escape the one obvious, glaring thing shining at me like a hundred watt bulb.

He raped me.

On my eighteenth birthday, Drake took me, and he raped me. He didn't ask if I wanted him to take me in the way that he did. He wasn't gentle. He wasn't sweet, and he certainly wasn't kind.

Yet, I can't help but want him. Now that three days have gone by, and the soreness I felt has eased, I can't help but yearn for his touch again. I have been sitting in my room for three days with nothing but the view of the pool and the thoughts in my head, and for three days I have been trying my hardest to get around these fucked up feelings inside of me. I shouldn't want him, but I do. And the only answer I can give myself as to the reason why is...

He's the only person I've got.

He's the only one who has looked after me since I was twelve. He's the only person who's made sure I've been looked after. He's the only person—up until this point—who has kept me safe.

I have to laugh when I think on this because he may have kept me safe, but not from the monster who lives inside of him.

"Do you know what happens when you rattle an animal's cage for years and then suddenly let him out?"

Those are the words that ring around in my head. At times, I hate him with a vengeance, but then I think of all the times in the past when he warned that I would make him go over the edge if I pushed.

And boy did I push. I pushed and pushed so much that the rattling cage rattled so much that the lock forced itself open with a violent break.

With a shake of my head and a sigh, I walk into my bathroom and take a contraceptive pill. I did at least *prepare* for Drake. I want to escape, but I have to cover all my bases just in case. After that incident in the car a few weeks ago after I ran away to that bar and got caught by Drake being chatted up by that guy, Chris, I booked an appointment with my doctor. This is my second course of pills, and I will be finishing them soon. Luckily, I still have another four months left before needing more. Hopefully, by then, I'll be let out of my cage.

Laughing at the irony, I head back to my bedroom and decide to watch some TV. I don't have much else to do since he has me locked in here. Luckily, I do have the TV, radio, and some books. Otherwise, I'd go crazy.

The only other thing I do is sleep. I sleep because I'm bored. I'm not used to being holed up like this with not a chance to at least walk around the house. Sure, I've been grounded before, but never like this. Never held prisoner against my will. At times, I think Drake bought me to help escape my parents, but now it seems he is worse than they are. Yes, they were cruel, and it's true that they didn't give two shits about me, but at least I had the freedom to walk around my own house.

As the hours progress, so does my frustration. Bit by bit, I watch the sun go down until it finally disappears over the horizon. Night is coming, and it looks as though I will be all on my own again.

Then, I suddenly hear a noise at my door, and it makes me jump. For a moment, I think it's the maid coming to bring me food, but when the door opens instead of the courtesy knock I always get, I know otherwise.

Drake enters, and following him are two guys with two plates of food, some champagne, and two glasses. Without a word, they place everything on the table in front of my bed and pour the wine once done.

"That'll be all," Drake says, dismissing them.

Soon, they are all gone and silence fills the room. He has his back to me at first and hasn't looked at me once. I can tell he's still angry. I can tell he's still reeling. But it's a good sign that he's here, bringing food and wine. He obviously wants to eat with me at least.

"You must be hungry. Come and sit, so we can properly celebrate your birthday together." He says it with an edge to his voice. He still hasn't turned.

With a trembling of my hands, I rise from the bed and watch him as I make my way to the table. He still hasn't looked at me, but I'm certainly looking at him. He's casual today in my favourite jeans. I'm not sure if he's wearing them for me on purpose, but I can hazard a guess that he is. As if that isn't bad enough, he's also got a nice, tight white t-shirt on which accentuates his toned physique.

As I walk, I wait for the feeling of nausea to come from the thoughts of all that this man has put me through—embarrassment, pain, and even trauma. I experienced all of that and more at the hands of this man. But the nausea doesn't come. Instead, all I feel is heat ... longing ... desire. Disappointment fills me when he still can't seem to look at me. When I finally approach the table, however, he has no choice but to turn his head. The reaction it elicits has my heart thundering and makes my knees weak.

He hitches in a breath as he takes in my short, summery, strappy peach dress. It curves to my body perfectly and accentuates my long legs. Despite the fact that we've already had sex twice, we still haven't seen each other completely naked. For some reason, I want to. For some strange, unfathomable reason, I yearn for it.

"Have you been sleeping well?"

And just like that, I remember all too well why I'm here ... being held prisoner. And the anger comes just as quickly. "Considering I haven't had a chance to do anything but, then yes."

I see when Drake's jaw ticks and wonder if I've gone too far. I'm rattling that cage again. I just can't help the injustice of it all. Is it too much to ask not to be owned by someone?

Drake walks to his chair, sits down, and pushes the champagne glass towards me. "Sit."

I know it's not a request, so I dutifully do as I'm told. Once settled, I pick up my champagne glass and take a sip. The bubbles are so nice that before I know it, I'm taking another sip, and then another until the glass is completely empty.

"Is this another attempt at defying me?"

His harsh tone sets my skin ablaze. "I didn't do it to—"

He puts his hand up. "Never mind," he snaps. He points to my plate. "Eat your food. It's risotto."

I pick up my fork and start eating while Drake fills up my glass again. "This is delicious." I'm attempting some sort of normal conversation ... that's if Drake and I can ever have one.

"You can have chocolate cake for dessert if you eat all your food."

Closing my eyes, I try not to let the anger rise, but it does. "Drake, I'm not a child."

He snaps his head to me. "And yet you continue to behave like one."

I almost say the words *fuck you*, but I hold my tongue. Instead, I carry on eating my risotto and drinking my champagne. Pretty soon, the risotto is finished and so is my second glass. Drake puts his fork down and refills my glass. My head is buzzing now in a lovely warm hum. In fact, it's not the only part that's humming. I'm not sure if it's the champagne, but the more I look at Drake, the more I want to climb onto his lap and ravish him.

Only because I hate him, of course.

"Are you going to talk to me?" I finally ask to break the silence. I'm not sure what's worse—having him angry with me or this near-silent treatment.

"What would you like to discuss?"

I leisurely trail the bottom of my flute glass and notice Drake watching me. There's something strangely erotic about that.

Rattle, rattle. Rattle, rattle.

"Did you know that approximately eighty-five thousand women a year are raped in England and Wales? And one in five women between the ages of sixteen and fifty-nine have experienced some sort of sexual assault. One in five, Drake. Don't you think that's a lot?"

Rattle, rattle.

"And your point is?"

I shrug my shoulders. "I'm just saying." I look away as if I'm casually throwing this out there for discussion. He knows I'm not, and he knows what I'm after.

"I didn't rape you."

My eyes snap to his. "What would you call it then?"

"Taking what is mine." He says it so matter-of-factly that it just seems to roll off his tongue.

I try to think of a comeback ... some sort of stab of retribution. But no words come out of my mouth. When Drake notices my silence, he speaks again. "But, I do have one regret about the other night."

I look up at him expectantly. "You do?"

He nods. "I didn't get to feel you shatter beneath me. I didn't get to give you your first-ever orgasm by a man ... by the *only* man who can give you one."

I don't want to feel wet by the prospect, but I give it away by uncomfortably shuffling in my seat. Drake notices and he smiles. "How can I possibly miss what I haven't had?"

Drake smirks. "Do you know how much it fucking turns me on to hear you say that?"

More squirming and shuffling. All of a sudden, the heat is turning up in here. Drake notices my flushed cheeks and leans forward, over the table. "I would like to have *my* dessert now."

"Oh," I say—a little disappointed. I was starting to hope that something else was on the menu.

Without another word, Drake gets up from his chair and then kneels on the floor. "What are you doing?"

"Stay still," he orders. "Don't move."

Suddenly, he disappears under the table, and I feel when his hands move up my thighs. "Mmm," he murmurs. "I can smell your arousal from here. Do you know how incredible that is?" I feel his head in between my legs, and I let out an incoherent squeal. "Grip the sides of the table with your hands. You're going to need to once I get started on you."

Heat flushes into my cheeks, and a need like no other pulses through me. I have no idea what he's about to do, but the expectation of it has me on high alert.

Obeying his command, I grip the sides of the table and hold my breath. I can feel my pussy throbbing as it agonisingly waits for whatever Drake is about to do.

Sliding my dress up my legs, I feel Drake tugging at my panties. I lift myself up so he can glide them down my legs and discard them. Once finished, I feel his hands back on my legs again, and then, soon after, I feel his lips on my skin.

Moaning, I throw my head back and grip the table a little tighter. "Drake, please."

"Please, what?" he asks, breathlessly.

"Please do something."

"Why? What is it you're feeling? Tell me."

Running his hands up my legs, he reaches my pussy and gently runs his finger through my folds. I jerk up, moaning. I feel like I'm on fire.

"I feel... Oh my!" I scream as he reaches my clit.

"Tell me, Evelyn."

Panting, I let out another moan before responding. "I feel like I'm going to burst apart if you don't relieve this pressure I feel. I want you to... I *need* you to do something to make it go away."

I hear Drake growl before he leisurely licks my thigh and up into the crevice of my leg. I jerk up again, panting and moaning.

"You're so fucking wet, baby. I'm going to make it all better for you now, okay?"

"Please," I urge.

And like a rocket soaring, I feel when his tongue darts out onto my clit, making me grip the table harder than ever. "Fuck," I breathe—unable to hide what it is I'm feeling.

"You taste incredible, Evelyn. I'm going to feast on you now."

And boy does he feast. He licks all of my juices around my pussy and between my folds before landing on my clit again. With careful precision, he works his tongue in slow, leisurely circles. It's so arousing, but at the same time, it's so frustrating because I can feel something building. I can feel it climbing higher than anything I've ever experienced.

With my hands still gripping the table, my mind wanders. A whirl of different emotions wants to burst through me like a tidal wave.

"Oh my God, Drake ... I'm going to ..."

Suddenly, he stops, but I have no time to show him my aggravation as he pushes my chair back, pulls me into his arms, and places me on the bed. "I could have made you come," he says, undressing himself. "But I have to feel your first time around my cock. I need to feel you come beneath me."

One by one, he discards his clothes before standing before me. He looks simply divine with his bronzed, toned chest and big, muscular arms. As I gawk at him a while, I fail to realise until the last minute that he has a tattoo of my name beautifully written in italics below his left shoulder. He catches me staring at him and smiles as he crawls between my legs.

"Your name is even carved over my heart. See how much I love you?" Instead of the words scaring me, they just make my body heat up with lust. "Now, lean forward a little," he commands, swiftly ridding me of my dress.

Once it's on the floor, he looks at my breasts with hooded eyes. It turns me on more than ever. "Please, Drake."

119

He chuckles under his breath. "Ever the eager one. Having you like this underneath me is all I've ever dreamed about."

With my nipples pert and ready, he takes one into his mouth, quickly followed by the other. My whole face flames with desire. I'm still on that precipice. I'm still feeling the effects of my lost orgasm.

And it's the most frustrating feeling on earth.

His head comes up and he positions himself on top of me before capturing me in another spellbinding kiss. After a beat, he pulls away and moves his hand down towards his impressive cock. "This won't hurt anywhere near as much. I promise. Are you ready?"

Smiling at his ironic choice of words, I nod my head. I'm still a little nervous, but the need to have him far outweighs everything else.

With a gentle shove, Drake settles in me pretty quickly. "That's better," he strains. "You're so wet, baby. So fucking wet for me."

With our breathing heavy, Drake starts to move inside of me. The discomfort that was there at first soon dissipates and replaced by it are waves upon waves of pleasure. My hands start to caress his back before pulling and scratching at him as the heat in my body rises.

"Drake, please," I urge again, moaning. I feel desperate for him to do something.

"You need to come?"

"Yes!" I scream, scratching at his back again.

Growling, Drake thrusts harder and faster inside of me, making the most erotic noises as he pushes. The sound of him, the feel of him, and the smell of him all bring my orgasm back with full force. "That's it, baby. I know it's coming. Let it go for me."

Bright sparks fill my head as my orgasm bursts open. I scream out his name and notice when Drake's movements become faster and more erratic.

"I'm going to come!" he shouts, biting the side of my shoulder.

And then, I feel it. I feel his hot liquid shoot inside of me, and it's a sensation that's surprisingly satisfying for me. Once calm, Drake pulls his head up and kisses me. "That's happening at least two more times before the sun comes up. Do you hear me?"

I don't get angry at his forceful words this time. Instead, I embrace them. I'm certainly not going to say *no* after that.

"I hear you. I hear you loud and clear."

And with that, he kisses me again, sending me into a frenzy. I guess round number two is going to come faster than I thought.

CHAPTER FOURTEEN

Present Day

The sound of the alarm going off early in the morning is an unwelcome one. I have my back to Drake as his arms move from cradling me. He turns, switching it off, and I, too, turn over to look at him. He has his back to me, and I see when he rubs his eyes with his thumb and forefinger. I look over his shoulder and see it's only six in the morning.

Groaning, I snake my arm through his and pull myself so that my breasts are pressed against his back. "It's way too early, Drake. You don't have to get up, do you? I can think of something else we can do."

I bite his shoulder, earning a low chuckle from Drake. Ever since our four encounters last night before we fell asleep from sheer exhaustion, I've been constantly feeling horny. I even dreamt that we had sex during the night and woke up wanting to start on round five. I didn't, though, as I knew Drake was sound asleep, and not even wild horses could have woken him.

"You're a little vixen. I knew you would be once you gave us a chance."

I smile at his comment and snuggle my face into the crook of his neck. "Is that a yes then?"

He quickly turns and has me on my back within an instant. "I would love nothing more, but your man has work to do. Otherwise, I can't keep you in the life you're going to grow accustomed to." He smirks at me, making my bite my lip. Right in this moment, I feel happy. For the first time, I have let my walls down and allowed Drake to take charge. Maybe not fighting him will be easier after all.

"How long will you be?"

"Ever the eager one, aren't you?"

"Mmm. Now that I've had a taste."

He presses his forehead against mine, and I feel him shake his head. "You're going to be the death of me."

As soon as he said this, he was off me like a shot and walking to the bathroom. I watch with fascination as his cock sways side to side as he walks. A little giggle erupts at the sight.

Drake turns to me and smiles with amusement. "Is something funny?"

"Watching your dangly bit tick-tock like a grandfather clock is highly amusing."

Drake stands stock still, and at first it looks like he doesn't know what to say. "Did I just hear correctly?"

I nod. "I think you may have."

He shakes his head as he disappears into the bathroom. "You're so childish."

"And you're no fun!" I shout from the bed.

I wait as he showers and when he appears dripping wet with just a towel draped around his waist, I suddenly want to pounce on him.

"You're making it way too hard to get ready when you keep

looking at me like that."

"I can't see why you can't skip work for one day."

Drake stalks towards me, tilting my chin up to meet him. He kisses my lips softly. "I would if I could, but I have important business to conduct. You'll just have to wait until I get back." He stalks back towards the bathroom. "Oh, and you're moving into my room by this afternoon. No arguments."

I won't argue with that.

"I'm thinking to call Mandy today. Maybe we can go shopping or something."

Deathly silence meets me, and I wonder whether to say anything. But then Drake emerges with a white shirt and black trousers, looking every bit the God that he is.

"You're not going anywhere for a while. You have free rein around the grounds, but you're not to leave this place. Not until I know I can trust you."

I close my eyes. I thought our little play of domestic bliss was too good to be true. "Drake, I'm bored. I need some stimulation. Otherwise, I'll go crazy in here."

Drake walks towards me, grabs my hair, and pulls my head back to meet his eyes. "The only stimulation you need is my cock inside you. You're staying here. End of fucking discussion."

He pulls away from me and wanders towards the door. "Fucking prick," I mutter under my breath.

Drake stops dead still. He's like that for a few seconds before he finally turns, walks towards me and rips the sheet from my body. I scream when he pulls my legs up in the air and covers his hand over my neck. He squeezes a little making me struggle for breath.

In an instant, he has his zipper down and his hard cock in his hand. With one big thrust, he pushes his way inside of me, not caring if I'm ready or not.

"Fuck!" he screams, before relentlessly pounding his way inside me. "Is this the way you wanted it, huh? Is this the way you like me treating you when you misbehave?"

A part of me wants to scream at him to stop, but another part of me is loving the way he feels inside of me. Different feelings are awash within me—not knowing whether to scream in pain or joy.

Bit by bit, Drake releases his chokehold, giving me some breathing space to be able to enjoy the experience. He's relentlessly grunting and thrusting his way in over and over again until he hits that g-spot and my orgasm starts climbing higher.

But, just as I'm about to come, Drake thrusts hard, groaning before stilling. "Fuck," he says pulling out. "You see what you did?" Quickly, he pushes his cock back in his trousers and zips himself up. "I'm supposed to be at a meeting in ten minutes. Now, I'm going to be late. Why can't you just do as you're told?"

How can this man make me love him and loathe him in one breath? I let my walls down to him, and this is how he treats me?

"I'm not a prisoner, Drake. You can't own me and tell me what to do."

Leaning over the bed, he grabs my chin. "Five million pounds tells me different. The sooner you realise who you belong to, the better. If you misbehave, I can make life a hell of a lot more difficult for you."

I want to scream at him, but I'm frozen in shock by his admission. He *paid* five *million* pounds for **me**?!

When I don't say anything, he moves towards the door. "In my room by six o'clock. Not a minute later."

He leaves with a slam of the door, making me jump. As the quiet descends, I look at all the luxury this place has to offer, and I wonder if in different circumstances I could be happy here. What woman wouldn't want to be taken care of, pampered, and given everything she could ever desire? It's just that there's a catch. All of this luxury comes at a cost. The price was my freedom. For five million pounds, my freedom was stripped away from me.

Now, my parents are rich, and I belong to a fiend of a man in gentleman's clothing.

As I think on all this, I get up and have a shower before wandering over to my wardrobe. I have a few clothes inside here already, but I can bet there's more in Drake's room.

Deciding on a pair of jeans, high heels, and an off-the-shoulder red top, I get to work on my hair and makeup before leaving my room for the first time in three days. As I pass the many maids and bodyguards watching me, I get to the kitchen where the smell of bacon and eggs hits my nostrils. George, one of the chefs I've known for a long time, is cooking up a treat that's making my stomach growl. He spots me the moment I walk in.

"Ah, Evelyn, you're looking very pretty today."

I smile. "Thank you."

"Would you like some bacon and scrambled eggs? I've just cooked some for the boys, but thankfully, there's plenty left over."

I take a seat at the island. "That would be lovely, thank you."

I watch as George gathers a plate and places some food on it for me. Once ready, he picks it up and places it in front of me. "Bon appétit."

"Thank you." I take a fork and start digging in, not realising just how hungry I am.

"You really are hungry, aren't you? I wonder what you were doing last night to work up such an appetite." George winks and places his finger to his nose, making me laugh.

"Can it make you this hungry?"

"What?" he asks as if he doesn't know.

I immediately turn red. "You know ..." I lean in to whisper and so does George. "Sex."

George pulls away chuckling. "Oh, yes. Sex can make you all kinds of hungry ... if you know what I mean." He suddenly shakes his head. "It seems like only yesterday that you were a child running around the grounds. Now, you're all grown up, living here, having sex, and getting married. Whatever next?"

I swallow hard at the marriage comment. It would seem that everyone knows about me and Drake, but then again, I suppose that's how Drake wants it.

I don't say anything after that. My eagerness to eat has diminished now that my forced marriage has been brought up.

"Good morning," a voice calls from behind me. I look at who it is and recognise it as Joe straight away. He makes a purposeful trail of my head down to my feet before looking up again. "I can see my morning just got better."

"Have you eaten yet?" George asks.

"No. Have you got any to spare?"

He motions to a seat next to me. "Sit, and I'll get you some."

Joe swiftly takes a seat next to me, but I ignore him and carry on eating my breakfast.

"So, you decided to join the big wide world this morning after being holed up in your bedroom for days. I wonder what you were doing all this time."

George walks over and places Joe's plate in front of him with a warning glare. I'm sure I wasn't meant to see it, but I did. But George's warning is temporary when a delivery man comes in with some boxes asking where George wants to put the stuff. George motions towards the pantry, and soon, they both disappear.

"What's eating him?" Joe asks.

"I don't know. Maybe your cockiness."

"You think I'm cocky?"

I look up from my eggs at him. "I'm pretty sure we've had a similar conversation."

He leans forward to whisper. "Have you been having fun up in your tower?" He wriggles his eyebrows at me.

"I see we still like overstepping the mark."

"I can overstep a lot more if you'll let me."

I sigh. "Can I just eat my breakfast in peace?"

"Sure," he replies, going silent.

For the next couple of minutes, we eat in silence together and when I finish, I get up and move towards the sink. In a flash, I wash my dish, dry it, and put it away.

"You seem to know your way around already."

I turn looking at Joe. "Well, I have been coming here since I was thirteen. You would think I would know my way about by now."

He frowns. "Doesn't it bother you that you've known Drake since then, and now you're ... what are you ... lovers?"

I show him my ring. "Fiancée, actually." I wouldn't normally show my commitment to anyone, but this guy seems to push my buttons in the wrong direction.

"Oh, yes. I always seem to forget that part."

"Yes, it seems you always do."

"So, doesn't it?"

"What?"

"Bother you?"

That part doesn't really bother me. It's more the fact that I'm being forced into a situation I can't get out of. Well, at least for now I can't seem to find a way out.

"No, it doesn't bother me."

"So, if I were to offer to take you away from all this, you would turn it down?"

I inhale a little at his question. Would I take it if someone gave me the opportunity? I suppose I would. I can't tell Joe this. For all I know, he could be secretly working as Drake's snoop.

"Yes, I would turn it down."

Joes stares at me for a moment before slightly shaking his head. "You and I both know that's a lie, but I'm sure one day you'll come to me asking the question."

"Ask you what?"

"To take you away. Give you your freedom back. I know as well as you do that you're being forced into this."

My heart starts beating rapidly in my chest. I guess everyone knows, but up until this point, only Joe has blatantly pointed it out to me.

However, I don't know this guy, and again, he could be secretly asking me this so he can report to Drake later. I suck in a breath, and I'm about to answer him when I hear a bellowing voice.

"So, where is she? I need to meet my soon-to-be daughter."

I frown at Joe, but all he does is smile at me. I walk out of the kitchen to see if it's who I think it is when I'm met with a middle-aged man standing tall amidst a couple of armed guards. They're Drake's guards, and they look a little out of sorts like they don't know what to do.

The man—who I now recognise as Drake's dad—stands regally in his three-piece grey suit, white shirt, and navy tie. His hair is still black, but it's now greying slightly at the sides. I remember meeting him once when I was thirteen, but I also remember Drake not being pleased by this. I doubt the situation has changed. Maybe Drake's dad knows he's not here and is taking the opportunity to see me knowing this. Maybe this is the reason why the guards are standing by him, looking like they're stuck between a rock and a hard place.

At first, he doesn't say anything. He creepily looks me up and down and then extends his hand. "Evelyn, how nice to meet you again. I don't know if you remember me?"

"I do."

He smiles wickedly at me. "Did I make that much of an impression?"

What a slimeball.

"Do you remember my name?"

I shake my head. "No. That part I don't recall."

"Sebastian."

As much as I don't want to, I offer him my hand. He leans over, gently placing a kiss on my skin. For some reason, the hairs on the back of my neck stand on end. I remember instantly disliking him when I first met him. Today is no different.

"You've turned into a beautiful woman. I can see why Drake wants to keep you."

Keep me?

"Why don't we go to the living area where we can have a little chat? Considering you're marrying my son shortly, I would like to get to know you better."

I nod my head curtly and lead the way into the living room. The guards follow every step of the way, and for the first time, I am actually quite glad of it. However, once we reach the living room, he motions for the guards to stay outside.

"We have our orders, sir."

"And what the fuck do you think I'm going to do in here?" he bellows. "Drake is my son, and this is going to be my daughter soon. I would like some fucking privacy."

He's so angry that I can feel the fear creep up my spine. I see the guards looking at Sebastian and then at me.

"Look, if it makes you feel any better, I'll leave the door ajar. Would that fucking suffice?"

"I'm going to have to let Drake know," the guard says.

"Let him know whatever the fuck you like." He then pushes the door violently until it slams shut. He turns and I notice that the guard opens the door again and leaves it ajar. At least I know they're out there if I need them.

Sebastian walks towards me and motions for me to sit down. I do so, and he helps himself to a brandy from one of the decanters before sitting opposite me.

He studies me for a moment as his clearly evil eyes assess me from head to toe. It makes me uncomfortable. I want to leave, but I know he won't let me go in a hurry. The silence goes on for a while, and I wonder whether I should say something—anything—to break this awkward silence.

"Tell me, Evelyn. Are you well educated?"

Okay... A bit of a strange question, but I will answer nonetheless. "Yes. Why do you ask?" In fact, with my A-level results in biology, physics, and English, I have been hoping to start university next year with a focus on either English literature or psychology. It's a bit of a wide range, but I'm hoping to figure it all out at some point. First of all, however, I need to figure out how to get out of the clutches of my mad fiancée.

"Why I ask doesn't concern you."

His stern voice makes my eyes widen. I thought Drake was bad. I suppose this is where he gets it from.

He takes a sip of his drink, seeming to compose himself before speaking. "You've known my son for a long time. How is your ... relationship?"

I frown wondering why he asks me such a question. We're engaged. Forcibly, but we are engaged. Shouldn't he already know?

"I don't understand your question."

He shakes his head as if I annoy him. "For a girl who's well educated, you sure have no common sense."

I inhale sharply giving away my annoyance. He stares at me again as if assessing my movements, my actions, and my words. He's assessing everything. It makes me angry that I feel under intense scrutiny.

"I have plenty of common sense. I just don't understand where your questioning is going. Your son and I are engaged. How much more do you need to know?"

I see his jaw tick and instantly regret snapping at him. I'm angry he is prying into our relationship, but I'm also scared by his sinister, evil-looking eyes. He could probably send a man to Hell with those eyes.

He takes a deep breath, narrowing those evil eyes of his before speaking again. "I know you two are engaged, but I'm struggling right now. You see, I was led to believe that a very large amount of money was paid for you. Money that once belonged to me. Therefore, I think I have a fucking say in this relationship. I also think I deserve a bit more fucking respect."

He leans forward, spitting the last sentence out. He wasn't loud enough for the guards to hear, but the message he was trying to convey came across loud and clear.

With my heart thumping rapidly, I watch as he gets up, walks over to the decanter, and with his back to me, I believe he's pouring another drink for himself. It's only when he turns around that I see it's an extra glass. He walks over to my seat and hands it to me. I shake my head. "It's too early for that."

His jaw clenches again. "It is not a request."

On a sigh, I take it from him and watch as he takes a seat opposite me again. "I don't know what the fuck my son has been doing with you. Obviously, the amount of time he's spent with you thus far has made you into this ... this insubordinate woman. Have you heard the expression 'familiarity breeds contempt?'"

"Yes, and I can relate to that right now."

Again, his jaw ticks. I don't know why I'm pushing his buttons, but the way he's speaking to me is like I'm a robot ... like I should say and do everything I'm told. For some reason, the song "Sit Still, Look Pretty" by Daya pops into my head.

"Drink your drink, Evelyn. When Drake gets back, I feel we will have a lot to discuss. Some training wouldn't go amiss for you."

Training? What does he mean by training?

Sit still, look pretty.

He watches as I take a sip of my drink, and on a satisfied inhale, Sebastian gets up and starts pacing the living room floor.

"You know, I have often wondered why Drake has had such a thing for you. It's almost like he's been obsessed. Something must be worthy of paying five million, but other than your obvious good looks, I can't think of what that could be." He turns, facing me. "Do *you* know what it could be?" He makes a sweep of my body and it almost makes me shudder. I take a gulp of my drink to steady my nerves and watch as he moves closer to me. Once by my feet, he kneels before me and stares into my eyes. "What is it about you that makes you so special, huh?"

As I stare at him, my eyes start to become droopy. My head starts lolling to the side, and I feel woozy. "What have you given me?" I slur.

He gives me an evil smile. "Just a little something to make you more compliant. Drake likes his girls compliant. We all do." I feel him run his hand up the inside of my thigh before squeezing hard. "Hmm... I bet Drake loves fucking you."

I want to tell him to fuck off and that he's disgusting. I want to ask how he could do this to his own son. I'm supposed to be his daughter-in-law soon, and this is how he respects that?

I feel fear deep in my gut as he runs his hands over my breasts and squeezes my nipples. I want to push him away—fight him—but I can't. I want to shout to the guards to help me, but no words come out.

Luckily, a noise sounds from outside, and Sebastian quickly gets up from his crouched position in front of me. The room is spinning. I'm trying to focus on what he's doing, but all I can see is his evil smile. "Your master is back. Now, you'll get to see what he's really like."

What is that supposed to mean?

My head lolls back. I'm trying hard to keep it upright, but all I want to do is sleep. I can't sleep. I won't sleep. I need to know what's going on. What's going to happen next. I can't lose focus.

I hear the door slam open and Drake shouting. At first, I can't hear what's being said, but then I feel him close to me. I watch with blurry eyes as he takes the glass from my hand and wipes my hair from my face. "All will be okay, Evelyn." He gets up, turning to Sebastian.

"What the fuck have you done?"

"Only what you should have done ages ago. She has a mouth on her, Drake. You and I have never allowed girls to speak to us in the way she spoke to me earlier. You're becoming a pussy."

Through my blurry eyes, I watch as Drake shoves his father up against the wall. "I'm not a fucking pussy."

Sebastian looks at me with an evil smile. "Well, now's your chance to prove that. I suggest you let me go now." With a grunt, Drake lets him down. He starts straightening his suit and tie out. "I'll leave now. I just thought I'd pop by and see how your little investment is going. Just make sure you control the situation. You obviously don't have a handle on it now." He pats him on the back. "You can thank me later." He turns to leave, and I watch as Drake walks towards me and picks me up. As my head lolls back, I'm out cold.

CHAPTER FIFTEEN

Present Day

I wake to find myself restricted somehow. My head is still fuzzy, and I feel I can't move. I try to pull my hand, but I can't seem to move.

Someone's pushing inside me, grunting, and making lots of noise. With as much strength as I can muster, I pull my head up and see Drake in front of me. His eyes are dark and sinister. His voice like an evil monster.

"I will make you submit. I will fuck you and make you submit." Over and over again, he pounds his way inside me. I'm strapped to something with my arms above my head, and it looks like I'm in some kind of basement.

"Drake?" I ask, not understand what's happening. Why are my hands tied and why is he doing this to me?

"Don't fucking talk. You talk too much. I am your master, and it's about time you realised this. Take my cock like the good little slut that you are. My fucking slut. My. Fucking. Slut."

Over and over again, he grabs at my hips and uses them to thrust his way inside of me. I want to tell him to stop. I don't want this. I don't want him like this. Why can't we be like we were this morning—

wrapped up in each other's arms after a night of spellbinding lovemaking?

This isn't lovemaking. He's taking again. Taking things without my permission. I want to scream at him to stop, but no words come out.

"Fucking bitch. Fucking whore. My fucking whore."

Who is this guy? I don't know him. I try to look into his eyes to find some sort of humanity in there, but all I'm met with are pools of black. He's like the devil himself.

"Fuck!" he screams, and I feel when he thrusts one last time before I'm out cold again.

My head is pounding and at first, I don't know where I am. I try opening one eye, and all I can see is black. I move my body so I can see better and feel the ache between my legs. I wince a little, grabbing myself down there. Why am I so sore?

I'm in Drake's bedroom on Drake's bed, but there's no Drake with me. I frown, confused as to what's going on. I remember Drake saying he wanted me here, but I can't seem to remember anything else. Where is he?

Holding my sore head, I look around the room and almost scream when I see a silhouette crouched in the corner of the bedroom by the door.

"Drake?" I ask, my voice croaky. He doesn't move. He is sitting with his knees bent and his face down in between his legs. Without seeing his face, I can tell he looks troubled, but by what?

Getting up, I go to him, crouching down beside him and touching his arms. "Drake, what's the matter?"

"You should take some tablets. Your head must be hurting by now."

I frown. How does he know this? What's going on? Why can't I remember anything? "Drake, I don't understand."

Finally, he looks up. It's dark in here, but not too dark to see the pain written across his face. "You're not meant to understand. You're only meant to comply."

I close my eyes, feeling the fuzziness of my head. I'm about to ask him what the hell's going on when he speaks again.

"Why do you always have to push, Evelyn? Why? Always disobeying. Always pushing, pushing, *pushing.*"

His last word was so venomous, I almost stumbled back. What on earth have I done?

"One day, you're going to get yourself into trouble. You need to learn to do as you're fucking told. If you just did as asked, then none of this would have happened."

None of what?

"Sit when told, stand when told, and obey when told. That's all you have to do."

Sit still, look pretty.

Suddenly, flashes of memories come back to me. I remember Drake's father visiting. I remember how nasty, vindictive, and arrogant he was. I remember feeling scared. Feeling his hands on me. I remember...

I shoot back, suddenly afraid of Drake. He notices my change in demeanour, and I see the look of pain cross his face. I can also see what looks like an apology there, but how can I accept what he did?

Again.

"You raped me." The words come spilling out of my mouth. I can feel that anger building again. How dare he?

I hear him sigh and dip his head low a little. "Evelyn—"

"You raped me," I say again, harsher this time.

My words must hit a nerve because soon he is up, stalking towards me. He grabs my hair, making me yelp, and pulls my head back. "You are mine to take when I want, however I want. Do I need to remind you again? Do you want me to get my cock out and shove it down your throat just to make you listen and shut that fucking mouth of yours?"

Tears pool in my eyes. What's happened to him all of a sudden? He watches me as a lone tear falls down my face, and for a moment, I see what looks like a flash of guilt in his eyes, but he quickly composes himself.

He pulls my hair again. "Well, do you?" I shake my head. "Well then, just do as you're fucking told." He releases his grip and stands upright. "Now, get on the bed and spread your legs." I start to shake my head again. I don't want him like this. "Don't make me ask you again."

With my legs shaking and my head still pounding slightly, I wobble towards the bed, get on it, and lie down. I'm naked, and I feel bruised and violated in every way possible. I can't understand how a man who once bought me ice cream, mobile phones, and even a horse could do such a thing to me now. I'm sore down there and certainly not ready for sex. In fact, I don't want him anywhere near my body again.

I watch as he climbs onto the bed. My instinct is to run, but I know for a fact I won't get anywhere. He's naked like me, and I can already tell his cock is hard.

As he settles himself between my legs, I close my eyes, biting back the tears that threaten to fall. I don't want to shed tears for this man. He is not worthy of them.

I don't open my eyes, but I can feel him manoeuvring. I can feel his hands on my skin and his heavy breaths against my thighs. I lie there rigid as he kisses up my thighs just like he did last night to me under the table. But this time I don't want it. This time, it disgusts me.

"You're so fucking sexy, do you know that? I can't get enough of you, Evelyn."

"Fucking bitch. Fucking whore. My fucking whore."

Those words from earlier hit me like a ton of bricks. I inhale sharply as a new set of tears sting my eyes. Why did he talk to me like that? Why did he make me feel worthless, used, and abused? Why did *he*—when he's the only man I've ever slept with—make me feel like the whore and the slut he made me out to be?

"So fucking perfect," he whispers against my pussy before licking my clit.

I don't want to react, but I can't help another sharp inhale take over as my body arches to his touch. Slowly, but precisely, he swirls his tongue along and around my clit. My whole body ached, but now all I feel are tingles all the way from my head down to my toes. I don't want what this monster's doing to affect me, but my body is betraying me once again.

In slow circles, he moves his tongue around my clit and then down towards my entrance. He moves it in and out, and I can't help but relish how soothing that is compared to what I felt earlier.

Closing my eyes, I feel when his tongue moves back up towards my clit again, making me moan as he flicks it quickly.

"That's it, baby. You know you love this."

I want to tell him to fuck off, but instead my hips move in tune with his tongue. Instead of trying to get away, I'm seeking out more of him.

As he carries on his relentless onslaught on my clit, I fist my hands in my sheets, trying desperately not to give him the one thing I know he's after. After what he did to me, I don't want to give him the satisfaction of making me come.

As if sensing that I'm holding back, Drake picks up the tempo, and my orgasm races to the surface quickly. Again, I try holding it, fisting the sheets even tighter this time and even pulling them to me. I start grunting as my heart beats frantically in my chest. I don't want to come, but again, Drake is forcing it out of me. Again, Drake is bending me to his will. I don't want to feel how incredible his tongue feels. I don't want to relish that feeling of pleasure when I know that hours earlier, all he wanted to give me was pain.

Drake, so desperate to win this battle, grips my hips tighter to him and practically buries his face into my pussy. His tongue is everywhere—in me, on me, racing to get me to that precipice. I know fighting it will be a losing battle, but I can't help trying to beat him. I can't help trying to will my body to do as I wish instead of as Drake commands.

But, it's a losing battle. As his tongue darts frantically around my clit, I feel that burning sensation in my cheeks. I feel the tingles rising and heading straight in between my legs. I feel pleasure building and building inside of me until it hits the point of no return.

With my head thrown back, I come harder than I ever have in my life. I see stars dancing before my eyes as my orgasm ricochets throughout my whole body. I feel myself go rigid as I grip the sheets and cry out from the most intense pleasure I have ever felt in my whole life. The orgasm just seems to go on and on until it gets to a point where it becomes too much.

"Please stop!" I cry, pulling myself away from him. Luckily, he does as asked and pulls himself up. I can see how hard his cock is still, and I'm frightened as to what he's going to do next. I'm too sore for that.

"Fuck me, that was sexy. I almost came just from the sound of your screaming." He positions himself between my legs again, and I wince thinking he's going to push it in. Drake looks up to me. "Don't worry. I know you're sore. But I need to come." I wonder if he'll order me to do a blow job on him, so I'm surprised when instead he starts pleasuring himself over my pussy. I want to look away, but I can't. My eyes are transfixed by the way he's pulling his hand back and forth against his shaft and by the way his eyes are hooded with pleasure. I don't want that to please me, but it does. For some reason, I'm finding watching this evil monster wanking himself over me highly erotic.

"Fuck, Evelyn. I wish this was your pussy. You're too fucking sexy for your own good," he pants, picking up the pace. His breathing is becoming heavier and heavier as he yanks on his cock back and forth, back and forth. His hips start to move in turn with his hand, and at one point, he throws his head back in pleasure before meeting my eyes again. He places his other hand on my body, trailing the contours before reaching up to my breasts and squeezing my nipples.

"Fuck, Evelyn, you're going to make me come."

He leans forward slightly and grunts as he spills his come on my pussy and stomach. "Fuck, that's so sexy." He coats the last drops on my pussy, spreading it along as if marking himself on me. I should feel disgusted. I should turn away, but I can't help but look at what this monster is doing to me.

Once he's finished, he rubs his come into my skin until there's nothing left. "Now, you can sleep with me on you as well as inside you." He presses himself against me and kisses me hard. "Who do you belong to, Evelyn?"

This time, I don't hesitate in replying. "You."

He kisses me again before starting around my neck. He finds a spot and starts sucking so hard that I almost cry out. Again, he is marking me. I know this is a show of his dominance. Tonight, I will let him have it, but I know once the morning comes, I will be just as disgusted with him as always. Maybe even more disgusted with myself for letting this go on so long. I should have known he was lying when he said he wasn't a monster. He *is* a monster.

And I need to find away to escape his clutches.

CHAPTER SIXTEEN

Present Day

Almost two weeks have gone by, and I feel more trapped than ever. I haven't been able to leave the house. Instead, all I'm allowed to do is walk around the grounds, ride on Ireland, and swim in the pool. Even then, I have to make sure I wear something that practically covers my whole body. None of the guards are allowed to see me in a bikini by the pool.

Unfortunately, for the last few days, I haven't been able to enjoy swimming as I've had a period. I'm finished now, and I'm due to start my next pack. However, once I shower this morning and get ready for my day, I go to get the next pack out of the bathroom cabinet when I find the whole lot missing.

Frowning, I walk out of the bathroom where I find Drake putting on a pair of shoes. "Drake, I can't find my pills. I could swear I left them in the cabinet."

He doesn't look up. He just carries on doing up his laces. "Well then, it looks like they're missing."

"I need to take one today. Otherwise, I could get pregnant." When he doesn't acknowledge me, I sigh. "Drake, this is serious. I need to go to the doctors and get some more tablets."

Finally, he stands, turning himself to face me. "You don't need to go to the doctors."

"How else am I going to take the pills? Could it have been one of the maids? Maybe I should ask them." I start moving towards the door when Drake stops me. I look up at him, frowning.

"There's no need to ask the maids. I already know what happened to your tablets."

I place my hand out. "Can I have them then?"

He shakes his head. "No, because I threw them in the bin."

"You did what?" I shout.

Drake pulls me towards him. "Keep your fucking voice down," he growls. "We're getting married two weeks this Saturday. It's perfect timing to start a family. I want six children, so we'd better start soon. Why not now? I know you've just had your period, so we get married, start the process of having a baby, and then, hopefully by the time we get back from our honeymoon, we can announce to everyone our baby news."

My eyes bulge out of my head. Did I just hear him correctly?

Sit still, look pretty.

For the past few days after what Drake did to me, I've been trying my level best to comply with his every demand until I can get him to trust me more. I need to escape, and the only way I can do that is to get Drake to let me out of the house. But this? This is going too far. I simply can't hold my tongue any longer.

"But what about what I want? I don't want a family yet. I don't even want to marry you. I want to go to university and study so I can make something of my life. I want to marry once someone asks me and I willingly say yes. I want to start a family once the person I'm married to is willing to start one when we're both able and ready. Not when I'm told to. You can't do this to me."

Within an instant, I'm held up against the wall by my throat. Drake's eyes are wild and dark as he glares at me. "I've tried being patient with you, but my patience is wearing thin. I tell you time and time again that what I say goes, and yet you continually want to fight and disobey me. You don't need to go to university to make something of yourself. You've already made something of yourself by getting to marry me. I will give you everything you ever ask for, so why bother with a university degree when you have all the money in the world that I can offer you? All you need to do in return is comply. Just fucking comply," he growls, thumping my head against the wall. He does it gently enough not to hurt me, but it's not his actions that are hurting me now. It's his words. He doesn't seem to understand that it's not about money. It's about me making something of myself. It's about me having a life outside of Drake's. It's about me having my own independence, and doing something I can be proud of. Right now, I'm not proud of myself. Sure, I achieved great grades in school and I was proud of myself for that. But what have I got to show for it now?

Sit still, look pretty.

My heart starts to beat rapidly at the injustice of it all. I don't want this life. I never wanted this life. But, what can I do? I know Drake can make life Hell for me now if I don't agree with him. Right now, I want to be as far away from him as possible, and the only way to do that is...

I nod my head. "Okay, Drake."

He frowns for a moment, assessing me. It's almost as if he can't believe that I've given in so easily. "Okay, what?"

"I'll comply." I'm not going to say I'm having his baby. That's one victory he doesn't get to have from me. I will go to great lengths to see to it that I don't have a baby with this man, but for now, I will be the dutiful little whore that he wants me to be.

With a victorious smile that I want to wipe off his face, he loosens his grip around my neck. He comes in to kiss me, placing his lips hard against my mouth and forcing mine open so he can stick his tongue in. I want to gag right now, but as usual, he forces me to comply. He forces his hands on me in a way he knows I'll like. I don't want to like when he brushes his thumb across my nipples through my shirt, but I do. They react instantly, earning a low growl from Drake.

"I want so much to make love to you right now, but I have to get going." He looks down, placing a hand on my stomach. "I can't wait to watch as your stomach swells with our baby. That'll be the sexiest fucking sight on earth." He leans in kissing me again as the fear of his words makes my heart thump louder than ever. "Soon," he says, rubbing my belly again. "We're going to have fun making him."

Him?

With that last word, he's out the door. No goodbye. No see you later. Just the fear of his parting words.

"We're going to have fun making him."

I shudder as the words roll around in my head. I feel the panic and the fear burrowing its way into my mind. I need to figure out what I can do to stop this. By the end of today, I will be unprotected. I can almost feel my womb dancing at the joy of it.

With my heart still thumping, I make my way downstairs to see George making me breakfast again. Like clockwork, Drake has left by eight, and like clockwork, George is busy frying up some bacon and eggs. I don't feel hungry today, though. Those parting words of his have made sure of that.

"Good morning," he greets cheerfully.

"Morning," I almost groan.

George frowns as he places my plate in front of me. "Ooh, that's not a good morning at all. Did you not get much sleep last night?"

I don't want to get into anything with George. He's nice, but he's also been Drake's employee for many years. "Something like that," I respond.

I start playing with my food, not offering any additional conversation, and I think George gets the hint that I'm not in a talkative mood as he leaves me on my own to eat in peace.

I eat a few bites, but it's more out of necessity than hunger. Normally, George's breakfasts are delectable, but today, it just tastes like cardboard. Feeling disgusted, I get up, taking my plate with me, and pour the contents in the bin.

"No appetite this morning, huh?"

Looking up, I find Joe standing in the doorway with a big grin on his face. I don't smile back. Instead, I take my plate and start washing it.

"So, what's the matter with Princess this morning? Did we have an argument with our prince?" I carry on ignoring him and concentrate on washing up. "Hey, what's wrong?" He sweeps my hair away from my eyes, trying to look at me.

I pull away. "Don't touch me."

He steps back with his hands in the air. "Sorry."

I see how genuine he looks and soften to him a little. "I'm sorry. I'm just not having a good morning I guess. There's no need to take it out on you."

Joe smiles. "That's okay. I'm here if you need me." I grab a towel and start drying the plate. I watch as Joe sits down by the island, and it's only then that it hits me. Without Mandy, I have nobody. No friends to talk to and hang out with. Joe may be a douchebag, but he's the only one—apart from Kane—who's willing to talk to me. None of the other guards are even willing to look at me. I guess it's because they're afraid of Drake. I should be afraid that they're afraid, but it only makes me angry. There was one thing Sebastian said that was right. Familiarity really does breed contempt.

I watch as Joe sits in silence. We're just looking at each other, but for once, Joe isn't looking at me like he wants to eat me. He's looking at me like he wants to be my friend.

And I could really use a friend.

Sighing, I place the tea towel on the counter. "What's Drake like as a boss?"

I think my question surprises him a little. At first, he doesn't seem to know what to say, but then he composes himself. "He's firm, but fair. I think that's the best way to describe him." I can't help the sarcastic laugh that escapes me. Fair, my arse!

"I take your laughter to mean you don't hold the same sentiment."

"Drake is not my boss, so I simply can't comment."

"Touché," he says in amusement. I smile back when he does. "I think that's the first I've seen you smile in days."

"Well, I haven't had much to smile about." I don't know why I'm suddenly opening up to this boy. I know nothing about him.

"That's a shame. A beautiful girl like you should be smiling all the time. So, why aren't you?"

"It's complicated."

149

"Try me."

It's tempting. It really is. But I'm at a loss for words. "What do you think of free will?"

He frowns at my question. "It's something God gave us ... something we should all have a right to."

"I didn't take you as the Godly type."

He smirks. "Ah, you see, Evelyn ... there's not a lot you know about me." We both chuckle at that. "So, are you going to tell me why you asked?"

Sighing, I look down at the black high heels on my feet. A pair I chose to wear today. At least I had free will as far as that was concerned. "Nothing, really. I was just asking."

"Oh, I highly doubt that, but I won't press you. I know you feel you have a crappy life here, but there are other lives that could be far worse than the one you have."

I look up to him then. "Are you saying that I should therefore be grateful?"

He puts his hands up again. "Whoa there, tiger. I didn't say that at all. I'm just saying that when you're in a shitty situation, the best way to look at it is that there are others who are worse off than you."

I think on that answer, and of course, he's right. I have a roof over my head, clothes to wear, and food to eat. Some people don't have those luxuries. I wonder, though, would someone without the luxuries I have *choose* to swap her life for mine? It's a pretty hard question to answer.

"I know you're right. I guess, selfishly, I don't look at it that way."

Joe gets up from his seat and walks towards me. He places a hand on my shoulder and smiles. "Listen, I know it seems pretty shitty now, but you can change things if you really want. I did offer you a chance."

I think back on what he said before, but I didn't think he was serious at the time. My heart thumps from the thought of it. "Actually, I do need help."

He cocks his eyebrow. "Go on."

I swallow hard, wondering if I can trust him, but also knowing that I have very little choice. "I need tablets."

He shakes his head. "I don't know anyone who deals in drugs."

I tut at him. "I don't mean drugs-drugs. I mean contraceptive pills."

"Oh," he says, finally smiling.

"If I gave you the name, would you get them for me?"

"I thought you wanted to escape?"

"I do, but this is urgent. If I don't have one within the next," I look at my watch, "ten hours, I'm unprotected."

"Is this purposeful?"

"Yes, and not by me. I had tablets, but they were thrown in the bin." I huff the last word out.

"I think I can help you."

My eyes widen, and a little ray of hope shines brightly inside my heart. "Really?"

"Yes. I also think I can help you escape, but I'll want something in return."

"What's that?" I watch as he leans closer to my lips and purposefully trails his eyes down to my cleavage. Immediately, I know. "You want me."

He steps away, laughing. "Hey, I'm just being honest. Would you want me to say I'll do all these things for you and *then* bring it up? You were worth a lot of money. Surely you must realise that every man who knows this wants to try a piece for themselves? It's like a woman seeing a five million pound diamond on display. It's just human nature."

Disgusted that I let him in, I push him away. "Forget I said anything."

I start to walk away, but something he says halts me. "So, you won't be wanting these then?"

I turn, noticing the packet of my tablets in his hands. My eyes widen as I stalk towards him and try to grab it out of his hand. "Ah, ah. Not so fast. You haven't agreed to my proposition yet."

"You make my skin crawl," I growl in his face.

"Or, I can crawl all over your skin. One night. That's all I'm asking. I will give you these and offer you a way out of here, but it will come at a cost. You're just going to have to let me know that you accept the consequences. At least you will have free will when you make your decision."

Yes, but at what cost? Am I so desperate that I'm willing to pimp myself out to this arsehole? Am I so desperate that I would sell myself like the whore Drake called me last night?

"Okay," I say timidly.

"Okay, what?"

"I agree to your terms."

"And you'll accept the consequences of your decision?"

I nod my head. "Yes. Can I have my tablets now, please?"

"Not so fast." Without warning, he grabs the back of my head and pulls me in for a kiss. At first, I try to push him away, but when I realise he won't give me the tablets, I relent, kissing him back. On a moan, he darts his tongue into my mouth and moves his hand from my head down to my face and then onto my breast. He squeezes hard before tweaking my nipple. He moans again before pulling away. "I have to stop. Otherwise, I'll push it," he says breathlessly against my mouth.

He steps away, allowing me room to breathe before giving me the tablets. I take them from him and move away. "I can't wait to try the rest of you."

A shiver crawls up my spine as I make my way up to my bedroom. I will need to take one and hide them in the bathroom somewhere. I don't want to sleep with that arsehole, but I would also much rather go through that than the alternative of getting pregnant with Drake's baby.

Feeling like I'm stuck between a rock and a hard place, I make my way into my room and very quickly open the packet. I pop the pill in my mouth and sigh as I look at my reflection in the mirror.

What have I become? I'm only eighteen, but I feel like I've already lived a lifetime. Closing my eyes, I let out the tears that have been threatening to fall for days. I'm not crying because of Drake. I'm not crying because every arsehole wants to use me to get their own thrills. I'm crying because of the situation I'm in. I'm crying for the lost girl who could have had so much potential ahead of her. I'm crying because no matter what life offers her in one hand, it's quickly stripped from her in another. I'm crying because of the love not given from parents who should have been there for her.

I'm crying for me.

CHAPTER SEVENTEEN

Present Day

Later on in the day, I fancy a swim, so I look in my wardrobe. But, when I see only the stupid, boring granny swimming costume in front of me, I slam the door shut. I'm eighteen and an adult now. I should be allowed to wear what I want to wear—not what other people are telling me I can.

Thinking about what I can do—because if I don't do something soon, I'll die of boredom—I come up with an idea to instead look through my underwear drawer. I know I have a black bra and matching black panty set somewhere that could possibly be worn as a costume. What does it matter if I do anyway? There are loads of people here, but they never acknowledge me anyway.

With my decision made, I get undressed and put the bra and panties on. The panties show half my arse, but at least it's not a thong.

Once satisfied, I open the bedroom door and start making my way downstairs. Nobody is around until I make my way through the hallway and outside to the pool. One of Drake's guards is there, and I expect him to ignore me, but when he spots me in the corner of his eye, he turns properly to have a closer look. I notice his eyes widen before trying to look away. I can tell he really wants to look, though.

Smiling, I walk the rest of the way through the kitchen and open the door outside. The sun is hot today just like I hoped it would be. Finding a sun lounger, I drape my towel across it and make my way into the pool house for some sun cream. I manage to find it, but once I turn, I find Joe standing there with his phone. He takes a picture and wolf whistles at me.

"Damn, look at you. I knew you had a rocking bod under all those layers. Decide not to wear the Burkini today?"

I race towards him and try and grab his phone. "You can't take a photo of me without my permission like that. Give it."

Joe starts laughing and holding it up in the air. "It's a free country. Besides, what do you expect walking around like that?"

"What are you going to do with it?"

"I don't know. Maybe I'll share it on Facebook and wank to it later."

"You're disgusting. Besides, if you post it to Facebook, Drake will find out and sack you."

Joe starts stalking towards me, so I start walking back. Pretty soon, I'm up against the wall. Once trapped, Joe leans in and trails a finger down my face. "You and me both wouldn't want that now, would we? Remember, I'm your only saving grace in here." He moves his hand until it's down towards my breast. I grab his hand, and he just smiles at me. "I thought we had an arrangement?"

"Yes, but you haven't carried it through yet, have you?" I seethe.

"You got your tablets back, didn't you? I should at least expect a blow job for that."

My heart starts racing. "We made a deal."

He pulls away. "So we did." He motions for me to pass him. "Enjoy your swim."

Glaring at him, I walk past him, but as I do, I feel the sting of a big slap. "Ow!" I protest, looking back at him.

Joe laughs. "Such a peachy arse. I simply couldn't resist."

Ignoring him, I make my way outside before I get into any more trouble. I really don't know how Joe does it. If it wasn't for the fact that he's my only way out of here, I would have told on him ages ago. He's an arrogant pig—especially since he wants to use me for his own pleasure as payment for my freedom. I've gone from virgin to whore in the space of a few weeks. How can it end like this so suddenly?

As I dive into the pool and start swimming, I think on my parents and also Mandy. I often wonder if they think of me. I doubt my parents do. They're probably lavishing it up on their world cruise and spending the five million that Drake gave to them.

I imagine that Mandy, on the other hand, would at least be wondering why I haven't called. I also imagine she's tried to call me, but since Drake's taken my phone from me, contacting her has not been an option.

As I swim, my thoughts drift away to a better place. A place where I get my degree, meet the man of my dreams, and start a family once my career takes off. Joe is offering me this chance. How I would be and where I would go frighten me beyond words, but at the same time, the feeling excites me. If I could withdraw the amount that's accumulated in my account, I could get a place, work in a bar somewhere at night, and study during the day. I picture myself owning a place near to the sea where I can take leisurely strolls in my free time. That's if I *get* any free time between school, studying, and working in a bar.

Once I've done fifty lengths of the pool and finished off dreaming of the life that can be, I get out of the pool, dry myself off, and sit down on the sun lounger. I make sure to lather on the cream before laying back.

I must have fallen asleep at some point because, all of a sudden, I feel something silky soft over my skin. I look up to see what's happening when I see Drake hovering over me, looking as deadly as ever. His eyes are dark—like the pools of black I stared into after his father drugged me. Instantly, my skin prickles, and my heart races a million miles an hour.

"Put that on now."

I grab the turquoise kaftan he threw on me and quickly place it over me. Once in place, Drake grabs my arm and hurls me to my feet. "So this is how it's going to be, huh? I'm obviously still too soft. Otherwise, you wouldn't have disobeyed me. Again!" Squeezing my arm, he pulls me towards the house.

"Drake, please stop. You're hurting me."

"You should have thought about that."

Holding me by the back of the neck, he pushes me until I almost fall onto the floor. I know why he's doing this. He's showing his authority to everyone in the house. That he's the boss. He's the boss of them, and he's the boss of me. He's humiliating me the only way he knows how just so he can assert his authority.

Grabbing the back of my neck again, he leads me through the kitchen and out into the hallway by the stairs. Guards are watching this time. I suppose this spectacle is too good to ignore.

As we reach the stairs, he motions to one of the guards to open the door. Once he does, he pushes me through and turns to the guard. "No one comes in or out. Got it?" The guard nods and shuts the door behind us. I'm lead down the stairs and into the basement where I find a big seven-foot frame with chains and harnesses attached. This must be where he took me before.

Feeling afraid, I back up, but hit a solid chest when I do. Drake pushes me again, and this time I land on the floor. "When am I going to get through to you? When are you going to learn to fucking submit and do as you're told?"

He's so angry—the angriest I've ever seen him. I've seen his Mr Hyde, but that version has nothing on what I'm seeing before me now.

"Get up!" he orders, but I'm too afraid to move. When I don't respond straight away, he stalks towards me and grabs my hair. I yelp, but I know he's far beyond caring.

He pulls me towards the bathroom and throws me to the floor. He stands by the toilet, staring at me with pools of evil. "You always think you can fucking outwit me, but there's one thing you need to learn. A player can't be played. You think I don't have cameras watching you when you're in your room? You think I can't see what you're getting up to?"

My eyes widen, and my heart starts hammering in my chest. Just how much does he know? Has he seen what Joe did to me in the kitchen today and again in the pool house?

"Yes, that's right," he says, pulling out the contents of his pockets. I watch as he pulls out the empty packets with one hand, drops them onto the floor, and then pulls out all the tablets from the other. He stands above the toilet, and I watch as they fall and he flushes it. I don't want Drake to see me cry, and I vowed I never would in front of him, but I can't help feeling the sting of tears that well inside my eyes.

"You fucking monster!" I scream, getting up and lunging for him. I know it's fruitless, but I'm angry. So fucking angry.

Pushing me away, he grabs me by the neck and pushes me outside into the basement where the harness is. I know he's going to strap me up there, but I don't want him to. "I tried to reason with you so many times. You're my fucking whore. Nothing but my whore. And I'm going to treat you like one now."

I start shaking my head, but he's restricting me. He pushes me towards the harness, pulls down one side, and then straps in one wrist before restraining the other. Once secure, he pulls me slightly up into the air. I'm suspended, and I can't move ... but I guess that's how he wants me. What happened to this man? I thought I knew him, but how wrong I was. This is nothing like the Drake I knew. This man—whoever he is—is worse than a monster. He's the devil himself.

I watch him as he assesses what he's done. I try to look him in the eye to reason with him, but all I'm met with is black. It's like a switch has been flipped inside of him, and all elements of the sweet Drake I've known are gone without a trace.

Turning, he walks over to a drawer and opens it up. I see when a pair of scissors come out, and I start wriggling. "Drake, you don't have to do this. I promise I'll be good. Please ... please don't hurt me."

Ignoring me, he stalks towards me, and a fear like no other crawls up my spine. I can't see any remnants of humanity in him at all. It's almost like Drake isn't here, and some void has taken over.

Once in front of me, he cuts into the kaftan, and I watch as it sinks to the floor. The next to go are my bra and panties. I'm naked. Completely bare to him. I want nothing more than to scream, shout, and to struggle with all my might, but I know it's fruitless. All I can do is accept my fate. I know what's going to happen next, so I gear myself up for it. I should be used to this by now, but I'm not. This is the only life I seem to know with him, but the fact that I know it can be so much better is what's making this so hard.

I watch as he undresses, and I want so much for it not to affect me in any way, but I can't help but watch him. I can't help but want him still. Is this fucked up? How have I gotten to this stage so fast where wanting Drake—in any form—is never far from my mind?

As he strips completely naked, I watch his cock, completely erect and ready, and I can't help my pussy from throbbing at the thought. My mind doesn't want this, but my body is betraying me. Somehow, the thought of him taking me like this where I'm completely restricted and at his mercy has the fires dancing in my belly. This isn't me. Surely not?

I can't keep my eyes off of him as he strolls towards the drawer again and this time pulls out a tub. He places some jelly on his hand and rubs it up and down his cock. He walks over to me, his eyes still black. I want to look away, but I can't. I'm transfixed by his beauty. Even the monster in him is beautiful.

"You will learn. And you will submit." Grabbing my legs, he hoists them around his waist and pulls my hips towards his cock. He places it at my entrance and with one big thrust, he pushes his way to the hilt. I throw my head back, screaming. "That's right, little whore. Take me. Fucking take all of me." His words sting me, but the feel of him moving inside of me makes the pleasure build. I don't want it to come, but it does.

As he pounds inside of me, he calls me names as if I wasn't the one here. I'm not his Evelyn anymore. I'm just a girl with a hole he can fuck.

The hurt pushes through me as I lean my head back and take

every thrust he can give me. I feel the tears slide down my face, but I also know an orgasm's coming at the same time. How fucked up is that?

Again, like last time, I try to hold it in. I try to fight it from coming, but the more I do, the more violently it reaches towards the surface. As if Drake's sensing that it's coming, he pounds faster inside of me. "That's it. Fucking take it. Take all of me."

I blow, screaming out his name as he comes with me. He wasn't gentle. He wasn't kind. Yet, somehow, he forced his way inside me just like he has always done.

He pulls out, stumbling back, but doesn't let me go. He doesn't even look at me. He turns, walks into the bathroom and slams the door.

As I hang there—feeling the drips of his come down my leg and the fading orgasm—the tears come again, and this time, they don't stop. How is it that I've gotten to this? How is it that Drake has gotten to this? This is isn't him ... this isn't us. A part of me wants to think he feels some sort of remorse for what he's just done and what he keeps doing. Is that why he walked away?

That and a million other things crawl through my mind. Drake was always a mystery that needed solving. Will I ever solve it? I don't know. Do I really want to know?

Hopefully, one day, I won't have to.

CHAPTER EIGHTEEN

Present Day

Drake kept me down in that basement for four whole days. Eventually, he brought a bed in for me to sleep in, but I was never let out of my restraints. I was either pulled up above the floor, or let down to the ground.

He repeatedly raped me. Sometimes, I came. Sometimes, I didn't. I got lost in an alternate reality—not knowing whether I was dreaming or living the experience. Unfortunately, my subconscious knew it was the latter. Once the four days were up, I was brought to our bedroom where he kept me under lock and key for an additional three weeks. Every day, he would force me and then tell me not to move for at least ten minutes afterwards. I knew why. He was desperately trying to get me pregnant.

A week ago, we got married, but it wasn't what I thought it would be. The priest came to the house, and all that were there were a couple of guards as witnesses. No friends or family. Just me and him, the white dress, and a black tux. I said *I do* because I knew that if I didn't, I would be forced into that basement again. Drake knew I never wanted to go back down there again and played it for all it was worth. He told me that once he knew I could behave, then we could have a proper, lavish wedding with a honeymoon.

His mood swings were constant. He went from evil rapist to adorable, caring Drake whispering sweet nothings into my ear. He constantly told me he loved me in one breath and then called me his whore in another. It was like he was battling something inside him every day, and it scared the shit out of me. During the night sometimes, I would wake to find him watching me sleep. He would have the saddest expression I have ever seen sprawled across his face. In those times, I would go to him ... give him the comfort he needed. He would wrap me up in his arms, kiss my head, and tell me that he loved me—that I was his sweet Evelyn, and he would never let anything happen to me. Strange considering he was the one to fear. Not the outside world. Him.

I had even started to submit to him. I battled inside my head all of the time. I'm still stubborn, but the fact that I knew he would keep pushing and pushing until I relented made me compliant. Compliancy was better than the alternative I was sometimes subjected to.

"What is the fucker up to?"

Drake is on the phone, and he's madder than ever. Someone's royally pissed him off.

"I don't care that he's gone silent. The mere fact that he's still close by makes me think he's up to something. In fact, I know he's up to something. Find out what the fuck it is before I break this fucked up treaty we have and go down and shoot them all to kingdom come." With a press of the button, he ends the call and throws the phone onto the bed. "Fuck!" he screams, running his hands through his hair. A part of me wants to ask what's wrong, but another, bigger part tells me to hold back. If I make a sound, he might aim his anger at me.

With a huff, he storms out, slamming the door behind him. I'm so engrossed in looking at the door and wondering what on earth has gotten into him that I fail to realise he's left his phone on the bed.

Hurrying, I run towards the bed and pick the phone up. I light the screen up, but it asks me for a pin number. Fuck! This is all I need.

I sit for a while, wondering what I can do. I have three chances to put this pin in correctly, and if I get two wrong and decide to go for the third and get that wrong too, Drake will know. If I use the phone—which I will—Drake will know. Whatever options, I'm fucked. And I know I'm fucked.

But, I miss my friend, Mandy. I haven't spoken to her in weeks, and just two minutes of conversation with her would be worth any punishment Drake may want to unleash on me later.

With that thought in my mind, I light the phone up again and have a think on what the pin could be. I put Drake's day and month of birth, but it comes up wrong, so I put my day and month in. That's wrong too. Shit. What am I going to do now?

I sit for a while, thinking, but the only alternative pin I can think of is my month and year of birth.

With shaky hands, I type out zero-six, ninety-eight and hover for a moment over the *Okay* button. With my eyes closed, I press *Okay* and open one eye to see if it's worked or not. To my surprise, it's correct.

With my heart beating frantically, I quickly dial Mandy's number. Luckily, I know it by heart. Otherwise, I would have had to search on Facebook, and I really don't want to have to do that on

Drake's phone.

Knowing that there's no going back now, I press *Okay* to call and wait as her phone starts ringing.

"Hello," she tentatively answers. I know she's wondering who this is, but I'm glad Mandy's predictably curious.

"Mandy, it's Evelyn."

I hear her intake of breath before she speaks. "Evelyn, how are you? Drake told me you were ill. Are you okay now? Fuck, Evelyn, I've been worried sick about you."

Ill? So, this is the lie Drake has been spilling to my friend as to the reason why I haven't called.

"Mandy, I'm fine. I haven't been ill—"

"Then why did Drake tell me you were?"

I love Mandy, but she's so frustrating at times. "Don't you get it by now? You know who Drake is, don't you? You yourself pointed out that he kills people. Whatever Drake wants, Drake gets, and I am and have always been at the top of his list. I don't want this, and Drake knows that, so he's kept me prisoner here. That's why I haven't called you."

"But you're calling me now."

I sigh. "Yes. Because Drake had a phone call that he didn't like, threw the phone on the bed with a huff, and stormed out of our room. If he knew I was calling you now, he would flip."

"Jesus, Evelyn."

"Exactly." I close my eyes, hoping that, now, I've finally gotten through to her.

"I ... I don't understand it. He loves you, and you were always so infatuated by him—"

"But he forces it. Don't you understand?" I ask, cutting her off.

"He forces me to want him, forces me to be with him, forces me to have sex with him, forces me to marry him, and now's he's forcing me to have his baby."

"Fuck." She goes deathly silent for a while before speaking. "Can you meet me?"

"I can't. I'm stuck here with armed guards. I've wanted to see you for ages, but Drake said I couldn't. Not until I could be trusted not to run."

"Oh my God."

I can tell she's shocked and unable to quite fathom what's happening. Normally, Mandy's a very vocal girl, but I'm not getting anything from her.

"When do you think I can see you then?" she asks.

I sigh, wondering whether I can trust Mandy enough to tell her. In the end, I know she's the only one I can.

Looking towards the door, I run into the bathroom and start putting on the shower and turning the sink taps on to muffle any noise. I know Drake can see me, but there's no telling whether he can also hear everything that's going on.

"What's that noise?" she asks.

"I've had to put the shower on," I whisper. "The bedroom might be bugged, and I don't want him to hear me."

"Oh," she whispers back. I can't understand why she's whispering.

"Listen, I don't know when I'll get to see you again, but I'm planning on leaving. I've got some help from the inside. He's promised me he would."

"Who?"

"His name's Joe. But please, Mandy. Don't say anything to

anybody about this."

"Of course not."

"Do you promise?"

"I promise. Just be careful."

I smile at Mandy's concern. "I will." I go to work, switching everything off before walking out to the bedroom. I sit down with my smile still plastered and ask her a question.

"So, tell me, what have you been up to? What have I missed these past few weeks?"

"Well, do you remember Reese?"

I frown, but then I remember him from the cinema. "Oh, yes, from that day when we all went out together. I haven't seen him around here."

"I think that's because he's doing some work for Drake elsewhere. I often asked him about you, but he says he has nothing to do with the house anymore."

"Oh, okay."

"Anyway," I smile at the excitement in her voice, "he and I have gone out a few times, and a couple of weeks back, we had sex." She starts giggling.

"Really? What was it like?"

"Oh, my God, he was something else. And the things he can do with his tongue."

I start laughing. "Okay. I think that's too much information."

She giggles again. "Sorry. He just has a body to die for. I can't seem to get enough of him now that I've had a taste. The only problem is that he's a little possessive of me."

I let out a sarcastic laugh. "Oh, I would know all about that."

"He thinks every man is looking at me. It's like being with a caveman."

"I already have my caveman." I look at the wedding ring on my finger. "In fact, I'm now married to the caveman."

She gasps. "When did that happen?"

"A week ago. He didn't invite anyone. He just ordered the priest round to marry us and made two of his guards be witnesses. No church, no beautiful dress, no fancy reception with champagne. Just a very quick marriage followed by quick sex." I remember Drake not wanting to wait any longer to fuck me after we got married. It was almost as if we weren't properly married until he pulled me into the dining room after and pulled my dress up and my knickers down before fucking me over the table. It was over with quickly, but I knew from Drake's excitement that he wouldn't last long. It was almost as if the whole marriage session was his foreplay, and I was his reward after.

"Oh, Evelyn, I just don't understand. I thought it was going to be a big lavish wedding with lots of guests."

"It was supposed to be, but because I wouldn't behave, he decided to force it on me, knowing I had no other choice."

"Why is he doing this?"

I shrug my shoulders. "I really don't know. I really wish I did know. Can you be that obsessed with someone that you're willing to go to such great lengths to have them at all costs?"

She sighs. "I suppose so, but this does seem a bit extreme."

I huff. "Tell me about it." I start feeling depressed again, but I don't want this call to end on a low note, so I decide to change the subject. "Anyway, enough about me. Tell me more about Reese."

I cross my legs on the bed and listen intently as Mandy tells me of her adventures with Reese and how she's enrolled in college to study Biology in September. A pang comes in my gut when she tells me this, but I push it away, opting to be happy for my friend. On the outside, the world is still revolving and other lives exist. Unfortunately, it's just not happening with me in it for now.

As we close on our conversation, I cling on to the hope that one day I will have the life Mandy has, and even though I will most probably never see Mandy again, I will cherish what we had together and cling to the fact that one day … just maybe … I may live a normal life.

CHAPTER NINETEEN

Present Day

I fret for the rest of the day, knowing that Drake will be back soon and will punish me for calling Mandy. I hate him for taking my friends away from me, and I also hate him for taking my freedom. But the part I hate the most about him is that he's here. He's always been here. He's the only person who has ever bothered to be here. True, I'm never safe with him, but he's made sure that he's been such a huge part of my life and had such an impact that I guess I've become ... reliant?

I spend most of my time in my room trying to figure out a way to get out of my current situation. I need to get out, and I don't want to have to rely on Joe, the arsehole, to help me escape. I form plans and strategies in my head until I come up with something so brilliant that I curse myself for not thinking of it earlier.

Thinking it's now or never, I walk to the bedroom door, and I'm surprised and delighted that Drake left it open today. I think that in his haste to get going, he must have forgotten to lock me in. I walk towards the stairs, clutching my stomach and groaning in pain. No one is around, but I suspect there are cameras. I start taking to the stairs one slow step at a time. I'm groaning louder now, and in the corner of my eye, I see someone nearing the stairs. I take that opportunity to fall slightly, screaming out as I go. I feel a set of arms around me and look to find it's Kane.

"What's the matter?" he asks, his deep brown eyes full of concern.

"I don't know." I moan again, gripping my stomach. "Something's not right. I feel like my stomach's going to explode." Okay, that was a bit melodramatic, but I have to be in order to incite some panic into the situation.

Pretty soon, George and a couple of other guards are by my side. "What's wrong?" George asks.

I start moaning again. "Please, you have to help me."

"It's her stomach. I think she needs to go to the hospital." Kane replies.

Bingo!

George looks uncertain, but I moan again, and he knows he has no other choice. "Okay, get Joe to bring the car round, and I'll call Drake to let him know. Take her to St Thomas'."

One of the guards talks into his walkie-talkie while Kane very carefully leads me to the front door. "Help me," I whisper into his neck.

"Don't worry, Mrs Salvatore. You'll be at the hospital in no time."

I silently celebrate as I'm led out into the hot, fresh air. I'm tempted to inhale my pleasure, but manage to hold it in. I need to play at being a great actress until I can figure out what to do once I'm there.

In no time at all, a car is driven round to the bottom of the stairs at speed, and I notice a couple of other men getting out to help me in. You would think I was made of china the way they're fussing over me. I'm bundled into the car with Kane by my side and another joins Joe at the front. I notice Joe looking at me in the rear-view mirror, and I could swear I notice a smile. Maybe he knows what I'm up to. I'm pissed that I also have him to outmanoeuvre when I'm at the hospital. Maybe this is a lost cause, but I'll have to at least try. Fuck the punishment if I'm caught. I need to do this.

I keep groaning all the way there for special effect, and I notice Kane getting more and more agitated. I feel sorry that I'm putting him through this, but if he knew the circumstances, then maybe he would understand.

We're at the hospital in record time and I'm carefully taken out of the car and ushered onto a bed straight away. It's like I'm a fucking celebrity with the amount of people fussing around me. "Tell me where it hurts," a young male doctor asks as I'm being wheeled in.

"She has acute abdominal pain," Kane answers for me.

"Any vomiting?" the doctor asks.

Kane shakes his head. "No, nothing like that so far."

I'm quickly wheeled into a room, and the young doctor turns to all the guards. "You can all wait out here."

Thank God!

He shuts the door behind him and peace is restored. I'm so thrilled that I forget to act ill. The doctor turns to me and frowns a little at my sudden transformation.

"So," he begins, walking towards me. "Can you point to where it hurts?"

I point to the middle of my stomach. "Here, but it seems to have died down a lot now that I'm here."

"Hmm," he responds. "For some reason, that always happens a lot around here." He points to my shirt. "Can you lift that up so I can feel around your tummy?" I do as asked and instead of moaning in discomfort, I start giggling because it's so ticklish. He frowns again. "It seems whatever it was has passed. Maybe just some IBS or gas." He pulls my top down. "I'm going to run some blood tests just to be certain." He looks up at the nurse. "Can I get full blood chemical panel and an AFP? Also, try and schedule an ultrasound as soon as possible."

Okay, I don't know what the hell that is, but the nurse nods and grabs a tray with a syringe and some vials. "As long as you're comfortable now, I'll be back once the results are in. Do you want me to ask anyone out there to come in?" I vigorously shake my head and he frowns at me. "Okay, I'll see you in an hour or so."

He leaves the room and the nurse gets to work taking the blood from me. I wince a little at the needle. "Don't worry, love. It'll be over before you know it." She smiles at me reassuringly, so I smile back. "There," she says, taking the needle out. "I'll get these processed straight away and get on with making a slot for the ultrasound, okay? You just sit tight, and I'll be with you shortly."

I nod my head. "Thank you."

She seems to like that because she beams at me. "You're welcome, sweetheart."

She leaves, and I'm all on my own in a box room. The only exit is where the guards are standing by waiting. I groan. Maybe this was fruitless after all. All I got out of this was a wasted trip to the doctors where I've so far had needles stuck in my arm. I know Drake will be here soon, so time is running out.

I drop my head back on the pillow with a sigh. I shut my eyes and pray that someone up there can offer me a miracle. I'm not sure how long I am alone with my thoughts of this, but the door swings open, and in pops the nurse with a wheelchair. "Come on, sweetheart. We have a very convenient slot for you now. I can take you up."

Smiling, I get off the bed and settle myself inside the wheelchair. No doubt, the doctors and nurses here know who I am because I seem to be getting the star treatment.

The nurse opens the door and wheels me out. I make a show of holding onto my stomach so the guards can see. Joe is smiling and Kane looks concerned. He places a hand on my shoulder as we walk. "Drake knows, and he's on his way. He should be here in ten minutes or so." I smile up to him, but once I turn my head, I bite my lip and close my eyes. I'm never going to be able to escape now.

Taking the lift up one floor, the nurse wheels me into a darkened room and tells me to hop onto the bed. An ultrasound machine is next to it, humming away. "Get yourself comfortable. The doctor should be with you in a few minutes."

"Okay, thank you."

She nods with a smile and makes her way outside. That's when I look and see another door to my right-hand side. I don't know what's through there or if anyone is in the room, but I have to try.

With no time to waste, I get up and move quickly to the other door. I turn as silently as possible and push it slightly open. It's an office and it's empty. I make my way in, shut the door behind me, and notice a set of scrubs and a chiffon scarf. I quickly put these on and wrap the scarf around my head. Once dressed, I open the door to the office, and without looking to my left, I walk out and start making my way down the corridor. At the end is a turning, and I have to utilise every ounce of willpower I possess to keep myself from running—lest

I get caught in my efforts to avoid detection. I get to the corner and run to the nearest fire exit. I rush down two steps at a time and nearly trip once I hit the bottom. I open the door to run out, and that's when I see Drake and a couple of other guards coming through the entrance. I quickly pull the door back and wait a few seconds before opening again. He's gone, but I did notice how upset and anxious he looked.

I push the door a little more and make a hasty escape. I can't help but peek a little behind me, and that's when I see Kane looking at me. My eyes widen, but he doesn't do anything. In fact, he just seems to pretend not to notice and carries on walking away.

Shit, that was close. Not knowing whether he's running to tell Drake, I run outside, and I don't stop running until my legs start to protest. I find a quiet street and pull the scrubs and scarf off me. It's way too hot for this.

It's then I realise I'm free. But just as the euphoria comes from knowing this, so too does the fact that I have no money and nowhere to go. Fuck, I'm such an idiot. I didn't want to come this far only to have it stripped from me.

So, I do the only thing I can think of. I'm sweaty, and I'm obviously distressed, so I make an extra effort by slightly tearing my shirt. I look onto the road and try to find someone I can stop. Someone who looks trustworthy. After only a couple of minutes, I see an elderly lady driving down the road.

I don't hesitate. I run out into the road and flag her down. I start crying and willing for her to stop. She must see the mess I'm in because she quickly comes to a halt. I run over to the passenger side and lean over to speak with her. "Please, you must help me. I need to get away. He's after me."

Her eyes widen, but she takes in the state I'm in and nods her head. "Quickly, get in. Get in."

I gasp with a half smile. "Oh, thank you! Thank you! You don't know what this means to me." I hastily get in, and thankfully, she drives away as soon as I do. I know Drake will realise I'm gone by now and is no doubt already on my tail.

"Shall I take you to the nearest police station?"

No, I don't want that at all. I just need to get far away from here. "Please, no." I try to think of an excuse as to why not, and in my haste, I come up with something perfect. "You see, the guy who did this to me is my ex and a police officer. Going to the police is the *least* safe option."

She looks ahead, and I notice her concerned frown. "Oh, dear. That's not good, is it? Has he done this to you before?"

I nod my head. "Yes. That's why he's my ex. But he won't take no for an answer. He'll be after me now, so I need to get as far away as possible in order to figure out what to do next." I look ahead at the road for a moment. "Do you mind me asking where you're headed?"

"I'm actually going to visit my sister's house in Reading."

Reading! Shit, that couldn't be more perfect. It's at least thirty miles away from here.

"Do you mind if I tag along?"

She shakes her head. "Of course not. Let's get you as far away from that horrible man as possible. What's your name, dear?"

I wonder whether to lie, but considering she's been so courteous, I decide to be honest with her. "Evelyn."

She smiles. "Ah, Evelyn. Such a beautiful name for a beautiful girl." She looks at me for a moment. "You're wearing such mature clothing for such a young girl. How old are you? Nineteen? Twenty

176

at most."

I look down at my white blouse and grey pencil skirt and think she's right. I look like a high executive woman in her thirties. Not an eighteen-year-old girl.

"I'm eighteen," I reply with a sigh. For some reason, an overwhelming sadness comes over me. Yes, I may be free for now, and yes, this is all I've ever wanted. But why is it that it has had come to this? I'm at a crossroads now, and I sure as hell don't know which one to take. Wherever it leads me could either be my downfall or my saving grace.

"At eighteen, you shouldn't have to be dealing with someone like that. I assume he's quite a bit older than you?"

I nod. "Yes. He's twelve years older. I've known him quite a while. He's always been ... how would you say ... possessive."

She nods her head with a frown. "Yes, it sounds like it, dear. It's just a shame you're the one that's running. He shouldn't be an officer of the law when he breaks the law himself." She starts tutting under her breath. "Have you got somewhere you can stay once we get to Reading?"

I nod my head. "I'm sure I can think of something." I can tell she doesn't like the answer, but she doesn't say anything either. "Can I ask your name?"

"It's Dorothy, but my friends call me Dotty."

I smile at that. "Well, it's nice to meet you, Dorothy."

"Please, call me Dotty."

"Okay, I will. And thank you so much for accepting me into your car. I could have been anybody."

She smiles. "Well, you left me little choice."

"I'm sorry."

She places her hand on my arm, and I notice how unusually cold it is next to the heat of the day. Mind you, she has the air conditioning on, and I'm only now reaping the benefits of it after running at least a mile without stopping.

"Don't be sorry. I'm just glad that I can help in any small way possible."

I shake my head on a sigh. "You have no idea just how much of a great help this actually is. I just need to put some distance between us, so that I can figure out what to do next."

"Hmm," she ponders. "I don't make no mind to gossip, but I have heard rumours of a certain gentleman. He once helped my friend Mabel's niece. She got herself into all sorts of trouble when she was a teen." She shakes her head, tutting to herself again. "She was mixed up in drugs and therefore mixed with bad people. The bad people tried to do all sorts of despicable things." She sighs, looking sad. "Anyway, this gentleman helped the parents get their daughter back and even paid for her to go to the Priory. I think you know just how expensive that is?" She looks at me for reassurance, so I nod my head. "Well, she was there for around six weeks—something like that. He got her into college, and she came out with a diploma in architecture. She then got herself a boyfriend and is living with him now. I believe she and her boyfriend are even trying for a baby." She smiled at that. "She owes it all to that man." She looks deep in thought for a while before speaking again. "Anyway, I did have a point to the story." She looks over to me, and we both laugh. "I have heard he's very influential around my way. If you need to, I can ask Mabel if she has his number still. Maybe he can help you."

I would have thought that I had heard of this man, but I haven't. There's only one influential man that I know around my way.

"Can you remember the gentleman's name?"

She frowns for a moment, staring ahead at the road. "Hmm... I think it's David. No, Drew. Maybe it was Jake." She suddenly gasps. "I remember now. It's Drake ... Drake Salvatore. I remember the surname because of a certain young chap in *The Vampire Diaries*."

She smirks, and her eyebrows curve up a little at her joke, but after hearing that, it's hard for me to muster up a laugh. I did manage to smile a little, but my heart won't stop thumping. Drake did this for these people? But at what cost? I doubt he did it for nothing.

"How long ago was this?" I ask.

She moves her head a little closer to me to hear. "What's that?"

"Mabel's niece. How long ago was it that this Drake helped her out?"

"Oh," she says, returning to her position, "I think this was five or six years ago now. My, how time flies."

So this was when Drake knew me. I don't understand it. He's always such an arsehole with me, so how come this other girl gets rescued and placed into college, but when it comes to me, he keeps me prisoner? I can't help but feel how unjust the world is. I should feel enamoured with Drake for how he helped that girl, but all I can feel is anger. Hot-blooded anger tinged with jealousy is flowing through my veins at the thought of how much he gave to that one girl—a stranger—while he did nothing but strip me of all my choices and free will.

"Would you like me to ask Mabel?"

I snap myself out of my daydream and shake my head. "No, that's fine, thank you. I would prefer to try and deal with this on my own for now."

"I understand. You're obviously very independent."

I chuckle. "I've been told I'm rather stubborn too on many occasions."

She laughs at that, and it makes me smile. "Ah, there's no harm in being a little stubborn. 'To those waiting with bated breath for that favourite media catchphrase, the U-turn, I have only this to say: You turn if you want; the lady's not for turning.'"

"That's a great quote."

"Yes, but unfortunately, it's not from me. It came from the late Margaret Thatcher—God rest her soul. But, there is also something else to say about being stubborn. No matter all the will and pride you have in this world, you will at some point stumble. Sometimes, you will fall. But it takes a great person to choke on their pride and admit when they need that offered helping hand to get back up."

I smile. "Also great."

She briefly looks at me with an amused grin. "That one was mine."

I chuckle. "Very good."

I'm starting to really like Dotty. She's obviously a woman of advanced years, but she's still a lot of fun. She looks to be around her late seventies with long, greying hair in a tight bun. I also notice she's wearing a wedding band. "So, do you not have a Mr Dotty to bring with you to visit your sister?"

"No," she says sadly. "My Henry passed some five years ago now. Cancer it was. First, his lungs, but once it spread to his liver, he quickly faded into a man I couldn't recognise. He didn't last long after that."

I feel an overwhelming sadness for her. "I'm so sorry."

"Don't be." She smiles towards me. "I had the most wonderful fifty-five years with him." She suddenly points to the glove compartment. "Open that up. In there, you will find my purse. I have a few pictures in it of him, my kids, and my grandkids."

I do as asked, pleased that she trusts me enough to handle her purse. I don't think I would have been as trusting if it were me. Pulling the handle, I see a load of papers inside, but also a big blue purse on top. I take it out, and she instructs me to open the zip. Once open, I see a clear casing with a black and white photo of a man who looks to be in his thirties in a soldier's uniform. His hair is dark and swept back, and his posture is straight and serious. He looks handsome, though.

"That's my Henry. This was taken a few years after I met him."

"He was in the army?"

"Yes, 1st Battalion Grenadier Guards. He loved it. I and our children led an army life for many years, living on the barracks. But after a while, our kids got tired of all the travelling." She then points to the purse. "At the back of that photo is another."

I pull the photo of Henry out and place it carefully on my lap. I look back at the purse and see three grown women and six children of all different ages. Four boys and two girls.

"Those are my daughters, Meredith, Katherine, and Susan. Meredith has three sons, Tim, David, and Mark. Tim is the cheeky little devil."

I look at the photo, and straight away, I see one boy who is smiling mischievously at the camera. "Is this Tim by any chance?"

She gasps. "Yes. However did you guess? I suppose it's something to do with that butter-wouldn't-melt expression?"

I chuckle. "Yes, I think it must be that."

"The other boy is Karl. He's Susan's son. The other two daughters, Beth and Michelle, belong to Katherine."

"Wow, you have quite the family. You must be proud."

"Extremely," she answers with a big smile.

I start putting the photos away and place the purse back in the glove compartment. I feel a sense of sadness, and I think Dotty notices.

"What about your family?"

Looking down, I start playing with my hands. "I don't have any."

"None at all?"

I shake my head. "I guess when life was handing out sugar to balance out all the lemons I got, it skipped that particular line with me." I try a chuckle, but Dotty looks sad for me. "Please don't feel sad for me. It's all I've ever known."

"But, how can I not feel sad for you? How can anyone with a heart not feel sad for you?" She shakes her head, and I can tell she doesn't know what to say. "I suppose when life gives you the downs, there's only one place left to go."

Wow, this woman is something else. I only wished she was my grandmother. "I take that to mean you're a glass-is-half-full kind of gal?"

She starts laughing. "Yes, I guess so. I've been tested a few times in my lifetime, but I have also been blessed. I always think of that when life decides to test me."

I nod. "I suppose it's better to look at it that way."

"Have you ever watched the film *Good Will Hunting*?" I shake my head. "You should. It's about a very gifted young man around your age trying to find his direction in life. You should watch it."

I nod. "I'll have to remember that."

We then start idle chit-chat about movies, songs, and even politics. I was so enamoured by her that I didn't even realise that we were in Reading until she stopped the car on a quiet street.

"This is me. Would you like to come in for something to eat? I'm sure Heather won't mind."

I shake my head and take her hand. "No, really. You've done more than enough."

She doesn't look very happy with this, but quickly leans over and gets her purse out. She pulls out a couple of fifty pound notes and tries to hand them to me. "No, I can't. Please."

She forces it in my hand. "I won't take no for an answer."

My God, I feel like a total shit now. "But I can't—"

"Yes, you can. Go find your sugar and make yourself some lemonade." I look at her sincere expression and an overwhelming feeling of gratitude builds inside me for this stranger, who has just in the last hour, become my only friend in the world. I can't help the tears that well as I nod my head.

"Thank you," I say softly. I'm trying hard not to cry, but the wetness still builds inside my eyes. "I will pay you back one day. I promise. Even if it takes years, I promise I will find you and pay you back."

She waves me off. "It doesn't matter if you can't. It would be nice for you not to be a stranger, though. Once you're settled, look me up on Facebook. It'll be under Dotty Fisher. I'm the one with a pogo stick." I look at her with widened eyes. "Don't ask," she says in response.

I start chuckling. "Okay."

She looks towards what I assume is her sister's house. "Are you sure you won't come in with me? Even for a sandwich?"

I shake my head. "No, I'm fine. I better get going."

"Okay, if you're sure?" I nod my head and pull the handle of the

183

car to get out. Dotty soon follows suit, and once on the pavement, I give her a big hug.

"Thank you so much for this. You really don't know how much it means to me."

She pats my back. "A good deed never goes unpunished. Just be sure to pass it on one day—once you've made your lemonade of course."

Pulling away from her, I chuckle. "I will."

She strokes my hair, and I can't help but feel so cherished by that one small gesture. "You take care of yourself, okay?"

I nod my head. "I will. Thank you again."

"Don't mention it, dear."

I move away, saying goodbye ,and once I turn, I realise that for the first time in my life, I've had some sort of normality. It was only for an hour, but how fantastic that hour was. Dotty is an amazing woman, and I'm determined to follow through with my promise. I will find her—no matter how long it takes—and I will pay her back.

As I reach the end of the street, I see another, busier one ahead of me. I'm not sure whether I should turn right or left, but I know I will have to make a choice. Suddenly, I start laughing. For the first time ever, I can choose my path.

I look left and then right. To my right, I spot a market stall in the distance called "Squeeze Me." I smile as it has me thinking of that lemonade Dotty told me to make for myself.

"Right it is then."

I just hope it's also the right choice.

CHAPTER TWENTY

Present Day

I wander around aimlessly, and I don't know for how long. At first, I just walk and walk, taking in the sights, smells, and people. I had been cooped up in a house for far too long, and I needed just a few hours to myself to wander and think. I knew as the hours passed that I would need to find somewhere to get my head down eventually. I found a fish and chip shop and had something to eat. I was starving by the time five o'clock came around. I hadn't even had breakfast today, so no wonder I wolfed it down like a ravenous animal. Even the guy behind the counter looked at me with an amused grin. "Hungry?" he asked. "Or is it that my fish and chips are that good? I hope it's the latter."

"The latter," I said with a smile. "But I'm also really hungry. I haven't eaten all day."

He shook his head. "You need to eat. Men like a bit of curves, if you know what I mean." He had winked and was quickly distracted by another customer. I carried on eating until it was time to leave.

Once outside, I take a look at my watch and find it's six o'clock already. If I don't start looking for a hotel now, I'll end up on the streets tonight.

With that thought and a shiver down my spine, I start making my way down the main strip and ask a couple if they know where the nearest hotel is. They give me a couple of names and point in the direction. I say my thanks and walk the five or so minutes until I turn a corner on a quiet street. I notice a couple of signs for B&B's in the distance, so I head that way. Both of them were over sixty pounds, and I had already cut into six pounds of my one hundred. I needed to save money for trainfare somewhere tomorrow and another night in a hotel before I can figure something out for the long term.

Feeling defeated, I turn a corner and notice an Ibis hotel a little farther down the road. I quickly rush towards it and see a cheery man behind the counter.

"Can you tell me how much for tonight?"

"Normally, it would be forty-four quid, but how about I make it forty for you?"

I smile. "That'll be great." I walk towards the counter, and he hands me a form to sign.

"Can you just fill this in? I will need to see some ID." I bite my lip and he notices. He also notices the ripped shirt. "You know, ID isn't really that necessary."

I breathe a sigh of relief. "Thank you."

"No worries, sweetheart. Just know we're not all like that." He points to my shirt and already he's jumped to conclusions. Of course, I'm going to let him. I need him to be on my side as much as possible.

"I know. Thank you. I appreciate this."

"No problem."

I sign the form and he hands me the keys. I then hand over two twenty quid notes and he puts it in the cashier. I grab the keys and say my thanks when he shouts after me. "Miss, your change."

Frowning, I go back to the counter and he's holding out a ten pound note. I frown. "I thought you said—"

"Special discount rates for employee's family. If anyone asks, you're my cousin from out of town."

I take the ten pound note from him and well up for the second time today. "Thank you."

"Don't mention it. I won't see you in the morning, but you have a nice night. I hope tomorrow will be a better one."

"Thanks," I answer and walk away. If I stay any longer, I'll probably ball my eyes out. I'm not normally the crying type, but today has been an exception. That's two people who have been generous today. I really do have a lot to pay forward.

I get into my room and smile when I see a nice, comfortable-looking double bed. I place my card inside, and the first thing I do is run a hot bath. I have no spare clothing, so I'll have to wear the same thing tomorrow. I hate it, but have no other choice.

Once my bath is run, I sink inside and close my eyes, thinking about the day I've just had and what tomorrow may bring. I contemplate where I can go next, and the only place I can think about that is as far away from Drake as possible is Scotland. I'm not sure if my money will stretch that far, but I'm sure I can ask at the counter tomorrow morning if they know where the nearest coach park is. It'll be the longest option, but the cheapest. At least once I'm there, I can find a place to stay and immediately start looking for work.

Thinking about it, the whole thing frightens me to death, but also somehow thrills me. For the last five years, I knew my path because it was chosen for me. Now, I feel like I'm on an adventure with no clue as to how things will turn out. Excitement bubbles, and

I smile at the thought. I'm being reckless and throwing caution to the wind, but I don't care.

"I'm free!" I scream at the top of my lungs. I splash at the water and shout again. "I'm free!" If anyone's next door, they'll think I'm mad. I start chuckling at the thought.

Once finished, I grab the offered dressing gown and put it on. I then jump on my bed a little before putting on the TV. I watch a couple of reruns of *Friends* before my eyes start to feel droopy. I look at the clock and find it's already ten.

Sighing, I get up off the bed and walk towards the TV. I turn it off, and I'm about to walk to my bed when a knock on the door sounds. I frown, wondering who on earth it could be. Maybe it's the receptionist's manager, and he's found out that I'm staying here and wants to check that I'm his cousin or something.

I hear a knock again, so I shout, "Coming," before walking quickly towards the door. I open it and gasp when I see who it is.

"Well, hello there, Evelyn."

CHAPTER TWENTY ONE

Present Day

As quickly as I can, I try to slam the door, but he's way too quick. I try and scream, but immediately, he has a hand over my mouth. "Not so fast, little one." Once he has me in place behind me he snuggles his face into my neck and inhales. "Don't you just love that new bath smell?"

"What do you want?" I muffle behind his hand.

"I'm surprised you don't know. I thought we had a deal?"

"I'm not going back to Drake," I muffle into his hand.

"Drake doesn't know where you are, but I do. I knew you were up to something from the very beginning. I kept my distance and followed you all the way here. Now, don't you owe me something?"

He takes his hand away momentarily.

"That was if you helped me, but I managed it all by myself. Besides, I wouldn't sleep with you if you were the last man on earth."

Joe sniggers at my neck and licks it. My heart starts drumming and with it so does the fear. With his body still fixed to mine, he places a hand inside my dressing gown and finds my breast. He hisses his pleasure as he fondles me. All I feel is sick.

"Hmm, I want nothing more than to take this further, but unfortunately, someone else got wind of your escape and demanded that I bring you to him."

My eyes widen. "Who?"

"My boss."

"But Drake is your boss." I'm confused. What's happening?

"Drake is not my boss. He was just my way in to get to you. My real boss is the one who's been desperate to meet you. He's also my father, but that's another story."

"What are you talking about?"

"I'm talking about Isaac Monroe."

My eyes widen in fear. Practically all my life I have been told to fear that name. I've been shielded from this man for years, but what is it that he wants from me? What makes me so special?

"What does he want with me?"

He starts fondling my breasts again, and I try pulling away. "I have a knife in my pocket you could meet if you're not careful." I immediately still. "That's better. You see, my father has known about you for quite a long time. You're the girl who the great Drake Salvatore has been salivating over for the last few years. He knows the price Drake has paid for you. You're worth a pretty penny now out there in the big wide world. Isn't that where you've always wanted to be? Out there seeing what the real world is all about? Well, you asked, and now you shall receive." A phone starts ringing in his pocket, and he sighs his displeasure. "That'll no doubt be my dad wondering what's taking me so long. For some reason, he doesn't want me to fuck you before I bring you to him. So much to do and so little time." I feel a syringe in my arm and scream out. He has his hand over me again, and within seconds, my legs feel wobbly and my eyes begin to droop. "That's it, little one. Sleepy time."

When I wake, I find I'm restricted on a bed. I don't have my dressing gown on anymore, but what I do have on is a white negligee.

I look around the room, but all I see are four white walls, a door, and a window. That's it. I think I'm all alone, but then, I hear a voice.

"Ah, she's awake."

I search the sound of the voice, and wish I hadn't. That scar that has haunted me since I was thirteen is staring back at me. The scar belonging to the man with the most evil-looking eyes. Drake never wanted me near him, and now I can see why.

"Why am I here?"

He starts tutting. "Such questions. Obviously, Drake didn't teach you well enough. You were always the light in his eye. You were the only one to ... soften him shall we say. Everyone was fascinated with you—including me. Unfortunately, he always kept you at arm's length. Such a pity really." His eyes snake the length of my body. "I could have gotten more for you if it wasn't for the fact he had gotten to you first. Do you have any idea what the going rate is for you now since word got around that you were bought for five million? Men have been practically banging my door down for you. Some have even offered five hundred thousand for just thirty minutes of alone time. Can you imagine?"

My eyes widen when I realise what he means. "You kidnapped me just to whore me out?"

"I wouldn't call it whoring. I would consider it more of a sex slave. You do as you're told around here, and in return, you get a roof over your head, clothes to wear, and three square meals a day. We are the ones who generate the well-earned cash for you all." He suddenly frowns. "Hasn't Drake already briefed you about this?" When he sees the confused look on my face, he shakes his head. "My, my, Drake really has softened up, hasn't he?"

He starts laughing and it maddens me. Suddenly, I want to stick up for Drake. "I am his wife, not a sex slave."

"So, he didn't lock you up and only let you go when he wanted to play?" When I look down, I hear his evil laugh. "I thought so." He gets up and walks towards my bed and sits down. I start straining against my restraints.

"Don't touch me."

He laughs out a throaty laugh again. "You think highly of yourself, don't you? Not everyone wants to fuck you, you know. But I know plenty who will." He looks up at my hand and rises to grab the rings. I struggle again, pulling my fingers into a fist. Normally, nothing would give me more pleasure than to snap those rings off my fingers, but not when he's doing it.

"Unclamp you fingers." I don't, and he struggles to unclamp them, but I'm determined. "Unclamp your fucking fingers now, bitch!" I scream out a no, and he slaps me really hard across the face. The sting is so bad that I gasp and momentarily forget my hand. Isaac has them off within an instant. "You may be married, but only on paper. I have plans for you, Evelyn. My son has been itching to go first, but you'll be glad to hear that I'm holding him off. He's a persistent little fucker, though." He shakes his head on a smile. "Like father, like son."

He gets up, placing the rings in his pocket. He then walks to the door and opens it. Joe is standing there, looking like the prick that he is. Isaac looks at Joe and then turns around to look at me. "If I get so much as a whiff that you've lifted that negligee of hers up, I'll cut your fucking fingers off. Tomorrow, I have waiting clients for her, but first she has to be prepped."

"Yes, sir," he answers as Isaac shuts my door.

For a moment, I'm alone. My face stings, and my eyes start to water with unshed tears. How did I manage to get that glimpse today—just to have it so cruelly ripped away from me? I thought I was doing so well, and then *this*? Who is this man? What does he want from me? And why do I need to be "prepped?" Prepped for what?

I go over everything he said in my head, and I wonder what it is that Drake's been mixed up in all these years. I may have known him for six of them, but I never really knew him at all.

Closing my eyes, I start to wonder if I did the right thing today. Maybe I shouldn't have fled when I had the chance. I certainly wouldn't be here now. I think about all the times when Drake told me he was keeping me safe, and I used to laugh at him.

I'm not laughing now.

My moment of alone time is soon over when Joe walks into the room and shuts the door a few minutes later. He stalks towards me with an evil smile on his face. It's then that I can see the resemblance.

"I always thought you were a twat."

He seems shocked by that. "Wow, we are a gobby cow, aren't we? Maybe I should shut that gobby mouth of yours with my cock. How's that?"

"Do that, and I'll bite it off." I'm trying to save face. I don't want this arsehole to see me weak ... to see me begging him to stop. Whatever he's going to do, he'll do whether I beg or not. Unfortunately, I know this too much from experience.

For a moment, I feel a fleeting wave of regret deep in my gut. I shouldn't have tried to escape Drake. Maybe he knew my fate all along, but for some reason, he didn't tell me, and it pisses me off. Maybe, if he had told me, I would have been more pliable ... more ... compliant with his demands. The things that man has done to me are fucked up and inexcusable, but I can't help feeling that little pang inside.

I miss him.

Joe deliberately stalks slowly around my bed, circling me like a lion. I know why he's doing it. He's trying to prolong my agony. Only he knows what he's about to do, and yes, it frightens me to death, but I won't show it. I'm determined not to let him see my fear.

Finally, he walks up to the head of the bed and unzips his jeans. I notice he's breathing heavily, and so too am I, but for a completely different reason. He's turned on, and the evidence of that is clear when he takes out his cock and near enough shoves it towards my face.

"Suck it, and suck it good."

"Are you an idiot? I already told you I would bite it. Are you a masochist or something?"

He smiles and then starts laughing. That laughter brings cold shivers up my spine. He tries sticking his cock in my mouth, but I clamp my lips down shut and violently move my head from side to side.

Within an instant, he has his fingers clamped down on my nose and I have no option but to open my mouth to breathe, but instead of air coming out, Joe's cock goes in. He pushes in so deep and so fast that I gag and start choking.

Joe pulls out laughing. "Not so gobby now, are you, cunt?"

I wince at that word, and I feel myself falter a little. Tears start pooling in my eyes, mostly due to him shoving something unexpected into my mouth, but also because I'm tired. I'm sick and tired of this shit.

"Aww, are you crying?"

I inhale a sharp breath and, with it, the anger comes. "You'd like that, wouldn't you?"

He takes his trousers off and climbs on top of me. I start to struggle, thinking he's going to do the worst, but also remembering what his father said.

"Your father said—"

"I know what my fucking father said," he replies in annoyance. He unhooks the ties of my negligee. "He said I couldn't lift your negligee up to fuck you, but he didn't say I couldn't pull it down." His evil smirk returns as I start to flex my hips to get him off of me. He's straddling me now, laughing like the evil monster that he is. Why I had never seen this part of him before I don't know.

He yanks hard until both my breasts are exposed to him. He looks down at them and starts fondling each one. I can see the want in his eyes, and it makes me feel sick. One by one, he takes each nipple into his mouth, suckling on them and moaning as he goes, but then he bites one of them hard, and I scream out.

Placing a hand on my mouth, he silences me. "Shh," he says, placing a finger to his lip. "You'll get to enjoy the pain at some point. All the whores do."

"There's no way any woman on earth would get enjoyment out of being held against her will and forced upon like this."

"All you sluts love it," he says, licking my nipple again. He then gets up and pushes himself up closer to me. I wonder what the hell he's doing until I see him positioning his cock on my chest. He starts to pleasure himself until a little precum forms at the tip. He rubs it in my chest together with some of his spit. I start to gag and look away, but all this does is make Joe laugh.

"You have perfect tits. I'll give you that, little one."

"Fuck you," I say, gritting my teeth.

"Oh, I would love to, but for now, I'll have to make do with a tit wank." With my chest wet from his spit and juices, he cups my breasts around his cock and starts pumping himself in and out. "Fuck. That feels even better than I thought it would. Look at me pumping my cock through your tits, Evelyn. Look."

I don't look. I do everything I can to turn my head away and close my eyes. I don't want to see the vile things he's doing to my body. I don't want to have any participation in this at all. I want my mind to leave my body, float above this bed, and leave my body behind.

Unfortunately, I can't shut off my hearing. I can't shut off the fact that he's grabbing my breasts and holding them together so forcefully that it hurts. I want it to be over, and the sooner, the better.

"You want this cock, don't you, little one? You want me inside your pussy, don't you? Say you want me inside that golden fucking pussy of yours."

I can feel the bile creeping up in my throat as he picks up his pace. The smell of his cock invades my nostrils, making them flare.

"Fuck, you're going to make me come."

He makes a loud groaning sound, and I feel when his come hits my neck and chest. I start to gag until I have no other choice but to turn my head and vomit over the side of the bed.

I hear laughter. "Oh dear. Look at the mess you've made." I lean my head back on the pillow and close my eyes. "My dad won't be happy when he sees all this mess. Maybe I should help to clean some up, shall I?" He starts rubbing his cum in all over my chest and breast area, making sure all of it is coated in. Once done, he inspects his work. "See, that's better."

Thankfully, he gets off me and places his now limp dick back in his jeans. He zips himself up and leans into my ear. I turn my face away from him, but not before I see him smile.

"Next time I get to you, you'll have no time to think about vomiting because you'll be too busy concentrating on my cock buried deep inside that delicious-looking cunt of yours. I already had a little feel while you were sleeping." He gets back up then and starts walking to the door. "I would stay longer, but quite frankly, you stink of vomit and come, so I'll think I'll pass. I'm sorry if that disappoints you."

I want to scream at him and tell him to fuck off, but I know he's expecting that, so I deliberately remain quiet. Inside, I'm dying from the violation. For some reason, Joe doing this to me is ten times worse than all the rapes I received from Drake. I don't know why that is. Maybe it has something to do with the fact that I've known Drake for what feels like all my life. He's familiar to me, and therefore I know his personality traits—all of them.

But, as the door closes, I can't help let the frightened lamb inside of me out. I thought punishments from Drake were bad enough, but this ... this is exponentially worse. My eyes moisten, and despite the fact someone might be watching me through a camera, I quietly let those tears fall. I thought I had no hope in the world and no future with Drake, but I would take a lifetime of that in exchange for getting me out of here.

As I close my eyes, I think about the conversation I had in the car with Dotty. She was the one who said that situations in life can always be worse than the one you're in, but right now, I can't think of what could be worse than this. I've been kidnapped, and no doubt being prepped for men who want to do vile things to me. There's also no doubt that they'll be worse things than what Joe just did to me on this bed.

I have no idea of time. I know it's dark, and I know it must be the early hours of the morning. I want to stay awake just in case someone comes into the room, but as the minutes pass, my eyes can't help lulling themselves shut for sleep. I want to fight, but right now, all the fight has been taken out of me. The smell of Joe fades, or it could be that I've just gotten so used to the smell that I don't smell him anymore. Whatever it is, I welcome it.

As I slink into unconsciousness, I can't help but cling onto a hope I thought I would never ever cling to. For years, I've wanted to run away from Drake Salvatore. For years, I have hated, lusted, and loved that man with a passion so fierce that it burned me from the inside out. I loathed his possessiveness and the power he held over me for so long that all I could think about was an escape. He told me countless times he was there to save me and to protect me like a man who loves a woman should.

So, I drift off to sleep with words I never thought I would utter in my lifetime playing on my lips. So softly, I say them like a prayer to a higher being.

"Come save me, Drake."

He is my only prayer.

He is my only hope.

Come save me, Drake. Please.

CHAPTER TWENTY TWO

Present Day

I don't know what time it is that I'm awoken with voices in my room. Initially, in my sleepy haze, I think I'm at Drake's, and for a fleeting moment, I groan at the thought.

But then, I remember. I remember the day before—fleeing from Drake and being taken against my will. I remember how much I enjoyed the normality of a car ride with Dotty and all the nice people I met on the way after. I remember being in my hotel room, and then, lastly, I remember what Joe did to me in it.

I'm about to reluctantly open my eyes when I feel cold water being thrown over my head. My eyes fling open, and I gasp for air. The water is freezing.

I hear laughter. "Wakey-wakey, Drakey's girl. It's time to get up, clean this fucking shit up, and get ready for later. You've been sleeping all fucking day."

Joe is standing above me smirking. Another guy, who looks like just as much of a douche as Joe, is laughing. "*Wakey-wakey, Drakey's girl*. That's funny."

Joe smirks, but doesn't acknowledge douche number two. "Did

you have a nice sleep, little one? Did our little adventure last night tire you? You'll be needing more stamina for what's in store for you." Douche number two laughs again as Joe leans over to release me from my restraints. "You're going to love what's coming next for you. Especially your bath. Fuck, I often have them myself they're so good."

I frown at him, wondering what the hell he's on about. It's only when he forces me to my feet and drags me out into this narrow hallway and through another door that I see. It's a massive room that is at once a bathroom and a bedroom. In the middle is a full bath with three naked women standing and waiting for me with sponges. I start to walk back, but Joe pushes me forward.

"I can't believe she wants to back out of this." He starts laughing and so does douche number two. "You can wait outside," he orders him.

I see the reluctance on his face, but he follows Joe's orders and backs out of the door. And then I'm left in this strange bathroom with just Joe and the three naked girls. I try to look at them to see if I can detect any sign that they don't want to be here as much as I don't, but they all look wooden. It's like they're robots. There's no emotion from them whatsoever. They're all beautiful, but they're all like statues. They all have perfect, flawless skin. One is blonde, one's brunette, and one has the blackest, silkiest hair that I've ever seen. They all look well taken care of and healthy, but I suspect they've been deliberately made that way. Just the way I'm now being made. The thought both scares and depresses me.

I'm pushed forward by Joe, and the one with the black hair starts to pull my negligee off my head. I don't move, prompting Joe to stick my arms up in the air. Once the negligee is off me, Joe moves closer to my back and reaches forward to touch the other girl's breast. She doesn't move. She doesn't even flinch. "This little one here is not like you ladies. She's got spunk and fight in her. I'm sure together we can help crack her." I turn my head to him, not knowing what he's talking about, but all I'm met with is his evil grin. "Time for your bath," he says, guiding me towards it.

"Get in and stand up," Joe orders.

I do as I'm asked as, quite frankly, I want nothing more than to be washed—especially after what Joe did to me last night. One by one, the girls dip the sponges in the water and rub soap into them before washing me. They're so gentle and soothing that I almost close my eyes. As the warm water hits me, I immediately feel the cold aftermath, and it makes my nipples pucker.

"Mmm. So sexy. Do you see those, ladies? All natural and ready for sucking." Joe stands in front of me and watches intently as the ladies wash under my arms and over my breasts before going down between my legs and in between my thighs. I can see how much this is turning him on. If it wasn't for the heated stare in his eyes there to let me know, it would definitely be the straining erection in his jeans giving me a clue.

"Sit down," he orders me.

I do as he says, and the blonde woman gently pushes my head back. They don't say anything, and they're not forceful. It's like they're used to this—like they've done this a thousand times already.

At a leisurely pace, the blonde girl washes my hair and works it into a lather as she rinses it off. Then, the brunette comes with a toothbrush and starts brushing my teeth.

This is so weird. I can brush my own teeth, but I somehow knew this wasn't what Joe was expecting. He wants them to do all the work. In fact, I can tell he's getting great pleasure in seeing them pampering me like a china doll.

Soon after, the girl with the black hair comes over with a bowl and I spit the toothpaste in. I hear Joe clap his hand, and it makes me jump. "Right. Now, on to the fun and games. I'm really going to enjoy this." I frown at him and he notices. "Oh, don't worry, little one. You're going to really enjoy this. In fact, I'm going to have so much fun making you enjoy it." My eyes widen in fear. What does he have planned for me?

In no time, the girl with the blonde hair has a towel and grabs my hand to let me out. She dries me off while the brunette gets to work towel drying my hair. Once finished, Joe motions me towards the bed. "Get on it," he instructs. I shake my head. "Get on it, or I'll make you." I stand still, refusing to let him win. He sighs, shaking his head, and grabs me from behind. I start struggling, but soon he has my hands locked behind me as he pushes me towards the bed. He shoves me down so hard that I have no time to react to the fact that he's now turning me over and putting me in more restraints. The bed is huge, and I notice I'm lying on silky red sheets. Any other time, this would have been a wonderful bed to sleep in, but I know that's not what's going to happen now.

Once my hands are tied, Joe pulls out some restraints from the foot of the bed. He pulls me down farther towards the bed until the restraints at the top start to strain. He then pulls one leg and straps me in at the ankle before moving on to the other. The girls just stand there, watching from the sidelines with still no emotion on their faces.

Once satisfied, Joe steps back and takes a look at what he's done. He shakes his head with a smile. "So fucking sexy."

Bit by bit, he starts to undress until he's completely naked. He clicks his finger to the black-haired girl, and straight away, she marches towards him and gets down on her knees. She immediately takes him into her mouth and starts sucking him. Joe hisses, grabbing her head and pushing her deeper. "Such obedient little sluts." He moans. "Fuck, her mouth feels good." He pulls her off him by the hair and clicks his fingers to the other two and points to me. They march forward and climb on the bed. I'm wondering what the hell is going on until it's plainly obvious when they lean forward and start stroking my skin. Goose bumps rise until my nipples pucker again. Then, they lean forward and start suckling. I close my eyes, not wanting this, but at the same fucked up time, they're so gentle that I can't help but react to it. Heat prickles my skin and starts heading to an area that it shouldn't.

"That's the sexiest sight I have ever seen." Joe walks over to his jeans and pulls out a condom. Once he has it on, he motions to the girl with the black hair. "This girl here," he says, looking at me, "is the best cock-sucker around. I've also been told she's the best pussy eater too."

When I realise what he means by this, my eyes start to widen. "Yes," he says with a smile. "Little Laney here is going to make you come, aren't you, Laney?" He moves over to her and pushes her hair away from her neck. He starts kissing and biting it until he pushes her forward. "Get to work, Laney. I want to see that bitch come hard. That should wipe the smirk off her face."

I start pulling on my restraints, but it's no use. In no time at all, Laney is between my legs licking and sucking on my clit. I have it from all sides. The two other girls are still sucking on my nipples and coupled with the fact that Laney is licking my clit, I can't help but feel it all. My face heats and, with it, so does my body. I want to moan with the pleasure so badly, but I also don't want to give Joe the satisfaction.

"I know you're fighting it, little one, but there's no use. Laney will make you come, and you'll have no other choice but to let out how good it fucking feels."

Joe stands behind Laney and leans forward to cup her breasts. He positions himself behind her, and I know the moment he's placed himself inside of her as Laney stills for a moment.

"Fuck!" he bellows, slowly pulling himself out and back in. "She feels so fucking good, doesn't she, little one? Doesn't she make you want to scream?"

I feel the warmth and tenderness of all their tongues on my nipples and clit, and it sends me into overdrive. I don't want to feel the pleasure, but I know it's building. It's building whether I want it to or not. When Laney flicks her tongue in slow motion over and over my clit, I can't help the moan that escapes my lips.

"That's it, little one. Enjoy it. Fuck, her pussy feels good. I want to see you come before I do," he pants.

I close my eyes trying to stop the sensations from invading my senses, but once I do close them, the feeling is heightened. I can here moans, I can here suckling, and I can hear the sound of Joe moving back and forth inside Laney. I want it to sicken me. I want it to make me feel anything other than this rushing heat of pleasure about to burst its banks. I have never been attracted to women, so I would never even think to do this. Yet, here I am, sprawled on a bed with three women pleasuring me. I don't want to be turned on by what they're doing. I want to be as disgusted as what they're most probably feeling for being forced to pleasure me. I look for the disgust in me. I look for anything, so that I don't feel this heat burning its way inside of me.

"I can see she's licking you good, Evelyn. You should see what I see. It would make you come in seconds. I know you're trying to fight it," he grunts. "But you can't avoid the inevitable. Come for my little Laney. Come."

I keep my eyes closed, but all I can do is feel. I can feel the warm, wet tongues gliding and sucking on both nipples at the same time. I can equally feel the warm, wet tongue of Laney licking her way up and down my pussy. I want to fight it, but they're making it feel too good.

With an orgasm building, my legs start to strain against the restraints. Laney can tell as her tongue starts to dart faster and faster over my clit. "That's it, little one. Let it come. Let it fucking burst."

My head pushes its way back into the pillow. I'm willing myself not to come, but the more I will it away, the faster it comes. Strangled moans escape my lips even though I'm trying my hardest not to let them escape. I feel the bed jerking as Joe picks up his pace. He's close too, and I hate the fact that he's going to get his wish.

"Agghhh," I cry as the feel of Laney's tongue hits new heights.

"That's it. Fucking come for me. Give it to me, little one. Fucking give it to me."

With both hands and feet, I pull at the restraints as Laney keeps working on my clit. It feels like it's on fire and about to explode at any moment. Bit by bit, the feel of her tongue lashing over my clit again and again and again makes my head dizzy and my knees wobble. It's coming, and I know the moment I let go. I scream out, and with it comes my orgasm, crashing down on me like a tidal wave. Laney slows, but carries on gently licking me as my orgasm violently jerks my body in response.

"Fuck, I'm going to come. I'm going to come!" I feel the bed jerk violently, and I know that's when Joe's found his release. As the girls stop licking and my orgasm fades, so too does my euphoria. I open my eyes and find Joe standing behind Laney with that cocky I-just-won look on his face.

"That has to be the best experience of my life. We'll have to do this again someday." He smacks Laney's ass as she stands up and licks her lips. Again, no emotion. No tell-tell sign that she either liked what she did or loathed it. I look away, disgusted with myself for not only enjoying the experience, but also for coming.

"Do you know women will pay ten thousand pounds to have done to them what you just experienced? You just got that one for free, and you look like daddy's just taken your toys away. You should be a bit more grateful, little one." He gets dressed, walks towards me, and grabs my chin. "You can't deny that what you felt was most probably the best experience of your life. I saw how hard you came. I saw the way you furrowed your brows and parted that gobby mouth of yours with bliss. You can't hide what I witnessed." He trails his hand down my body until he reaches my pussy. He feels around my wetness before sticking a finger inside me, making me gasp. "So fucking wet I could slide my cock in that tight little cunt of yours with no problems. You're still full and swollen from your orgasm, little one. Feed on the euphoria." He pulls his finger out and then walks over to the girl with blonde hair. "Taste her juices for me. I bet they taste incredible."

She immediately complies, putting her mouth over his finger and starts sucking. "Hmm, this is making me hard again." He then looks at me. "Do you fancy round two?" My eyes widen and he laughs. "Maybe not. One freebie today is enough, but definitely another time.

That was seriously fucking hot. Every man's dream come true." He pulls the head of the blonde towards his lips and kisses her. "Come. I have plans for you, blondie." He smacks her arse and opens the door to the awaiting douche number two. "Make sure the girls clean her up good for tonight. No touching."

Douche number two looks disgruntled, but nods his head. "Yes, sir." I guess Joe is the boss whenever Isaac isn't around.

It's then that I feel it … the disgrace for letting myself let go. Joe wanted that victory, and he made sure he got it. I hated him for making me feel he was the only way out, and I hate him for taking me and forcing me into this. I thought Isaac was supposed to be the evil one, but so far, it's only been his son. It makes me wonder if Drake knew Isaac even had a son. He obviously didn't know who Joe was. Otherwise, he wouldn't have let him anywhere near me.

I don't know what kind of game Joe is playing. I'm sure his father didn't plan for what just happened to happen. I feel that he forced it. I feel sick that I was made to go through that, but most of all, I feel sick that he made me enjoy it. Maybe he knew that, and that's the reason why he did it. No doubt now he's having sex with the blonde girl who, only minutes ago, was sucking on my nipple. Closing my eyes, I feel sick. Those girls most probably hated every minute of that, yet I was as high as a fucking kite on euphoria. What does that make me? Again, I suppose Joe knows this, and again—because let's face it, he's a sick fuck—he made it that way.

Nausea builds up at the thought that one day, Isaac's aim is to make me just like one of those girls. A virtual zombie, void of any emotion. No pleasure taken—solely given. For the first time, I feel real fear. I don't want to be one of those girls. I don't want to stare down at another girl like me in a few years time and make her come like I was made to. I don't want someone like Joe thinking they can make me do things like a lap dog. Just yesterday, I was someone's wife. True, it was not under the best of circumstances, but at least it was Drake and Drake alone. It's funny how I can now curse myself for not listening to Drake and not following his rules. Look where I've ended up because of it. Did Drake always know this may happen? Is that why he kept me prisoner—to keep me safe?

Lots of questions. Questions I'll probably never have answers to. I would rather die than be here forced into things that I don't want to do. I don't know for sure what Isaac has in store for me later, but I can hazard a guess.

And the thought petrifies me.

The girls unhook me from my restraints before I'm led for an all over makeover. I'm waxed all over until there's virtually no trace of hair on my skin. I'm then plucked, manicured, and pedicured before finally my hair and makeup are done. And then, eventually, I'm dressed in a see-through baby-doll camisole before being led into a darkened room where Isaac is waiting. My eyes widen when I see he's standing in front of a virtual replica of what Drake strapped me into in his basement.

CHAPTER TWENTY THREE

Present Day

My heart starts thumping when I look around and see a pair of red velvet curtains covering what I can only assume is a window.

"Come," Isaac shouts, making me jump. I look back at him and see him smile. "I have a feeling you've seen one of these before. Did Drake let you in on his dark secret after all?"

I frown. "What is that supposed to mean?"

He starts shaking his head and tutting. "Drake really did keep you in the dark, didn't he? I thought you may have been used to this by now, but it seems we have a lot to teach you."

Before I can respond, two men grab my arms and force me into my restraints again. Is this how I'm going to live the rest of my life? Tied down and forced into situations beyond my control? "Drake's going to kill you!" I seethe, straining against my restraints. My wrists are sore from earlier, but I still pull on them nonetheless.

Isaac walks up close to me and nods his head to the man on my left. He yanks the rope until I'm suspended in air. I can't move. I am completely immobile. My heart starts beating, thumping through my chest until it's ringing in my ears.

"Drake can't kill me if he doesn't know where I am. Besides, he'll eventually find another plaything to replace you. You're all replaceable."

He and I both know that's not true. Drake would stop at nothing to get me, and he knows it. For some reason, Isaac doesn't seem to care. In fact, I would go so far as to say that he welcomes it.

He deliberately roams his eyes up and down my body. "Oh, well. What's Drake's loss is my gain. You look simply stunning this evening. I've got a line of very wealthy men behind that curtain who are dying to see you. They know you come from a good family and were hoping you were a virgin, but never mind. You've only had the one, so at least they know you're a good girl. They like the virginal-looking type, and you have that written all over that pretty little face of yours."

I want to know more about what he meant about Drake, but my eyes follow towards the curtains in front of me. Knowing that there are men waiting to see me behind that curtain makes the bile rise inside of me.

"Ben," Isaac says, making me jump. I look towards Ben, and he's coming towards me with a needle. I start to struggle again.

"I have a feeling you're going to want to talk and struggle, and I know my clients prefer the quiet types."

I start straining again, shouting and screaming. "You'll never get away with this. Drake will find me and he will kill—" I feel the needle going into my arm and cry out.

Isaac is beside me. "Hush now." He starts stroking my hair. "Soon, it will all feel like a wonderful dream."

Immediately, my eyes begin to droop, and I feel light-headed and fuzzy. Isaac smiles and motions to someone to open the curtains.

Once they're open, I find around nine men—all in expensive business suits—lined up, straining their necks to see me.

"Good evening, gentlemen. I've invited you here this evening for a rather special event. As you all know, this young lady—who has only recently turned eighteen—comes from a very prestigious upbringing. She was brought up pure of heart and of body. Unfortunately, I can't offer her to you as a virgin today, as again you already know that she was bought for five million a while back. The person who bought her has been her only sex partner. Unfortunately, he's dead, but I've luckily acquired her for myself."

I want to scream and shout out that Drake isn't dead. He's very much alive, and he's coming for me. My mouth parts, and I try to speak, but no words come out. I want to feel the fear and adrenaline pump through me enough to strain, kick out, scream ... do anything. But I can't move. I can't speak. I can't do anything, but listen to the lies Isaac spews out of his disgusting mouth.

Isaac points his hand to me. "You can see how beautiful she is. I'm sure whoever wins her tonight will get the night of his life." He smiles back at them all through the window. They don't have much of an expression—just one of interest.

"Now, would you like to briefly come through and have a few seconds to look before we begin?"

My head starts to lull back. I try to keep my focus, but whatever drugs he's given me have rendered me unable to care. A part of me wants to sleep, but another part is telling me to keep awake. I know my subconscious is fighting this, but for some reason, I don't feel fear, anticipation, or anger. I just feel ignorantly blissful.

I watch in a haze as the men walk through and come towards me. At first, they just look. Then, they pull my head back and inspect my face before hands are touching me. I feel them on my breasts, squeezing my nipples, and down towards my pussy. Several of them—I don't know how many—stick a finger inside me. I should react, but I don't want to. Again, I don't care. Again, I don't speak. I just let them because I know I can't do anything about it.

"Very pretty," one of them says. "Five million, did you say?" Isaac nods. "Hmm. Was she so good that she killed him?"

They all start laughing together like this is some big fucking joke. I want to laugh too at the craziness of it all, but no sound comes out. Again, I don't care.

"You never know," Isaac replies. "I believe it actually *was* a heart attack."

Liar, liar, pants on fire.

More hands are on me. I can feel some big, some small, some hot, some cold. All of them are exploring my body. All of them breathing heavily as they do. My head lulls back again, and I close my eyes. I don't want to shut down, but I'm fighting a losing battle. I can feel every pinch, every grope, and every glide of their hands on my skin. One hand, two hands, three hands, and then it feels like a dozen of them feeling their way around. At one point, I think I feel a tongue on my nipple, followed by a quick nip. Again, I don't care. I suppose that's what the drugs are for. I'm just how these men want me. Compliant. Quiet.

Sit still, look pretty.

"Stunning," one of them says breathlessly.

"Isn't she?" Isaac asks proudly. You would think I was a prized possession the way I'm being treated, touched, and looked at.

"Would you gentlemen like to take your seats for the bidding?" He motions for the men to go back to their chairs, and in a fuzzy haze,

I watch them walk back to their seats.

Once settled, the door is shut again, and Isaac addresses them all. "Now, let's start the bidding at two hundred thousand." Immediately, all the men put their hands up and Isaac acknowledges. "Okay, now three. Who will give me three?" A few hands go up again. "Okay, let's make this a little easier on everyone. "Who will go for five?" Three men put their hands up. This goes on and on until it reaches seven hundred and fifty thousand pounds.

"Sold to Mr Thomas!" I hear Isaac shout. "Mr Thomas, you have all night with the young lady. To the rest of you gentlemen, I bid you a good night."

I must pass out at that point because I don't remember them leaving, and I don't remember this Mr Thomas being in the room with me. When I try to focus, I find I'm still tied up like before, but Isaac isn't here. It's just me and this strange, overweight middle-aged gentleman in a navy suit. I watch as he comes closer to me, taking off his jacket and loosening his tie as he does. Once in front of me, he lifts my head up and forces his rancid tongue down my throat. He moans, grabbing my nipple and squeezing it hard. Again, I don't care. Again, I take it. Again, I say nothing.

"I'm going to want you on a bed, but I couldn't resist fucking you tied up here first. I want to feel your long legs wrapped around me as I bury my cock inside you." He plunges a finger inside of me. "Hot, tight little cunt. I can't wait to get in balls deep."

With some fight coming back, I manage to lift my head away from him in defiance. I don't look at him. I know that if I do, he'll disgust me. I can feel him, though. I can feel his hands all over my skin. On me. Squeezing me. Inside me. I can hear him as he moans and breathes his hot breath against my neck.

"I can't wait any longer. I'm going to fuck you now."

I hear the zipper of his trousers and feel when he pulls my legs up to position me in the right spot. It's only when I feel something push at my entrance that I suddenly find the strength.

"Drake," I whisper.

I feel him stiffen. "What?"

"I'm Drake's." I manage to look him in the eye and see him swallow hard. It would make me smile if I could muster one.

"Drake who?"

"Salvatore's wife."

Within an instant, he's off me, pulling up his zipper. He looks like a frightened lamb about to be slaughtered. Again, I want to smile but I can't.

"You're ... You're Drake Salvatore's wife? You're Evelyn?"

This time, I manage a smirk. "Yes, and he's going to kill you," I sing. I throw my head back, and suddenly find my laughter. Man, whatever drugs he's given me are making me all kinds of fucked up.

This makes him flee. He's across the room and banging on the door quicker than a tramp on chips. He starts frantically banging on the door before someone answers. "I demand to see Isaac," he bellows. Soon after, Isaac is inside the room. He looks at me and then back at Mr Thomas. "What is the trouble?"

He points to me. "The trouble is that you lied to us. Her master isn't dead because this is Evelyn, Drake's wife. If I had known this, I would never have bid on her."

Isaac grits his teeth as he looks at me. At one time, his look would have made me cower, but again—because of the drugs—I don't seem to care. Instead, I smile at him.

Isaac sighs his displeasure and shakes his head. "Come," he says, placing a hand on Mr Thomas' shoulder. Let's discuss this elsewhere."

The door is quickly shut behind them, and I'm left all alone, hanging from this contraption. I want to sleep still, but every time my head lulls back, I'm snapped out of it again. I start swinging, and once I start, I can't stop. Laughter erupts as I sway back and forth. For a few fleeting moments, I feel like a child.

That is until Joe walks in. "Having fun, are we?" I start giggling and throwing my head back again. "You are, aren't you?" I'm stopped by a grip of two hands around my hips. "My father's going to be real pissed at you. What use are you now if word gets around that you're Drake's?"

"Why do you think I told him, dumb-arse?" I start giggling again, but sleep takes a hold of me quickly as my head lulls to the side again.

I feel his hands push my hair back. "Maybe I can convince my father to make you my own personal slut. He's preoccupied now, so I can do anything I want with you." He pushes my head up and darts his tongue into my mouth. At first I let him, but a little fight left in me comes to the surface. I bite his tongue causing him to scream out. "Fucking bitch!" He slaps me across the face, but I hardly feel it. Again, I don't care.

"Someone needs to teach you a little lesson." I feel him biting me on the shoulder and my brain knows it's hard, but doesn't react. I know he wants a reaction, but I'm not going to give him one. When that doesn't work, he pulls a condom out of his pocket and starts undoing his jeans.

"I'm going to fuck you. I'm going to fuck you so hard you won't be able to stand for a week."

I should care, but somehow, I don't. In a sense, I'm glad that I'm drugged, so I won't have the emotion that comes with being raped. My mind knows he's going to rape me, but it's also shutting down any feeling that will come from that thought.

I just don't care.

It's like I'm completely detached from my body. Almost like I'm floating above and looking down at the scene. Joe is frantically undoing his jeans. He's in a hurry because he knows his father will be back shortly. I watch as he places the condom on his erect penis, and I watch as he pulls my legs up, and positions himself between my legs.

I feel when he pushes in and my head lulls back again. "Drake," I whisper, feeling something wet fall from my eye.

"Drake doesn't exist anymore, little one. It's just Joe now. Only Joe. Fuck, you feel tight. Fucking incredible."

I feel when he starts moving inside of me, and that is when I will the sleep to come. I close my eyes and try not to feel the invasion. I can feel it though. I can feel and hear him as he thrusts his way inside of me.

And then I hear a loud noise like gunshots. Joe's invasion disappears, but I don't look up to see why. I hear some more gun shots, shouting, and loud bangs, but I'm already falling.

I'm floating away on a distant cloud, and the more I welcome it, the more it comes. I feel blissful and euphoric. Pretty soon, all sounds are gone, and all that's left is a sea of calm washing over me. Then, the blackness takes over.

I can't fight it anymore.

CHAPTER TWENTY FOUR

Present Day

"Drake," I whisper, feeling a set of arms around me.

"I got you, babe. Fuck, why did you leave me, Evelyn? Why did you run away?"

"Drake," I whisper again. I feel I'm being carried and on the move somewhere, but I can't open my eyes. I don't seem to want to open my eyes.

Darkness comes again, and when consciousness finds me, I'm lying down somewhere with a sheet over me. I feel something restricting my arm, so I try and pull away."

"Evelyn, stop. The doctor needs to examine you."

I moan, but I still can't open my eyes. I feel myself slipping again when I hear a voice. "She and the baby seem fine. Let her sleep it off. I'll take the bloods to the lab and call you if I need to."

Baby? What baby?

"Thank you, doctor. You don't know how much of a relief that is."

"You're welcome. If she has any bleeding, bring her straight in to see me. Otherwise, I'll see how she is in a couple of days."

"Thank you," Drake says again with relief.

Baby? Bleeding?

Darkness comes again, and for how long I do not know. When I eventually come awake, light is shining in my eyes, so I turn away on a moan. My head is banging. It feels like I've got a raging hangover.

I manage to open one eye and then two. I'm in Drake's room, but Drake is not in the bed with me. How did I get here?

I feel confused. I can't remember anything from the moment I was brought into that room and hung on that contraption. I move again and wince when I feel a pain in my shoulder.

"The doctor said you'd be sore there for a couple of days. You were bitten quite hard."

Bitten? I push my hair out of the way and sure enough there is a bite mark with a big angry bruise around it.

Frowning, I turn towards the sound of Drake's voice. He's sitting on the chair, looking nothing like the man I used to know. His hair is dishevelled, and his shirt, which is normally crisp and buttoned up, is creased with three buttons undone. He looks like he hasn't slept in days. He also looks like he hasn't shaved in days.

He doesn't look at me. He's staring into space as if I'm not there. Is he angry with me? Of course he is. I ran away, but then, how did I end up back here?

"What happened?" I ask in a croaky voice.

He grits his teeth. "Isaac happened. He took you. Don't you remember?"

My heart sinks. He still won't look at me, and for some reason, I feel the stinging rejection. "I got a lift from a really nice lady. She took me to Reading. She gave me some money, and I managed to get a hotel room. Later that night, Joe knocked on the door, but I thought

POSSESSION

it was the manager. He injected me with something, and the next minute, I was tied to a bed with Isaac there."

His jaw ticks, and I watch as he grips the arm rest with his hands. I can see that anger in him. I know when he's about to blow. But I can't help but want to go to him. And I can't help but want to seek his forgiveness.

Throwing the sheet off me, I scoot out of the bed, noticing how every muscle aches. I want to moan with the pain, but I keep it down. As I walk towards him, Drake still won't look at me. A part of me wonders if I should do this. He may throw me off of him, but I need him. I really need his comfort.

I straddle him, placing my arms around his waist and snuggling my head into his neck. He smells musky—all man. I want to savour the smell, but I can't as Drake won't return my affection. I snuggle again and wiggle myself a little on his lap to get him to do something.

"Drake, please," I urge.

He visibly sighs, but snakes his arms around me before kissing the top of my head. This is the Drake I know and love. Not that monster he became.

"I should have known," he whispers into my hair. "I should have kept you safe."

Is he actually blaming himself for this?

"Drake, please. It's my fault. This was all my fault. I shouldn't have run, but you should have told me."

I feel his heart drumming, and he squeezes me to him a little more. I can feel the rage building inside of him again, so I do something I hope will calm him. I start laying gentle kisses around his shoulder and then his neck. I start on one side and then the other. I feel Drake growing beneath me, and it spurs me on. I start breathing

219

heavily and so does Drake. I can feel he wants this, so I push further and start kissing his lips. His eyes look lost, but glassed over as I come in for one kiss and then another. "Drake," I whisper at his lips as I plunge my tongue in. He accepts me, moaning as he places a hand behind my head. "I want you," I say, going in for more. It's only when I start trying to undo his trousers that he stops me.

"Evelyn, no."

Pulling back, I look at him confused. "What's wrong?"

Drake huffs and shakes his head. He looks me in the eyes, his expression angry. "You don't remember, do you? You can't. Otherwise, there's no way you'd want to do this."

I frown, shaking my head. "I don't understand."

Immediately, Drake gets up and carries me towards the mirror. He pulls my shorts down and then motions for me to look. When I do, I see bruises everywhere. All over my hips, thighs, and legs. I pull one leg up and notice the bruises on the inside.

I cover my mouth with a gasp. "What happened to me?"

"You don't remember?"

Tears pool my eyes, so Drake comes over and puts my shorts back on for me. He sits me on the bed. "I remember being tied to the bed. I remember asking Isaac why I was there, and he said that he was always trying to get to me, but then you got to me first. He said I was going to be a sex slave and that I should be used to it with you." I turn to him with a frown. "Why, Drake? Why did he say that?"

His jaw is ticking again. He's so angry. "I kept telling you, and you wouldn't listen."

"But why hide this from me? Why?" I ask, a little louder.

Drake quickly gets up from the bed and snakes his hands through his hair. "Because I was trying to save you from all this. From that fucker, Isaac. From my past. Even from me. But you had to push it, didn't you? You had to push and fucking push until the monster I used to be came out."

My eyes start pooling with tears. "What do you mean?"

He stares back at me with only anger in his eyes. "Don't you see that this was what I was protecting you from all this time? If you were to see me—truly see who I once was—you would never love me. You could never love a monster like me."

Wetness trickles down my cheeks. "Drake, please. I need to understand. You have a responsibility to tell me. I'm your wife."

"That's right. You are my fucking wife. But why would a wife run away from her husband?"

Feeling my anger rise, I get up. "Because you forced me. Don't you understand? Ever since I was thirteen, you forced your will—your *everything*—on me. The lady who drove me knew about you. She told me about her friend's niece you saved. She told me you got her off drugs, put her in college, and placed a roof over her head. Why couldn't you have done that for me?"

Walking over to me, he grabs my shoulders. "You were in danger. I couldn't let that fucker, Isaac, take you."

I look into his eyes, and I know that's not the only reason. "There's more to it than that. I can tell. What are you hiding from me?"

He grips my arms tightly and then lets go. He starts pacing the room before looking back to me. "Okay. You really want to know the truth?" I nod. "I was once Isaac. I was once that monster who took girls and made them do things they didn't want to do."

I cower back, shaking my head. "I don't believe you."

"Believe it because it's fucking true." He walks closer to me and points. "Do you know what my father gave me for my twelfth birthday?" I shake my head. "He gave me a drugged up whore to fuck. She was taken just like you were. Strapped up just like you were. I was only twelve—a virgin. He made me fuck her. Told me I needed to be a man. How is becoming a man fucking some drugged up girl against her will? How is it, Evelyn? Tell me!"

I step back, trying to fight the tears. I feel desperate. How do I answer something so fucked up as that? I stare at Drake dumbfounded. He's not looking at me with the same daring prowess and confidence he always exudes. Instead, he looks lost—broken even. I think back to when I was drugged by his father and Drake took me to the basement and called me his whore. He didn't look like my Drake then.

"You were just a boy."

He inhales sharply, still not able to look at me. It's almost as if he feels embarrassed to. "Yes, I was just a boy, but I could have said no. I even tried to say no. Instead, my father gave me that big man speech, and because it was my father, I believed him. I ended up losing my virginity to that woman, and I bet she didn't remembered it for a while. It does come back, though." He looks over to me as if trying to get me to remember. Remember what, though? My head is still fuzzy from the last twenty-four hours.

"I cried that night. And I cried several times after. But, I became immune to them after a while. Once I turned sixteen, he stopped drugging some. I thought I wouldn't be able to do it with a conscious woman, but I did, Evelyn. Again, I told my father no, but he forced me, saying that otherwise he'd kill her. So, I fucked her. I fucked her as she cried and told me everything was going to be okay. That she wouldn't blame me. Can you imagine what that does to a sixteen-year-old boy, Evelyn?" He looks at me then. I see the pain and the desperation staring back at me. Now, I understand him better. I want to comfort him, but at the same time, a part of me feels like I should be disgusted with him.

Against my better judgment, my feet move, and I go to him, placing a hand on his cheek. Drake closes his eyes and cups his hand on mine. "You were just a boy," I say again, hoping that it'll sink in.

Drake opens his eyes and stares into mine. "But that boy became a man."

I wince when he says this. Was he still doing these things after we met? "When you met me ..."

"I stopped. One look at you, and something snapped inside of me. You were only twelve, and yet you captivated me. I took one look, and what I saw in myself when I looked at you terrified me. You made me see the man I had become, but you also made me see what I could be. I couldn't possibly let you go."

I place my hand on his chest, and he takes it off and instead places it in his. "But what has this all got to do with Isaac?"

Drake closes his eyes. "My obsession with you became his."

"But why?"

"Because one of the girls I fucked was his sister." Gasping, I step back. "See?" he asks, with a snarl. "That's the kind of man I forced you into being with. That's the kind of selfish man who made you be with me because you were like a cure to my addiction. I tried to make you like one of them, but you wouldn't listen to me, would you? You wouldn't just do as you were fucking told. Isaac knew he couldn't kill me, but he made me pay the price. He killed my best friend in retaliation. But I always knew it wouldn't satisfy him. I always knew he would be waiting for an opportunity." He then looks at me. "He must have been fucking ecstatic when I met you. You were my one saving grace, but because of my selfishness, I made you a target. I tried to stop being that monster. In fact, for years, I managed to not even look at a woman again. But you ... you wouldn't listen. You kept pushing and pushing until I snapped."

The tears start running down my face, and I can't seem to stop them. Surely this isn't real? I can't form words. I can't even form thoughts. They're scrambled all over the place in one giant fucked up mess. I want to go to him, but the part that tells me of his past is what holds me back.

"See, how can you love a monster like me?" I stand there—my mouth agape. What can I say? How do I form words to answer such a question? In the end, I don't have to because he motions me forward. "Come. I want to show you something." He walks towards a red silk gown over one of the wardrobe doors and puts it over my shoulders before taking my hand. Silently, we walk out of the room and down the stairs towards his basement. For a moment, I pull back, but Drake tugs me forward. "It's not what you think."

Trusting him, I nod my head, and we make our way down the stairs and into the room I spent a few days tied up in. But instead of me, or any other girl tied to the contraption, it's Joe.

I gasp when I see him. He's tied up just like I was, but instead, he's fully clothed. It looks as though he's been used as a punching bag because his face is swollen all over with bruises, and he has several cuts on his face. He seems unconscious as his head lulls forward, and I watch as a drop of blood falls from his swollen lips.

Rooted to my spot, Drake walks up to him and pulls a gun out from his back. He points it at his temple and pushes his head. "Wake up, fucker."

He groans, but moves his head up. He spots me straight away and smiles. "Have you come to finish off the job I started, little one? We were so rudely interrupted."

My eyes widen, wondering what he means when Drake lashes out, smashing the gun over his face. Joe screams before spitting some blood out. "Ouch! That really fucking hurt."

Drake grabs the back of his head and pulls him up to look at me. "Say sorry for what you did. Say it!" He tugs at his hair.

Joe smiles again, showing me two missing teeth. "I ain't sorry. I'd do it all over again if I could."

Drake hits him again, making me wince. I look away. I don't know why I did, considering everything Joe has done to me. I should want him to get the beating of his life. I should want him dead. But looking at him now—strapped up and beaten—is eating away at my insides.

"Evelyn, look at me."

Slowly, I turn my head towards Drake. He's standing there with the gun to Joe's head. His eyes are blazing, and his breathing is heavy. This is the Drake I fear. This is the Drake who haunts me. But a part of me thinks he knows this. A part of me thinks this is exactly his plan. He wants me to see the monster in him. He wants me to fear it.

"What did he do?" Drake demands.

With my nerves shot, I lick my lips. Joe notices and smirks at me. "If you don't want to tell him, I will."

"Shut the fuck up," Drake growls.

"Why are you doing this?" I ask Joe. "Why aren't you scared?"

Joe starts laughing. "You are as innocent as you look, aren't you? One way or the other, I'm a dead man. I may as well go out in a blaze of glory." He winks at me before turning to Drake. "I gave her a tit fuck, rubbed my cum all over her chest, and later, I made her cum using Laney—one of my girls. I fucked her from behind and watched it all. I watched as she came. "Beautiful fucking sight. You must come a bucketful every time she does." I look away, feeling embarrassed. I don't want Drake to look me in the eyes and see the truth.

But then I hear Joe laugh. "The best fucking bit was when she was hanging all drugged up and smiling. She was like a beautiful siren. I couldn't resist, so I fucked her." My head snaps back to him with a gasp.

He did what?

But then it all comes flashing back. All the men with their hands on me, the auction, the winner who almost fucked me, but he didn't get a chance to when I told him I was Drake's. Then, there was the argument with Isaac about it before I was left in the room on my own. I remember Joe coming in soon after and that's when he... I feel the bite mark on my neck and remember it was him. He did this before he raped me.

Fresh, hot tears sting my face and run down my cheeks as the memories of that night come flooding back. I stare back at Joe and start shaking my head, but all he's doing is smiling at me.

"My only regret is that I didn't take the opportunity to go into that room sooner. I would have had the time to pull out before coming all over that sweet pussy of hers."

And then Drake does it. He pulls the trigger and blood sprays out before landing on the floor. Joe's head falls forward, and when Drake looks at me, I start stepping back. Before I know it, I'm running up the stairs, taking two at a time and fleeing to the room I used to sleep in as a child. Once there, I run to the en suite and vomit up bile after bile. My head pounds. My eyes pound. Everything pounds as image after image of what happened at Isaac's and just now wash over me. I don't want the images to come, but they do. One after the other, I'm being taken to a place I never want to see again. If I could bleach out those images, I would.

After emptying everything I can, I grab a glass by the sink and fill it up with water. I take two paracetamol from the cabinet and pop them before drinking all the water. I walk to the bed and climb in wondering if Drake will come after me. For some reason, I already know the answer.

And it's not the answer I would ever have imagined.

CHAPTER TWENTY FIVE

Present Day

Three days go by and no word from Drake. I had meals brought up to me, but always from one of the maids. The next day, I went in search of him, but I couldn't find him anywhere. The same on day two. I asked one of the guards where he was, and all I was told was that he was away and should be back soon.

Yesterday, I had a visit from the doctor who was pleased with my recovery after my drugging and raping incident. In the end, he told me I could only take paracetamol for any pain, which I thought was weird, and that I had to come in for a scan in six weeks time. I thought that was weird too, but then I thought maybe it had something to do with the fact that I had run out at my last one. I told him I was fine, but he insisted, saying it was normal procedure. Whatever the hell that means.

I didn't question him, as he is a doctor after all. I just thought a lot of fuss was being made over nothing. I know I was raped and bruised, but the physical scars are healing well. It's just my emotional scars I'm unsure I'll get over.

As I take a leisurely stroll on top of Ireland, I stare at the grounds ahead. The house that stands tall on them doesn't look as huge as it once did. I guess, after living here a while, it seems familiar and therefore doesn't seem as big as it used to be.

I rub my hand up Ireland's neck before patting her. "You're the only girl who listens to me without judgment, aren't you, Ireland?" I rub her fondly with a smile, but feel when the tears begin to fall. I don't want to miss Drake, but I do. I understand him now, but that means I also know the truth. He hid it from me, and I can also understand why, but it doesn't stop me from hating him for what he did, and it doesn't stop me from asking the same damn question over and over again.

Why me?

Out of all the women in the world, why did he choose the twelve-year-old girl who hadn't lived her life yet? Why did he love her so fiercely and so strongly in all the wrong ways imaginable? Why did he choose to put that same girl in danger—so much so that it led her into that same danger he was trying to protect her from? All those questions and more roll around in my head. He was a monster who was trying to better himself, but because of my stubbornness, I kept pushing until he cracked. Does this excuse his behaviour? Hell no. Does it make me want to leave and say a big fuck you? Hell yes.

But there is this part of me … a big part of me … that can't help yearning to be with him. I tried to find the logic in that, and the only explanation I could come up with is that he's all I have. He is all that I've ever had. My parents hated me enough to agree to sell me, knowing what the consequences would be. I was a virgin. An innocent child who longed for dates, time out with friends, and the freedom to choose her own path in life. Was that really so much to ask?

Feeling a breeze against my skin, I close my eyes and savour the moment. It's August now, and the heat is sticky, so this breeze is a welcome one. As I open them back up again, the realisation that I have no clue what happens next hits me like a freight train. I have no clue as to whether there's a threat anymore. If there isn't, does this mean Drake will let loose on the reins a bit? Does this mean he'll even want me still? He knows what happened to me while I was with Isaac, and a part of me worries that he won't find me desirable after what happened. I shouldn't care, but I do. That man over the years has become both my enemy and my saviour. My fissure and my bond. My sickness and my cure. My destruction and my salvation. I have even come to terms with the fact that Drake will probably insist on forcing us. So be it. I have nothing and no one else left. At least here, I know I'm safe. At one time, I wanted so badly to run away from this place. But now I feel like it's the only safe place I have left. How fucked up is that after everything he's put me through?

Wiping my eyes, I pat Ireland one more time before saying, "Come on, girl." She immediately complies, and we head back to the stables. As I near, I notice Mandy standing by the stable door waiting for me. When I see her, I practically fall off Ireland to get to her.

Mandy laughs and opens her arms to grab me. We embrace, and that's when the floodgates really open. I hadn't allowed myself to cry since all that has happened. Sure, I've shed a few tears, but now I'm balling, and I can't stop.

"Hey, hey," she says, stroking my hair. "Please don't cry."

Sniffling and wiping my eyes, I pull away to look at her. "How are you here?"

Pushing my hair away from my face, she smiles. "Drake called me this morning and asked me to come over."

My eyes widen and my stomach flips. "You spoke to Drake?" She nods. "How did he sound?" I don't know why I care, but I do. She sighs. "Broken. It was a shock to hear him actually. Normally, he sounds so self-assured, so confident." She searches my eyes as if trying to find something. "What happened?"

"Did Drake not tell you?"

"No. He just said that he thinks you'll need me and to make sure I give you a hug when you do."

I start laughing. "He actually said that?"

She nods her head. "So, what's been happening?"

"A lot," I sigh. "Too much to say standing here. Tell you what... How about we get Ireland settled, and then you and I can go grab some lunch?"

She smiles. "Sounds good to me."

Mandy helps me with Ireland before we head back to the house for lunch. I asked George if I could rustle up something for us, but he insisted on doing it himself. "That's what I'm here for," he protested. He gave me a look as if to say don't argue with me, so I shrugged my shoulders and headed outside with Mandy.

We sit at the table by the pool under a nice bit of shade and relish the welcome breeze that's blowing in from the west. Soon after being seated, one of the men comes out with a jug of fresh lemonade and pours us a glass each. Mandy seems beside herself. "This is the fucking life," she sighs contentedly behind her mirrored shades.

We both take a sip of our cold drinks, and it's a welcome feeling in the heat. Once Mandy places her glass down, she leans forward. "Are you going to spill the beans now?"

So I do. I tell her the part about trying to flee and the subsequent kidnapping afterwards. I leave out the gory details, but Mandy gets the gist of what happened to me. Once I reveal the story to her, Mandy sits back stunned into silence. At first, she just stares ahead open-mouthed. But then, she looks back at me.

"I feel like the worst friend on earth. There you were trying to tell me, and I just kept pushing you."

I shake my head at her. There was one time I used to blame Mandy for pushing Drake and me, but how can I when I never told her all the facts. "I never let you in on the full details, so don't worry about it."

"What will you do now?"

"I don't think there's much I can do. I'm stuck, aren't I? I never thought I'd say this, but Drake's won. If he wants to fight, then I'll give in. After everything that's happened, I'm just too tired."

Mandy runs a hand through her red hair and bites her lip. She looks like she's trying to think of what to say. "Okay, I'm not going to tell you how to live your life. I think I've done enough of that already. But what I will say... No, what I'll ask is: If faced with the choice to stay or leave, which one would you choose?"

CHAPTER TWENTY SIX

Present Day

Mandy stays for a couple more hours, and by the time she leaves, I'm exhausted. I don't know what's wrong with me lately, but I feel constantly tired all the time. I keep putting it down to the after effects of the drugs and all the shit I was put through in the small time that was spent at Isaac's.

With a shiver down my spine, I go up to Drake's bedroom and fall asleep. I'm not sure how long I'm sleeping before I feel a set of arms around me. His smell hits my nostrils, and for now, it makes me smile. My monster, my saviour ... my only salvation is here, and in this moment, it is all I could ask for. I want to be held. I want to be loved. And after all the shit that life has dealt me, I don't feel it's a lot to ask.

My back is pressed against his warm frame. He's dressed—unlike me—but he doesn't make a move to touch me. Instead, he snuggles his arms through mine and holds my hand in a tight embrace. The fact that he's not pushing this makes me want to push him. Knowing he's here makes my body instantly react. His touch, his presence, and his smell all warm my insides like nothing before.

So, I turn. I turn to face my handsome monster, and I find that I'm not staring at a monster at all. I'm staring at a man. A man who looks both broken and lost at the same time. He is still my Drake, but it looks like the light has died in his eyes, and that thought near enough breaks me.

And then, he says something that becomes the catalyst to my undoing. Just four words, and that dam I had built because of him comes crumbling down in a catastrophic collapse.

"I'm so sorry, Evelyn."

Gut-wrenching sobs wrack my body. Drake holds me throughout, not saying a word, but saying everything. I know through his words and actions that what he said is true. It's written all over his face. I believe he's truly sorry for everything, but what now?

And that's the part that scares me to death. I have no idea how we move on. I have no idea even how to start. But what I do know for now is that I need his comfort. I need to feel our connection between us no matter how fucked up that connection is.

So, once I calm my tears, I stare up to Drake's emotion-filled eyes, and I know right there in that moment that it's the right thing to do. Later on, tomorrow, and the day after is a different story. For now, I feel I need this. For now, I want this.

Leaning my head toward him, I capture him with my lips. At first, he doesn't do anything, so I lean in again, but this time so he knows exactly what my intentions are. I prop myself up and try to get on top of him, but he halts me. "Evelyn, don't you think that you should—"

"Don't you want me?" My heart beats a million miles an hour at the thought that he doesn't want me like that anymore.

"Of course I do. It's just that you've been through a lot and—"

"And I need this. I need you. Drake, please."

On my whispered beg, Drake captures my mouth with his and rolls over until he's on top of me. Our kisses aren't like the ones we shared before. These kisses are raw, passionate, and so tender that it makes my insides burn. "Drake, please," I beg, flexing my hips up to meet his erection. I'm undressed, but Drake isn't, and I need his clothes off of him quickly.

On a breathless moan, Drake pulls up a little, unbuttons his shirt, and pulls it off his head. As he's unbuttoning his trousers, I take my time feasting on the man in front of me. His body has never failed to spark a reaction in me. He's so toned, so flawless ... so perfect. As he pushes his trousers down, I trail a line in the middle of his V, making him hiss.

"Evelyn, you drive me crazy," he whispers. His trousers are soon off and then he's back to snuggling in between my legs, kissing from my neck to my shoulder before taking a nipple into his mouth.

Cupping his head, I thread my fingers through his hair on a moan. "Drake, please. I need you."

Drake listens to my pleas, positioning himself at my entrance. I'm so wet that he slides in with ease as we both moan out in pleasure together. As he starts to move inside of me, he lays gentle kisses all over my face before tenderly kissing me. This is a new side I've seen of Drake, and it's like I'm sleeping with him for the very first time.

"I love you," he whispers, flexing his hips deep inside of me. "I love you so much."

I cry out, loving this feeling inside of me. The connection between us is so strong that I almost say those words back. I do love Drake in my own way, but I can't say those words until I know I can give myself freely to him. I know Drake wants to hear them back, but this is one act of free will he can't force from me. This, at least, is something for me and only me to decide.

As he picks his pace up and flexes his hips in deeper, I gasp, clutching on to his hips and squeezing him into me more. "Drake," I cry, throwing my head back into the pillow as I allow myself to feel every tender caress, every kiss, and every thrust. I start moaning, and soon, I can't stop. It's like the noises have a mind of their own. Sex with Drake has always been mind-blowing in one way or the other, but this ... this is more on a nuclear scale. I know it because I feel it deep in my soul. *This* is what it feels like to be loved.

And with that knowledge, my orgasm rises, nearly robbing me of my sight. I scream, scratching his back and calling his name.

"Fuck, Evelyn, you're going to make me come." With one final thrust, he arches his back and releases himself inside of me on a long drawn out moan.

He says nothing as we calm, and he doesn't say anything when he pulls out of me and positions himself behind me again either. Instead, he pulls me closer to him and we spoon until we both fall asleep. I know we have a lot to say, and I know I need to find out what's happening next. But, for now, I will sleep. For now, I will savour this moment in his arms. A place I know I belong in this moment. A place I should have been all along.

Is it too little, too late?

CHAPTER TWENTY SEVEN

Present Day

I don't know how, but we both managed to sleep right through the afternoon until morning. When I woke, it was from the sound of the shower from the en suite. Turning, I take a look at the clock on the bedside and see that it's seven in the morning. No doubt Drake is getting ready for work and will leave me soon for another day to enjoy on my own. I start thinking that he's trying to avoid the inevitable talk, but at the same time, maybe being alone for a little while longer with my thoughts isn't such a bad idea after all. I still have no clue as to how I feel about Drake or the situation I'm in. I also still have no clue as to the possible danger I'm in. At some point, I will need to know.

I hear the shower turn off and soon after, Drake walks into the room dripping wet and still flawless. No matter how big or small my reaction, I find I always do react to him. It's like he's become a master magician at it.

Once he sees me propped up with my hand holding my head, he smiles. "Good sleep?"

I nod. "The best in a long time, actually."

"Good. You need your rest." He says this as though it saddens him.

"Are you getting ready for work?"

"I will be visiting a few of my companies today, but first I wanted to take the morning off and take you somewhere."

I rise up in surprise. "Take me somewhere?" He nods. "Where?"

"I don't want to say yet."

"So, it's a surprise?"

His face is impassive as he answers. "Sort of. It's hard to explain, but you'll see once we get there." He looks so sad still. Surely, it can't be a good surprise then. My face falls at the thought. Drake notices. "Don't worry. It's nothing bad. I promise."

"Okay," I say, swinging my legs over the side of the bed and standing up. "Shall I get ready?"

He walks towards me, cups the back of my head, and tenderly kisses my forehead. "Please," he says, lingering a little longer. Something's wrong with him, and I don't know what. "I'll meet you downstairs for breakfast."

He leaves the bedroom without looking back, and I know for certain something is wrong. I know I'm not in danger because Drake would never put me in harm's way, but there's definitely something not right about this surprise. In fact, I don't think I've ever dreaded a surprise so much.

Needing to know one way or the other, I quickly dress before meeting Drake in the kitchen. He's sitting by the island, drinking a black coffee and reading the *Financial Times*. He smiles as I walk in, but I can see sadness in that smile.

"Come and sit," George chimes. I didn't even notice he was there until he spoke.

"Good morning, George."

George smiles brightly. "Good morning, Mrs Salvatore. How are you this fine morning?"

Biting my lip, I look across at Drake. It's sometimes hard to remember that I'm his wife. Drake looks impassive, so I turn to George with a smile. "I'm fine, thanks. And you?"

"Enjoying the sun while it lasts." He motions to the chair next to Drake. "Sit, and I'll get bring you something. You must be hungry."

I assume that means he knows I haven't eaten since yesterday at lunch time. I suppose everyone in this house knows everything I'm getting up to on a day to day basis.

I take my seat next to Drake, but he doesn't stop reading the paper. I know something's up, but I'm guessing he's deliberately leaving it until he shows me whatever he has in store.

George places a plate of brown toast, scrambled eggs, and strawberries on the side before wishing me bon appétit and leaving me and Drake alone. Once he does, the silence is deafening. My stomach rolls with nausea at the thought of what might be in store for me today.

I eat the toast, but I can't stomach the eggs. Drake notices of course. "Are you not hungry?"

I look across at him. "No, not really. I actually feel a bit sick."

Placing the paper down, he cups my stomach with a frown. "Are you okay?"

I chuckle at his excessive concern. "I'm fine, Drake. What's gotten into you today?" I smile at him, and he smiles back, but I can tell it's forced.

"Nothing. I just worry about you."

Staring at the truth in his eyes, I can't help but feel how different this man before me is. Why is it only now that I'm being treated with kid gloves? Because I've been abused? Violated in the worst way possible? Wanting him this way is the only thing I have ever dreamed about, but now that it's here, I find it odd. This man looks like Drake, but he has someone else's personality entirely. It's like someone else's soul has entered his body. I don't know how I feel about it.

Sighing, Drake stands up. "Are you ready then?"

I frown, but nod my head—unsure if I really want to know what's going to happen next. "Okay. I'm ready."

He doesn't take my hand like he would normally do. Instead, he motions for me to walk ahead, and I do so, taking tentative steps. Once in the hallway, we see Kane. "We're ready now."

Kane nods. "Yes, sir. The car is waiting out front."

Drake nods and presses his hand into the small of my back. He leads me outside and into the waiting car. Kane gets in with another guard, and we drive in silence for around ten minutes until we reach a beautiful area of Sutton Scotney. We approach a gated community, and we're let in straight away. Once past the gates, Kane finds a parking space and stops. The whole time I'm sitting there, frowning and wondering why we're here.

"Do you trust me?" Drake suddenly asks. "I know I haven't given you a reason to, but can I ask that of you now?" I nod my head, knowing he's sincere, and he gets out of the car. Pretty soon, my door is open too, and Drake leads me up the two small steps until we reach the front door of the building. Drake enters a code, and when we walk in, we're met by a security guard who acknowledges Drake straight away.

"Good morning, Mr Salvatore."

"Good morning, Sam." Without another word, Drake moves us

towards the lift and we get in. He pushes a key inside the lock and presses the button for the top floor.

Once the lift opens, we're met with a vast lighted hallway with a huge mirror and a vase filled with sunflowers. Beside the vase is one door. Drake puts the key in the lock and pushes through. Once inside, Kane stands by the door and lets us have our privacy.

Turning, I look around, taking in the huge living room and adjoining dining area. It has all the mod cons of an upscale apartment with its white walls, plush beige carpets, and stunning views of the city outside the balcony doors. As we walk farther in, Drake places the keys somewhere, and I hear the clanking sound. Turning, I find an open-plan kitchen with black granite work surfaces and white cupboards. The place looks beautiful. Frowning, I notice two big manila envelopes next to the set of keys. That's when I finally turn to Drake. "What's going on?"

He waves his hand around the apartment. "This is all yours."

My eyes widen. "Mine?" I almost screech. "Drake, I don't understand."

He sighs, closing his eyes, and then I see that jaw tick I'm so used to. He's either angry or finding something really difficult. I'm guessing that under the circumstances, it's the latter.

"When I went away for those few days, it was so that I could think because I needed to figure out what to do next. You see, the moment I met you, I thought I knew my purpose in life, and that was to make you mine at all costs. I didn't think—or even care—about the consequences because, Evelyn, I'm a selfish man. A ruthless, selfish, despicable man who will stop at nothing to get what he wants. I thought I had a handle on things. I thought I knew my purpose." He sighs, looking away for a moment.

"Something's changed. What is it?"

Drake looks back at me with a pained expression on his face. "Seeing you strapped up ..." He grits his teeth, turning away from me and taking deep breaths as he paces. After a beat, he turns to me. "I always knew that what I did was wrong, but I couldn't help myself. You were all I ever needed ... all I ever craved. I knew I would stop at nothing to get my way. But when I saw you that way that night, you made me see all those girls my father had made me ..." He looks down, shaking his head. "It's like a switch was flipped." He looks back up, and I see the turmoil in his eyes. I almost go over to comfort him, but a part of me realises that this is not what's he's after right now, so I stop myself.

He shakes his head, offering a false smile. "You know how I reasoned with myself? I told myself that I was keeping you safe. I told myself that I was your salvation. I convinced myself that in return for my protection, I was entitled to have you all to myself. But then, what happened with Isaac happened, and I took in what you'd said about the girl I helped." I frown and he notices, but carries on. "Her name is Bettina. She was the first on my path to finding some sort of redemption for all of the shit I've done. She's a success story. She has a life and is doing well for herself." He finally looks at me and smiles. "And I want that for you, too."

I can't keep my eyes away from Drake. It's starting to dawn on me what he's saying, but I need to hear those words. I need to know if what I'm thinking is right. "You mean all this—" I wave my hands at the apartment.

"Is the start of your new life."

I look back at him confused. "But I thought you—"

"Were never letting you go?" He shakes his head on a smile

again. "Believe me, this is the fucking hardest and most selfless thing I have ever done. A part of me wants to pick you up, drag you back to the house, and force you to stay."

"So, why aren't you then?"

He sighs, looking defeated. "You must have heard the axiom that if you truly love someone, then you'll let them go?" I nod my head, noticing a tear falling down my cheek. "This is me letting you go." He croaks the last word, and it almost makes me fall to my knees. I have hardly any time to take in everything he's just said when he starts to talk logistics to me.

"You don't ever have to worry about Isaac and his men again. I sorted that problem out once and for all. Having said that, because of who you are, I'm not going to take anything for granted. These apartments are the most security tight apartments in the whole of England. Not one burglary ... not even an attempted one. The only way into this apartment is through a security guard and a key to both the lift and this door. Cameras are everywhere—even outside on your balcony—so if someone tries to get in, either I or security will know about it." He walks over to the kitchen counter and picks up the two envelopes. "This envelope contains a college placement for this coming September. I've enrolled you in psychology courses, but you can change that if you want to. The other envelope I request you open once I'm gone." I watch in shock as he walks over to the table and picks up my old handbag. "Here's your stuff. You have access to your bank account now, and your phone is inside. You also have clothes in the wardrobe and all the toiletries you like in the bathroom. If there is anything else you need, don't you dare hesitate to contact me. I'm still going to be a big part of your life—there's no denying that now. But I'm trying to be a better man, Evelyn. I figured this would be a start."

With my mouth agape, I watch as he walks up to me and places a tender kiss to my forehead. He lingers there, allowing me to take in his musky scent. I close my eyes and allow myself a moment to surrender to him. I know I'm in shock as I can't think of what to say or do. I know I should say something, but no words form or leave my mouth.

"I love you, Evelyn. I know you don't think that's true, but it is. I just didn't show you in the right way, and because of that, I ended up pushing you away. Because of that, I endangered you in the worst way possible. I will never forgive myself for what I've done." He kisses me again, and I feel his warm breath against my temple. "All that I ask is that you take care of yourself for me and allow me to be a part of your lives. I want to be there every step of the way."

I frown, not understanding what he means, but soon, he kisses me one more time before moving quickly to the door. He's out of here so fast that I have no time to react. Instead, I just stand there—for how long, I don't know—and wonder to myself what in the hell just happened.

Once my mouth starts drying from keeping it open so long, I finally snap myself out of it. I walk over to the envelopes and pull out the contents with the college details. I should smile. This is all I've ever wanted. So why is it that I feel empty and dead inside? Why is it that I feel more alone than ever?

Placing that envelope down, I pick up the other one and slowly tear it open. Once I pull out the contents, my knees buckle, and I fall to the floor.

CHAPTER TWENTY EIGHT

Present Day

"You should really try these tacos. They're awesome."

My stomach rolls as I watch Mandy eat a taco. For some reason, my stomach has been off lately. I try to eat, but then nausea hits me like a bitch.

I rub my stomach in discomfort and Mandy notices. "Have you still got this bug? I thought you would be over it by now. How long has it been? Over a week?"

It's been three weeks since Drake walked out the door, and I miss him more than anything in the world. For the past week, I have felt constantly sick and constantly tired. I've gone off some of my favourite foods, and I feel crabby at times. I'm putting it down to the fact that I can't get over Drake. I don't know if this is love I feel, so I'm giving myself a chance to breathe without him. I find at times that my finger hovers over the button of my phone—desperate to call him and ask him to come over. But I know that if I do, I will get lost in him. If I allow myself to get swept up by him again, then what? He'll take me back to the house and lock me up? I can't go through that again.

"Something like that," I answer, looking over at the envelope. Mandy catches me and stops chewing.

"Have you signed them?" I shake my head. "Do you want to?"

I sigh. "I really don't know."

"You're hesitating for a reason. Is it because you actually love him despite all the shit he's put you through?"

"I can't answer that either. My head won't stop spinning. Do you know how many times I've found myself almost on the phone or at my door, getting ready to go over to him? I don't know what the fuck this is, but I can't seem to get him out of my head. I'm trying so that I can think clearly, but he always manages to find a way back in."

Suddenly, Mandy starts laughing, so I frown at her. "He's a clever fucker. I'll give him that."

"What is that supposed to mean?"

Placing her taco down, she wipes her hands before speaking. "Reverse psychology. He's doing all the things you never expected him to, and now it's confusing the fuck out of you. He's either genuinely giving you time, or he's playing a very shrewd game. My money's on it being a bit of both. I reckon he's doing it partly because he knows that this is what you want, but also partly—and this is the biggest part—because he hopes that you'll realise that you can't live without him."

I had thought of this myself, but hearing Mandy say it out loud makes it sink in even more. Maybe he is playing a very shrewd game. I groan. This is why I know I need more space and time away from him.

"I know. I think I just need to figure out whether this ... I don't know what to call it ... obsession with him is just that or more. Apart from you, he's all I've ever known. He's the only person who has taken care of me like a lover should, and sometimes, even like a father should. I have to try to separate those feelings out somehow to see how I *truly* feel."

Mandy looks at me for a moment. Her face crinkles like she's in deep thought. "Okay. I'll ask you a question to put it into simpler terms." I nod my head in agreement. "Imagine life without him, and then imagine meeting someone else. Someone who you think can make you happy. Someone who you think will love you unconditionally. Someone who maybe one day you will want to marry and have kids with. Can you imagine that in your head? Can you see that picture?" I try to, but when I do, all I feel is a pang in my stomach. Admitting the truth, I shake my head no. "Well then, that may be your answer. Sometimes, life isn't about fairytales and finding that perfect someone. There's no such thing as perfect. We all have our flaws. Drake just seems to have some rather large ones. It's whether you think you can cope with them or not that matters."

"What do you think I should do?"

She starts laughing. "Don't ask me that. I can't tell you what I think you should do. It sounds as though you've had that all your life. It's time to start thinking for yourself."

"I know what you're saying, but a friend's advice is always welcome."

She laughs again. "Only in some situations ... when asked."

"Well, I'm asking."

She sighs and stares ahead for a moment. "I know I used to push you two together back when I thought it was more innocent than it really was. As a friend, I should tell you to run and to run as fast as you can, but then it's easy for me to say that when I have no romantic feelings involved in this situation. All I can offer are words. You are

247

the only person who can look inside yourself and see how you truly feel. You are the only person who can see whether or not Drake holds a huge piece of your heart. Therefore, my advice is to carry on doing what you're doing and take time out to see how you really feel. You've done well to not call the moment the urge comes. Keep doing that until you are one hundred percent sure whether you can really love him like he's asking you to."

I chuckle a little at that. "At one point, it wouldn't have been a question. He was always trying to force me into loving him."

"But he's not now. I'm not saying that's a reason to return to him. I'm just saying it's a start. And by the sounds of it, that's one major step he's made." She shakes her head on a smile. "Either that or he's one shrewd, manipulative bastard."

We both chuckle, and I watch as she picks up the taco and starts eating again. The spices hit my nostrils, making my stomach roll. I screw up my face, and Mandy notices. She starts laughing. "Anyone would think you were pregnant the way you're carrying on."

Suddenly, I feel like the wind's been knocked out of me. I had been so busy concentrating on Drake and getting over what had happened to me that I had completely forgotten about the fact that before I was taken, Drake was desperately trying to get me pregnant.

Heat flushes my skin, and nausea rolls again in my stomach. I vaguely hear Mandy asking what's wrong when I remember something that was said after Drake rescued me.

"She and the baby seem fine."

Before I know it, I'm rushing to the toilet and hurling up the banana I'd managed to eat half an hour ago. Mandy follows in hot pursuit, rubbing my back as I hurl.

Once I'm done, she hands me a tissue. "Evelyn, is there

something you're not telling me?"

"I'm pregnant," I blurt.

She frowns. "But you told me it was a bug."

"I thought it was, but when you mentioned being pregnant just now, I suddenly remembered what I heard the doctor say after Drake rescued me. He said, 'She and the baby seem fine.' Oh God, Mandy. What am I going to do?" I start freaking out and hyperventilating.

Mandy grabs me by the shoulders. "Okay, calm down. We can figure something out. First of all, you need to sit down and breathe." She leads me out to the sofa in the living room and sits down next to me. "Just close your eyes and breathe." I do as she asks and try to calm myself. "That's better."

Once I open my eyes, something dawns on me. "Why hasn't he said anything?" I think back, remembering when he said that he would be in *our lives* no matter what, but not once did he bring up what we were going to do. How is it that he's let me go knowing this?

"Do you think he's just trying to give you space to get used to the idea?"

I shake my head. "I really don't know." I place my head in my hands. "I just can't get my head around this. He enrolled me in college knowing that I'm pregnant."

"Women can be pregnant and still study, you know. It's not the end of the world just because you're having a baby. Which leads me to my next question: Are you going to have this baby?"

Looking up to her, my expression must be one of shock. I haven't even gotten round to accepting the fact that I'm pregnant yet—never mind my choice of whether or not to keep the baby. Jeez, what a mess I'm in. What a mess *he's* put me in.

I suddenly realise I have no other choice but to confront Drake about this. That means I have no other choice but to see him. Closing my eyes, I sigh. I was hoping to keep my distance until I was sure, but this news has to be addressed. I need to know why.

I get up quickly and try to locate my phone. "I need to call Drake about this."

"But I thought you said—"

"I know what I said, but this is huge, Mandy. I can't ignore this. I need to know why."

"Why what?" she asks, shocked.

"Why he made me pregnant. Why he's suddenly letting me live my own life. I just don't get it, and I need answers." I flip cushions up from the sofa and lift papers and magazines off of the coffee table. Nothing. "Ugh! Where's my fucking phone?"

Mandy places a hand on my arm. "Calm your shit. Listen, I'll ring it, and then we should be able to find it from there."

Nodding my head, I watch as Mandy punches in her pin and starts calling. Pretty soon, the sound of "Close" by Nick Jonas starts playing. It's muffled, so we have to lean forward a bit more to trace where the sound is coming from.

"It sounds like it's coming from the sofa," Mandy says, walking towards it.

"But I just checked there."

She gets on her knees and looks underneath. Before long, she's pulling out my ringing phone. "How did it get there?"

"You must have dropped it and accidently kicked it under." She ends the call and hands my phone back to me. "Are you going to call or text?"

I bite my lip. The coward in me wants to text, but I know he'll worry if I do. "I think this has to be a phone call." Mandy nods her head and gives me a sympathetic smile as I dial Drake's number. On the second ring, he answers.

"Evelyn, is everything okay?"

"Everything's fine. I just need to speak with you about something. It's important."

"I'm on my way."

He hangs up straight away. "He's coming over."

She rubs my arm. "I'd better go then." She walks over to her taco and starts wrapping it up to take with her. Once she's gathered her bag, she turns to me. "Call me once you've talked?"

I smile. "Of course."

She sighs. "It looks like you've got something else on your plate now."

"This is huge, Mandy."

She nods. "I know."

"I'm only eighteen."

She nods again. "I know." She notices my sad expression and nudges my arm. "But hey, look at it this way: When the child is older, you'll be known as the super hot, young-looking mum who picks her kid up from school." She starts laughing, which makes me smile. "You decide. It's whatever you want to do. Having a child is a huge responsibility, but at the same time, you'll have someone who loves you unconditionally. You can't ask for better than that."

I think on Mandy's words, and I know what she says is true. I would want nothing more than to have unconditional love in my life after being raised in such a loveless home. I would never want any child to grow up like that—let alone my own child.

Grabbing Mandy, I take her in for a hug. "Thank you."

She strokes my back. "Don't mention it." She pulls away,

grabbing my hands. "Don't forget to call."

I nod. "I will."

"I'll see you on Friday. I have to do the lunch and dinner shift tomorrow because Bob is short staffed." She rolls her eyes, making me laugh. She's been working full-time at a restaurant just until she starts college in September. I was so happy when I realised she would be going to the same college as I.

"That sucks," I say, genuinely feeling bad for her. I know how much one shift tires her out. I thought about getting myself a job too, but I've been too busy trying to heal myself. Now, with this extra news, I really don't know what I'm going to do.

"It does," she sighs. "Listen, I'd better go. I hope you get the answers you're looking for, but girl … don't you let him into your knickers or I'll hit you. Stay strong."

She fist pumps the air, making me laugh. "Okay. I think I can resist … especially under these circumstances."

I watch as she leaves and waves goodbye from the lift. I barely have five minutes to myself to think before the sound of the door knocking makes me jump. "Evelyn, it's just me."

Running to the door, I take a peek inside the spy hole and see Drake with Kane behind him. I immediately open up, and when I do, my skin heats.

Drake is casual today in a pair of loose jeans and a tight-fitting navy polo shirt. His hair is spiked up today, showing off his piercing brown eyes. He looks tired, but it certainly doesn't hide the fact that he's sexy as fuck.

For a brief moment, I forget why he's here. It's like my woman parts have come alive … as if lust has suddenly clouded everything.

So much for restraining myself.

"Hi," he says, his lip curving up into a heart-stopping smile. I'm not sure whether it's because he's pleased to see me or if it's because he's noticed my reaction to him. I'm guessing both. Drake always did have this uncanny knack for knowing exactly how I feel all of the time. But then he *has* had six years of studying everything about me.

"Hi," I say back, trying to snap myself out of this lust-filled haze. "Do you want to come in?" He nods and walks through, but Kane remains where he is standing. "Hi, Kane," I say, smiling.

"Hi, Evelyn. How are you?"

"Hanging in there." He gives me a knowing smile as I shut the door and walk back to the living area where Drake is standing and obviously drinking me in.

"You look beautiful today."

I feel my face flush a little. "Thank you."

"What is it you wanted to see me about?"

I motion to the sofa for him to sit. "Please, take a seat." I wait until he's seated before sitting next to him. When I get a whiff of his aftershave, I decide to move farther away from him. I'm already losing my concentration as it is without adding something else to the equation.

Taking a deep breath, I wonder how to begin. I decide to get straight to the point. "I'm pregnant."

Drake frowns. "I know."

I shake my head. "Why didn't you tell me?"

He looks confused. "I thought you already knew? The doctor came and examined you and everything. Did he not mention it then?"

"He mentioned me having to come for a scan, but I thought he was being overly cautious because of you." I close my eyes. "How far gone am I?" I can't believe I'm asking Drake this.

253

"You're around ten weeks. That's why you have to go for a scan in three weeks time. It'll be the first scan of a few."

I shake my head, unable to take it all in. When Drake reaches forward to take my hand, I pull back. "Why?" I ask, surprising him.

"Why what?"

"Why did you do it? Why did you force me into having a baby with you?"

Running his hands through his hair, he sighs. "I knew that if I got married to you, and you were carrying my child, then it would mean you were untouchable—safe. I was trying to prevent you from going through the one thing you did. I know it sounds fucked up, and I know I did wrong, but at the time, it seemed like the only way. There was that and the fact that having you bear my children would be just about the greatest gift I could ever imagine."

I briefly close my eyes. "Don't you know how fucked up that sounds?"

"Yes, but I've already told you that when it comes to you, there is nothing I would let get in the way. Not even you."

"I'm married to you and having your baby, and yet you're just letting me go? I don't understand it."

He shakes his head on a sigh. "I don't fucking understand it either, but I know that's what you've always wanted. The only thing I can't abide is you not letting me be a big part of our child's life. I admit that I'll want to ask you to move back in once the baby's due, but doing so at all would be completely up to you. If you do decide to come back, it will be completely on your terms, and it will last only as long as you wish. You can even live in your old room if that's what you want. I'll take anything I can get just to have you and the baby close to me for as long as possible."

254

I swallow hard, not able to comprehend everything he's saying. "You'd do that?"

Grabbing my hand, he moves closer to me. "I'd do anything for you. You know that."

He swipes his other hand over mine, gently gliding it across my skin. Heat prickles and descends to a certain part of my body. I don't normally get so turned on just from hand holding.

As he swipes his hand again, my lips part, and my breathing becomes heavier. *Focus, goddammit. Focus!*

Standing, I start pacing the floor and wiping my brow. Drake immediately gets up and walks to me. "Are you okay?"

"I'm fine," I reply, a little flustered. "I just feel a bit hot."

He places his hand on my forehead. "You feel cool enough."

My God, I wish he would stop touching me. I pull away from him again and sit down. "I'm fine. I just... I suppose it's the pregnancy."

He sits down again, and this time, he's closer than he was before. "Do you want me to ring Dr Philips and ask him to come and see you?"

I shake my head. "No, it's fine. I'm fine." I see his concerned face, so smile. "Honestly, I am." I sink back into my chair and sigh. "What am I doing? I don't even know where to begin."

"Hey," he says, cupping my chin. "Whatever happens, you'll have me. You've always had me. That will never change. We can do this, and we'll do it together. Every step of the way."

He locks me with those big brown eyes of his, and for that moment, I melt into him. Every touch he gives me is like a firework going off inside of me. Logical thought goes out the window, and everything I want to say and should say gets stuck in my mouth.

Without thinking, I lean in to him, kissing him on the lips. When he doesn't pull away, I straddle his lap, pulling his head towards me. I devour his mouth, and it makes the fires burn hotter than ever. If I don't feel him inside me soon, I'm going to burst.

As our tongues dance, I moan against his mouth and start frantically pulling his polo shirt up. I feel wanton. I feel crazy with lust. All I can think about now is how much I need to feel that connection we have. All I can remember is how good it feels to have him inside of me.

But, as I start yanking at his top, Drake grabs my head. "Stop, Evelyn."

His words only seem to drive me forward. The more he protests, the more I want to push it. He grabs me again, but this time by my roving hands. "Evelyn, stop!" he growls.

I do as asked, but feel confused and rejected. Drake breathes heavily against my own breaths as he leans his forehead against mine. I see the rise and fall of his chest. Closing his eyes, I see the strained frown on his forehead like he's trying to calm himself.

"I can't do this with you."

"Why?" I ask breathlessly.

"Because if I do, then I won't hesitate to bring you home. If you do this with me, then that's it. It's your choice."

I close my eyes when I hear that word. My *choice*. That's all I've ever wanted, but now that it's here, I want to throw it out the window.

He cups my face, making me look into his eyes. "I want you to want this one hundred percent. I don't want fifty, sixty, or seventy percent of you. I want you all in. Do you understand?"

I do ... despite my loins screaming otherwise at me. In the end, I nod my head. "I understand."

Regretfully, I get off his lap and sit down. I move my hair out of my face and straighten my clothes. I'm trying to compose myself, but failing miserably. "Are you okay?" he asks.

I look at him and nod my head. "I'm fine." I clear my throat. "What about college?" I almost squeak.

He frowns, leaning forward. I can tell he's trying to hide his straining erection. It only makes my situation worse.

"What about college?"

"How will I fit the baby around my studying?"

He smiles. "Well, that's what you have me for. I know this wasn't what you wanted, so I'm going to do everything it takes to make your life as simple as it can be."

I huff a little when he says this. My life is anything but simple. "You make it sound so easy."

"It's as simple or as difficult as you want to make it. Just know that I will always be there. That's one hundred percent guaranteed. Have I ever let you down on a promise before?"

I think back to our complicated six years and shake my head. "No, you haven't."

"Well then," he says, taking my hand, "this baby's not going to want for anything. You're not going to want for anything. I promise you that too. You will get to go to college, study, and have this baby at the same time. Nothing about it has to be complicated. Nothing needs to get in the way. I'll make sure of that." I smile, and he smiles too, but then he looks away and notices the envelope on the coffee table. "Is that the—"

"Yes," I answer.

He swallows hard. "Have you signed it?"

I shake my head. "No."

He visibly sighs his relief. "Does that mean there's still hope for us?"

Closing my eyes, I swallow hard too. "I honestly don't know. I just know that until I'm sure, I'm not going to sign anything."

He nods his head in resignation. "Okay," he answers. "Just know that no matter what, I'm not going anywhere."

That thought never even crossed my mind.

CHAPTER TWENTY NINE

Present Day

Another three weeks go by, and I use them to think harder than I ever have in my life. I still don't know what I'm going to do, and the fact that Drake's been nothing but sweet doesn't help matters. Since our talk about the baby, I've been finding myself drawn to him more than ever. We text and call each other all the time. We've even been out to dinner together on occasion. It's like it's been a date, but without the kissing at the end of it. And, believe me, I want to kiss him so badly. Every time I'm with him, I feel like I'm this ball of hormonal mess. Like right now. Drake has taken me out for a meal again, and he's looking as sexy as ever. He has a black suit on with his signature crisp white shirt. His hair is spiked up in the normal style I love to see, and as usual, it's making his gorgeous brown eyes stand out even more. To top it off, he's sporting a nice five o'clock shadow. I find myself fantasising about what it would be like to lick it if I had the chance. And boy do I want to have the chance! Ever since Drake told me that I can't have sex with him until I become his again, all I've wanted to do is jump his bones. I think Mandy's right. If he's using reverse psychology, then it really is working.

"Are you playing a shrewd game?" I know I need to ask this. If he is playing a game, then there's no way he'll admit to it, but at least I can gauge his reaction to my questioning.

Drake frowns. "What do you mean?"

"I just find it so hard. For years, you kept telling me that I was yours and no one—not even me—would get in your way. Now..." I sigh. "Now, you're letting me live my own life, giving me a place to stay, and setting me up in college. It's all I have ever asked, and it's all that you've ever begrudged me. Why is it now—especially since I'm also pregnant with your baby—that you're deciding to give me my free will back? You've even signed divorce papers."

"Have you signed them?" He looks worried for a moment.

"No, but that's not what I want to discuss right now."

"You think I'm playing a game?"

"Yes. No. I don't know. I just find it all hard to believe. Are you trying to make me fall in love with you or something? Did you think that by giving me everything I have ever wanted that you would end up having me to yourself again? To lock up—never to see the world?"

"Number one, I would never lock you up."

"You did once I turned eighteen."

"Things were different then."

"How?"

He sighs. "Because I knew Isaac was after you, and I knew why. He's not an issue now. I've made sure of it. We once had an understanding, but I knew after what I did, he would never let it lie. He must have had the biggest hard-on when he found out about you."

It makes me shudder to think about that man. "I always thought that he was the main reason, but I also think there was another."

He frowns. "What?"

"Control. You have a desperate need to control everything—including me."

"There's no denying that."

"And yet, here we are. We're married, I'm pregnant with your baby, and once we finish this meal, you will be going your way, and I will be going mine."

His jaw clenches. "You don't need to remind me of that."

"Then, why do you do it?"

"Because, contrary to what you believe, I am trying to be the man you want me to be. I'm trying to give you the breathing space you need in order to make your choice."

"And you will respect whatever that decision is?"

"I won't like one outcome, but yes, I will respect it."

"No kidnapping me and locking me in your room?"

He shakes his head. "No. As much as I will want to, you have my word that I won't." I frown as if I don't believe him. Drake notices. "I know I haven't given you cause to trust me, but your safety and protection have always been my number one priority."

I take my time thinking on what he has just said. I don't doubt that what he says is true. I do believe that he genuinely wanted to protect me. He just failed to protect me from himself.

"But how do I know I'm safe around you?"

Drake sighs, places his napkin on the table, and leans forward a little. "I have demons, Evelyn. There's no denying that I do. There's also no denying that I've done some unspeakable things. Things that I deeply regret. The way I handled the situation with you being one of them. I was brought up in a world where control was everything and weakness had to be eradicated. Weakness was and never can be allowed in my world."

"Aren't you worried about what people may think of our current situation?"

"To be honest, nobody really knows. The only people who do are a couple of trustworthy guards and the security at your apartment. They get paid handsomely for their discretion."

"Mandy knows, but I trust her to not say or do anything that might put me in danger." Even as I say the words, I wonder which of us I am trying to reassure more.

I know he's trying to contain the situation, and knowing that I'm not his must be driving him crazy. A part of me wants to believe everything he says as he may be able to silence everyone, but he can't silence me. I could easily tell everyone where we live about our situation, but the fact that I don't want Drake to look or seem weak is what will hold me back.

It's a strange situation—wanting to protect the man who put me in harm's way. He may have been my protector, but he was also someone from whom I needed protection. I know he had his reasons for doing all the things he did. I know that he wanted to be my first because he knew some other random scumbag would pay a fortune to be otherwise. I know he forced me to marry and become pregnant in order for me to become untouchable.

But now I find myself in this strange and fucked up situation. Could I ever forgive a man who took from me without asking? Drake has been my world since I was twelve-years-old. I know now that he came into my life to protect me from my parents and the disgusting people whose company they kept. I'm no stranger to the types of people they mixed with. I was an inconvenience to them, but at the same time, I was also their path to infinite wealth. It disgusts me to think that they're now living a life of luxury without a care in the world for their only daughter. I bet as their days go by, not a thought about me enters their heads. I'm probably just a distant memory to them now.

And I hate every single bone in their bodies.

"What are you thinking about?"

Shifting in my seat, I look up at Drake. "I was just thinking about my parents."

Drake looks disgusted. "Why the fuck would you want to think about them?"

I shrug. "I don't know. I know they're not thinking about me."

"They aren't worthy of your thoughts. They are not and never were worthy of you."

"Then, why did you associate with them?"

"Because I have a lot of business ventures, and I was told that your father's expertise in the field of law was second to none. He's a ruthless lawyer. I will give him that. He's just a fucking scumbag."

"Is he still your lawyer?"

"All ties were cut the moment you turned eighteen. After meeting you and knowing how they treated you, my interests changed. My only goal was to make sure you had a proper upbringing."

"Why me? Why not someone else?"

Drake smiles. "Because I could see the innocence in you. Despite the fact that your parents were despicable people, I could tell that their influence hadn't rubbed off on you. I wanted to keep it that way. One look from you, and I knew I had to protect you. I saw something in you—something that told me you were just as invested in me as I was in you. I knew by the way you looked at me. It was almost as if your eyes were pleading with me to help you. How could I not have answered your call?"

I think back to that memory as a child. I will always remember our very first meeting because it was the first time that I felt a real connection to another human being. Drake's right. There definitely was something there between us. Throughout everything we've been through together, there's always one thing that's been constant in our lives.

Our connection.

"Do you love me, Drake?"

He frowns. "That's a very odd question to ask. I would have thought it obvious. I've also told you often enough."

"That's not answering the question."

Grabbing my hand, Drake strokes it tenderly with his thumb. "Despite what you think of me, my love for you is undeniable. I have never loved—nor will I ever love—anyone as fiercely as I do you. The only one who will come a close second will be our baby."

He smiles a big, heart-warming smile, and I make an effort to bite my lip to hide mine. It's useless, though. I don't know if it's the pregnancy or not, but I want to cry and crawl onto his lap and hump him all at the same time.

"And despite the fact that you haven't told me, I know that you love me too. You're just too stubborn to admit it." And with that, he orders the cheque, and I'm left as dumbfounded as I normally am with him. How quickly he can turn my emotions upside down.

CHAPTER THIRTY

Present Day

It's scan day today, and for some reason, I'm as nervous as hell. I have found myself in a situation where I know I need to start reading up on the pregnancy and preparing myself for what's to come, but I always seem to find an excuse. Studying is definitely one of them. I started college a few days ago, and everything's going extremely well. The only problem I have is that people tend to either walk the other way when they see me or they act extra nice. Even the teachers are giving me preferential treatment, and I hate it. It's actually gotten so bad that I've had to have a talk with my tutor to request that I'm dealt with in the same manner as everyone else. Of course, I tell people that Drake and I are together as I feel I have to out of some strange, deep sense of loyalty towards him. He is never far away. He drops me off at college every day and picks me up afterwards. I know it's partly for show, but I'm also certain that he wants to make sure I'm safe. No matter the reason, all I know now is that my feelings for him aren't going away in a hurry. A part of me wants them to so that I can put all the things that have happened to me in the past. I should close that chapter in my life and move on with a brand new, fresh start.

But, I can't. I can't move past the fact that I not only need Drake, but I want him too. I miss him when he's not here, and I find myself randomly texting him for no reason. I could deny him and the feelings I have for him, but I won't. Despite the circumstances, we're married, and we're about to have a baby together. My head says that I can do this on my own, but my heart wants the marriage and the family life. A life that I was never truly blessed with as a child.

"You're fidgeting."

I look across at Drake, who's sitting beside me in the car. "I guess I'm nervous about the scan results. I also need to pee really badly."

Scooting over to me, Drake takes my hand. "Everything will be fine. I promise."

I start laughing. "I know you like to control everything, but some things are just beyond your control. What if something's wrong with the baby? Look at all the drugs I was given when I was pregnant at the beginning. What if they've had an adverse effect on the baby's development? What if—"

"Shh," Drake whispers, stroking my hand. "Stop worrying. Everything will be fine."

"Easy for you to say," I mutter under my breath.

"We're here, sir."

I look out the window and see the clinic. My nerves kick up a notch, so I take a deep breath.

"I'm here with you every step of the way, remember?" I nod my head and he smiles. "Come. Let's go and meet our baby."

We get out of the car and make our way inside. Drake talks to the receptionist because my mouth is too dry to even utter one word. My hands are clammy, and my body trembles as we're ushered in to take a seat. There are two other couples waiting, and they smile once they see us. I know the gossip will start from today. There will be no hiding the fact that Drake and I are pregnant anymore. It makes me wonder how he'll spin this.

I feel an arm around me as Drake pulls me to him. He places a kiss on my head and whispers, "There's no need to be nervous, baby. I got you." I instantly relax and lean in to him for support. I know the other couples are watching our every move, but for now, I don't care.

"Mr and Mrs Salvatore?" We both look up. "Dr Taylor will see you now."

Drake helps me up, and we both make our way inside the room where Dr Taylor awaits us. "Ah, Mr and Mrs Salvatore. How are we today?"

"Evelyn's a little nervous—anxious to get this done."

The doctor looks at Drake and nods his head. "I understand. Why don't we skip the formalities and head straight to it then?"

I nod. "Yes, please. I also really need the toilet."

He starts laughing. "Okay. Just go through that door and lie down. I just need you to pull your jeans down a little so we can begin."

Nodding my head, Drake and I head through the side door and see the big scanning machine next to the bed. I take a deep breath and climb on top. Once settled, I undo my jeans, which are getting a little tight for me now, and I notice the relief I feel once I pull them down. It's amazing how much they were actually pressing on my bladder.

Straight after, Dr Taylor comes into the room and starts preparing. He gets a tube of lubricant and squeezes it on my belly. It makes me jump from the cold.

"Sorry. It can be very cold once it goes on. It'll warm up soon enough." Grabbing the scan probe, he holds it over my belly. "Okay, let's have a look."

Drake is right beside me, holding my hand. When he places the probe onto my belly, at first all I can see are a load of blobs. But as he presses down a little more, the shape of a tiny baby begins to emerge.

"Now, here's the head, and you can see the arms and feet there." The doctor points to the screen, but all I can do is stare. It looks amazing. "Now, if I move this a little ..."

All of a sudden, there's the sound of a loud heartbeat. The doctor smiles, I gasp, and Drake squeezes my hand. "Do you hear that?" I ask Drake, feeling absolutely overwhelmed. Drake stares back at me with the most heart-warming smile.

"I do, babes. Isn't it the most beautiful sound? Look, you're giving life. You're such a clever thing."

I beam back at Drake, but I need to see the baby, so I turn again and see the doctor making outlines. "What are you doing?"

"Taking measurements. It's imperative to make sure that the baby is growing. It also gives us an indication of how many weeks along you are."

I bite my lip, getting worried. "Is everything okay?"

The doctor looks back to us and smiles. "Everything's perfect. The baby's heart and lungs are fine, and he or she is growing well. I'd say you were around fifteen weeks."

A gasp of relief leaves my lips. "Oh, thank you, doctor." He smiles, and without a thought, I turn to Drake and pull him to my lips. I kiss him like I've never kissed him before, pouring into it the immense happiness of knowing that despite all the shit this poor baby's been through, everything will be okay.

After a few seconds, Drake pulls back. "Wow! If I had known you would kiss me like that, I would have brought you in sooner."

The doctor starts laughing. "I will give you two some privacy. Evelyn, you can use the toilet now."

I sigh in relief. "Thank God!"

I'm quickly handed some tissues from a smiling nurse, and I wipe myself down before pulling up my jeans and rushing to the toilet. Once I'm finished, I rush back outside where I see Drake in a heated discussion on his phone. Once he spots me, he quickly hangs up, and I run straight into his waiting arms. "I'm so happy the baby's okay."

He squeezes me to him. "See, I told you everything would be okay."

"Who was that on the phone?" I ask, pulling away.

He smiles down at me and kisses my lips. "No one important." He kisses me again and rubs his nose with mine. In this moment, I couldn't be happier.

"Would it be okay if you came round to my place for dinner? I don't really want to let you go now. Besides, I think this is cause for a celebration, don't you?"

I bite my lip, silently wondering if I should go. I haven't been to Drake's since I left all those weeks ago. It's crazy really because I've been pining over Ireland, and I'm desperate to see her.

"Okay," I answer without a moment's hesitation.

Drake smiles, takes my hand, and leads us out to the waiting car. "Oh, what about another appointment?" I ask as we're nearing the car.

"Don't worry. I sorted that when you went to the toilet. You have to go for another scan in about five weeks. It's then we can find out the sex of the baby ... if we want."

I get into the car wondering if that is what I want or not. I decide finding out is easier because at least I will know whether to shop for a boy or a girl that way.

"Where to, sir?" Kane asks as we settle in the car.

"Home, please, Kane. Evelyn and I are celebrating." Drake looks across at me with a smile, and it's then that I feel my heart ache for this man. All this time I have been trying to deny my feelings, but I know that in this moment, I definitely have them.

As we drive back, though, I wonder to myself whether or not I'm just getting caught up in the moment. Do I want Drake, or am I just being swept away by this awesome and precious moment between us? Right now, a big part of me just wants to take Drake into my arms and tell him never to let me go. But, come the light of day, would I end up regretting that decision?

"We're here," Drake announces.

I look out the window—only now realising just how deep in thought I really was. In front of us, the all too familiar gates open and we drive through. A little pang hits my stomach as we approach the stairs that lead toward the entrance. A small part of me feels like I shouldn't be here, but this is the first step towards trusting Drake, and I believe him when he says that he won't hold me prisoner.

"Can we go see Ireland first?"

Drake smiles. "Of course. I know she's missed you." I bite my lip as the guilt washes over me. "Come," Drake commands. "Let's go inside."

We get out of the car and make our way into the house. Some guards I recognise are here, and they greet us as we walk in. "Where's George?" I ask, looking around. I've actually missed him in my own way.

"George is taking some time off, but he will be back this evening to make us dinner. Do you have a special request?"

I smile. "How about steak?"

Drake smirks. "I thought so, but I wanted to be a gentleman and ask." He then takes my hand and immediately leads me out back towards the stables. I practically run towards Ireland, kissing that little map on the top of her nose. She nuzzles into me, and I inhale, taking in her smell.

"I've been regularly exercising her in your absence. Every time I take Max out, she comes with us."

"Thank you," I reply, kissing her head again. "I suppose I shouldn't ride her now ... just in case."

Drake frowns. "Hmm. Until you have the baby, I think that's wise. We can't have anything happen to either of you." He walks up to me and places a hand on my belly. When he captures my eyes with his, lust like never before courses through me. I find I can't look away. Visions of him ripping my clothes off and taking me in the barn run through my head. Right now, I don't care about the consequences of demanding that he does exactly that. I just know that if I don't, I will burst.

Gripping his shirt, I pull him towards me. The air has shifted between us. It almost feels like a huge electric charge, and I'm burning from the inside out. I need to have him inside me at any cost.

"Drake," I say breathlessly as I pull him even closer to me. I feel once his erection presses into my stomach, and I know he wants this just as much as I do. "Drake, I—"

"Sir, you have Mr Montgomery waiting for you in reception."

All lust leaves me at the sound of my father's name. What in the hell is he doing here? I look up at Drake and see the annoyance in his eyes. "Okay. I'll be right there."

The guard nods. "Very well, sir."

The guard leaves, and Drake turns to me, leaning his head against mine. "I'm sorry about this. If you want to stay out here until he leaves—"

"I want to come inside with you."

"Are you sure?"

I nod my head, but I can't believe that Drake is letting me choose. He takes my hand and leads the way. All the while, my heart is thumping in my chest. What on earth could he be here for?

Once inside, I see my father pacing in the reception room. He spots us and lifts his head, but he is obviously surprised when he sees me. "Brought her in to gloat I suppose?" he sneers at Drake.

"I don't know what you mean," Drake responds.

"You know exactly what I fucking mean."

Drake storms towards him and picks up his collar. "Don't you fucking dare come into my house and talk to me like this. You seem to keep forgetting who you're talking to.

"You must have known. You *must* have! Why would you give us all that money only to make us lose it all?" My eyes widen, wondering what the hell he means.

"Because it was never about the fucking money. It was always about Evelyn." Drake turns to me with a smile, but my father looks like he wants to kill me.

"I should have sold you to Isaac when I had the chance."

In no time, Drake punches my father, and he lands in a heap on the floor. My father cries out, and I see when blood starts to drip from his nose. He tries to get up, but Drake holds him there by his foot. "I'm going to tell you what's going to happen next. First, you're going to leave my house and never return. Second, you're going to take your penniless, worthless fucking arse out of this town and preferably out of this country. You are not to come within ten miles of this town. Ever. Again." Drake bends down and grabs him by his collar again. "Be grateful to your daughter because if it wasn't for her, you would have a bullet in your head by now. Got it?" My father vigorously nods his head. "Now, get out of here before I squeeze you by your scrawny little neck until there's no life left." Drake pushes him away, and we both watch as my father gets up, stumbles, and then walks out.

At first, I don't know what to say. Drake's just standing there, looking angry. Thoughts of when he hit that pervert, Charles, come into my head, but this time, it's different. I can really feel the murderous anger pouring off of him. But despite all his anger, I need to know.

"What happened?"

Drake inhales sharply before walking over and pouring himself a glass of bourbon. He takes a swig and then pours another before turning to me. "I like to play with the stock market at times, and people—including your father—know I've gotten good at it. There was a company called Briars, which was once a blossoming company. I got word that they had made some bad business decisions and were about to go bust. I just thought it was a good idea to convince your father to invest all the money he had left into it. I told him he would be set for life if he invested. He believed me as he had no reason not to. He invested all his money a few days ago and just found out this afternoon that he's lost the lot. As you can tell, he is rather angry." He finally smiles at me.

"Did you do all that for me? But all your money—"

"You heard what I said. It wasn't about the money. It never was.

Things changed for you in a dramatic way, and while you got the shit end of the deal, they were left lording it up like they were a king and queen. How was that fair to you? Something had to be done."

My eyes start to water immediately at his words. I know Drake has always been there for me, but I never thought he would do something like this. Does this mean he truly loves me? He must. Mustn't he?

Without another thought, I walk up to him and place my hand on his arm. "Can you get your driver to take me home? I would like to freshen up for our dinner."

"Of course. Do you want me to come with you?"

I shake my head. "No. I will only be an hour tops. Stay here, and I will be with you soon."

Drake nods and asks Kane to escort me home and wait for me once we get there. Once home, I take a quick shower and slip into the one dress I can still fit into. It's long, red, and coincidently one of Drake's favourites. Once I'm ready, I slip into my high heels, walk over to my coffee table, and deal with something I should have dealt with ages ago. Once done, I grab my bag and head outside to where Kane is.

"Are you ready?" I nod. "You look beautiful."

I smile. "Thank you." It's then I remember something, but I just haven't had the chance to ask. "Erm, Kane?"

"Yes?"

"That day at the hospital—" I notice his sad expression, so I stop.

"I will always regret that day. I wanted to help... I thought I *was* helping. But, I only ended up leading you into danger."

Grabbing his arm, I squeeze. "You can't blame yourself for that day. I would have run no matter what. I was pretty determined." I chuckle and he laughs too.

I often think back on that day and of Dotty. A couple of weeks ago, I managed to find Dotty on Facebook. It was pretty easy to find her, considering she was clutching that pogo stick she'd mentioned. I got in touch with her, told her I was safe and happy, and asked for her address so that I could send her a card to properly thank her. She was over the moon that I was finally settled and requested that I keep in touch. I sent her the thank you card along with a hundred pounds. I also included a hundred pound gift card for Marks and Spencer. She contacted me via Facebook Messenger a couple of days later, telling me how naughty I was and that she never expected the money back. I assured her that I still intended to pay it forward. The very next day, I gave a homeless woman one hundred pounds. It felt extremely rewarding. The homeless woman couldn't believe it and wanted to hand some of it back. I just told her the same as what Dotty had told me. "Keep it, and pay it forward." She had smiled and promised that she would.

Once back at Drake's house, I place my bag and envelope down and join Drake in the dining room. He's changed too and is looking as sexy as always. He has his back to me, but as if sensing me, he turns towards me, and when he does, his eyes widen. "Wow, you look … stunning."

"Thank you. I wanted to make an effort this evening."

"You never need to make an effort, but I appreciate that you did. You've always been a beautiful woman, Evelyn. Always."

Just then, George walks in with our plates of food. Once he spots me, his smile spreads wide. "Evelyn, how are you, my dear?"

I start laughing. "Fine, thank you." I look at the food, and my stomach growls. "This looks and smells divine."

"Well, I hope it tastes just as good." He places the food down. "Please, sit, and bon appétit."

"Thank you," we both say in unison.

We both sit down, and I immediately tuck into my meal. It does indeed taste as good as it looks and smells.

"You look like you're enjoying that."

I smile. "Oh, I am. George does cook a mean steak."

Drake smiles, and we watch each other as we eat. I think Drake realises that conversation comes last when I'm this hungry. Once I finish, I place my knife and fork down and watch as Drake does the same.

"Dessert?" he asks as he takes a sip of wine.

"Not now. In fact, I need to discuss something with you."

He frowns. "Oh yes?"

I nod. "Well, first I have to show you something." I get up from my chair and walk out to the hallway. Once there, I pick up the envelope and bring it back in. Drake is watching with quiet interest, but when he sees the envelope in my hand, his eyes widen slightly.

I sit in my seat and carefully push the envelope towards him. "This is what I wanted to show you."

Drake doesn't move at first. He just looks down at the envelope and then at me. Finally, he leans forward, grabs the envelope, and turns to the last page. I see the moment when his face falls and his mouth parts. "You signed it."

I grip the table as my heart starts beating rapidly in my chest. "Yes."

He places the papers down on the table. "So, that's it then."

"Not quite." He looks up at me with a frown, so I continue. "Do you still have my ring?"

"Yes. It was one of the things I managed to obtain from Isaac once I shot him between his eyes." I notice the slight growl when he says this.

"Can you get it for me please?"

"Why?"

"You'll see why in a bit. Please."

Sighing, he gets up and walks towards a giant painting on the wall. He pulls it aside, and a safe is revealed. He punches in some numbers, takes out a box, and closes the safe. Once the painting is back in place, he walks towards our table, sits down, and places the box in front of me.

"Ask me," I simply say.

Drake frowns. "Ask you what?"

I motion with my head towards the box and back up to him. "I want you to ask me like a man *should* ask a woman."

It finally dawns on him what I mean, and with renewed hope in his eyes, he picks the box up and gets down on one knee in front of me.

When he looks up at me, I smile, and it encourages him enough to return the gesture. "Evelyn," he starts, taking my hand, "I know I'm not the man of your dreams, but dreams are called such for a reason. I *am* your reality, however, and I can guarantee that I will love you more than any man could ever love you. I'm not perfect, and, realistically, I never will be. I just ask that you take me as I am—flaws and all. I promise to love and take care of you till the end of my days." As my eyes water, Drake clears his throat. "Evelyn, will you marry me?"

"Yes," I croak.

Drake beams a wonderful smile, but everything becomes blurry as the tears start to fall. In no time, Drake has the ring on my finger and me in his arms. The feel of him against me does nothing to aid my hormones.

"Erm, Drake ..."

And without hesitation this time, he answers, "Yes?"

"About that dessert." I give him a mischievous grin, and in no time at all, he has me in his arms and is making me squeal.

Once snugly there, he kisses me hungrily and smiles. "I thought you'd never ask."

EPILOGUE

Three Years Later – Drake

How much has changed since almost three years ago. I look back on those times with quiet frustration. I always knew from the moment I met Evelyn that she was meant to be mine. I was right in what I said. No one was going to stand in my way. Not even Evelyn herself.

See, I may have changed just enough to give her the idea that I am a changed man. I guess, for Evelyn, I did change somewhat. But, old habits die hard. I knew Evelyn was going to fight me at every turn, so I came up with a plan. A plan which—I am glad to say—worked. I never intended to let Evelyn go for a single moment. If she had resisted in the end, I would have gone against my word and kept her. I very nearly lost it when she brought the divorce papers around. In fact, I was seconds away from revealing my true self when she asked me to get the ring. It was pure intrigue that made me go along with it and play her game. If she had tried to leave with that ring, then I would have acted. I can only be grateful that I played my part so well and for every occasion that I was able to hold my tongue.

I did what I did simply to make life easier and to give off the illusion that she had all the control. Evelyn has never had control. I've just simply allowed her the time to eventually bend to my will. It took every ounce of willpower inside of me not to take her whenever we were together. I knew she wanted me. I could tell by the way her breathing hitched whenever I touched her or by the way her pupils dilated whenever I kissed her skin. That's why I added the immense frustration of not giving her what she wanted unless she agreed to be mine. Again, it worked, and again, it all added to her list of reasons why she was being stupid by being apart from me. I could tell the wheels in her brain were working overtime to figure out what she wanted. I was quietly convinced that she would choose to be with me. I just had to let her come to that conclusion on her own. That day when she had her first scan, I could see it in her eyes that she knew what her choice was. The final nail in the coffin was when her dad came round and she found out what I'd done. Again, this was all carefully orchestrated so that I would seem like her hero rather than her monster.

Of course I am a monster… But only when it comes to her.

"Daddy, look!" little James cries from the table. He holds out a drawing to me of the three of us holding hands in a garden. We're all stick men, and our hair looks like a collection of bushes rather than hair.

"Wow, that looks awesome, little buddy. Wait till Mummy gets home, and you can show her." I smile, thinking of where she is. She's at the doctor because she's been feeling sick. She says she can't be pregnant because she's been taking her pills regularly. She doesn't want another baby for a while as she's taking time out to concentrate on James and her career. She's a psychologist now, and with help from me, she has an office in one of the buildings I own. I don't like it, but it's one of the things I allow her. Knowing that it's my building and that there are cameras everywhere helps me feel that bit better. At least then I feel like I'm in control. I can watch how her patients interact with her, and if anyone tries to get a little friendly, I have a little word in their shell-like.

The sound of a car pulling up outside alerts us that Evelyn is back. "Mummy's back!" James cries as he runs out of the room into the hallway.

Smiling, I get up from my chair and walk out towards the hall where I find James desperately handing Evelyn the drawing. She looks down at him and smiles, but I can tell it's a strained smile.

"Wow, James. That looks so nice. Is that the three of us together out in the garden?" James nods. "It's so pretty. I love it."

James beams and once Evelyn kisses him on the head, he goes running back into the room to carry on drawing.

"Is everything okay?" I walk up to her and place my hand on her arm. She looks pissed.

"No, everything's not okay. I've just found out I'm pregnant again. How did that happen?" She throws her arms in the air.

"Baby, that's great news!"

"No, it's not great news!" she snaps. "I've only just settled in to my job, and James is still so small. I was hoping to wait at least another two or three years before having another baby. This just puts everything out of sync."

"Come here," I pull her into my arms and squeeze her tightly to me. "I told you the first time around that it didn't have to affect any of your work, and I was right, wasn't I? James is flourishing, you're at work doing what you love, and life is wonderful. Just think of it as an added bundle of joy to enter into our lives."

She sniffles into my chest, so I know she's crying. "You think so?"

I gently stroke her hair. "I know so."

I take her head and cup it in my hands. "This baby is only going to add to our family unit. I, for one, can't be happier with the news. Nothing needs to change, Evelyn. As always, I've got you, and I am here."

She smiles, giving me what I'm after. "You must have super sperm," she jokes, making me laugh.

"Well, what do you expect?"

She hits me. "Typical male ego." She starts to walk towards the reception room, but turns to me. "Once this baby's born, I'm getting sterilised."

She disappears, and I'm left with the biggest smirk on my face. She won't get sterilised because I will never let her. I wanted her to have another baby soon after James was born, but she refused. I knew taking her pills away wouldn't work, so I did the next best thing. I replaced them with placebos.

See, I own her heart, body, and soul, and I think she secretly knows it. I just like to give her the illusion of choice. I'm quite proud of myself really for all of my achievements.

Maybe I am a fucking monster after all.

COMING IN APRIL 2017

A Surrogate Love Affair

I never believed in fate. Destiny was something magical, something written in the stars. I was a world away from having that kind of excitement in my life.

I was alone, praying for a baby, that little miracle I could hold in my arms. My husband fought me at every turn, but I knew I would break him down one day. It was just a matter of time.

In the end, fate took the shape of my best friend and her husband, who were desperate for a baby. Desperate for that miracle, that hope, that joy in their lives. I wanted to give that to them. I wanted them to have the family they were striving for.

With my help, they would finally have everything they ever wanted.

On the day I found out their little miracle was coming, fate intervened again. It would turn my world upside down, shattering my life into a million pieces. It was on that day I realised things were about to become really complicated.

EXCERPT

"I can be your surrogate."

Those were the five words I uttered tonight. Five little words that stunned everyone into an awkward silence. My husband, Kyle, looked at me like I had grown an extra head. Sarah, my best friend, stared in disbelief, and her husband, Ethan, looked about ready to burst. What he wanted to say, I couldn't tell. Everything after that seemed to be a blur.

"What were you thinking tonight, Alice? I know you want a baby, but this is going too far."

As I sit at my mirror, Kyle angrily hovering over me, I slowly take off my earrings. We had just returned from a dinner party with our friends. An innocent dinner party that suddenly ended when those five words left my lips.

Blowing out a breath, I look at him. "This isn't about me wanting a baby, Kyle. This is about me giving my best friend a special gift. You haven't been there when she's cried to me about not being the woman she feels she needs to be for Ethan. I've had to sit there and comfort her, telling her she is all woman and more. I'm the one who has had to listen to the heartache in her voice when yet another IVF treatment doesn't work. I want to do this for her. I want to do this for *both* of them."

Kyle paces the room. I watch as the man I married fights the urge to scream and shout. I know he's angry, but I also know he's trying his hardest to keep it together. He spins toward me.

"Don't you know what this means? It means you will be pregnant with *another man's* baby! You will be the mother and Ethan will be the father. It will kill you to see another woman raising your baby." When my shoulders sag, Kyle kneels in front of me. "See? You know it's true, honey. How on earth will you manage to cope with that every day? And what about me? How do you think it would make me feel, knowing you're carrying another man's child?"

When a tear slides down my face, Kyle wipes it away. "It's been over five years, Kyle." I see him sigh, making me angry. "You said we would try for a baby after we've been married three years. It's been over *five.*"

Kyle sweeps his eyes over my body. "Your body is beautiful, Alice. You've always looked so young and vivacious. Having a baby would just—"

I gasp, standing up. Kyle stands slowly, too. "So *that's* what this is all about? You're afraid if I have a baby my body will be—"

"Ruined. Yes," he blurts out.

My eyes bulge. I can't believe what I'm hearing. "You selfish prick."

Kyle offers me his hand, but all I do is look at it in disgust. "Oh, come on, Alice."

I step back and walk toward the bed. "I can't believe you're saying this. So the reason you won't have a baby with me is because you're afraid I'll get stretch marks and saggy breasts?"

Sighing, Kyle throws his hands up in the air. "It's not just that. I've heard it from my mates at work before. There are countless times I've heard them complain about their wives being too tired to have sex after having a baby. Many have gone as far as to say dinner's sometimes not even ready when they get home. They're jealous of me, though. Jealous of the fact I have a hot wife who gives me everything I need." Holding his hands out, he walks closer to me, but I flinch away.

"Oh...my...god... I can't believe these words are coming out of your mouth. Seriously?"

Kyle sighs again in obvious frustration. "You should be happy that other men think you're hot."

I huff in disgust. I can't believe I've never seen this side of him. I already knew Kyle was a little reluctant about having a baby, but I never knew how deep it went. It made me see him in a completely new light.

I narrow my eyes at him. "What would make me happy is to have a husband who supports me. What would make me happy is to seal our unity of marriage by starting a family. Isn't that the way life goes? Isn't that the life we agreed on?"

Kyle shakes his head. "Honey, plenty of couples get married and don't have children."

My eyes widen. "So *now* you're saying you don't want any kids? Isn't this something you should have told me...I don't know...eight years ago when we first got together? Eight years ago when you told me you wanted the house, the wife, the white picket fence? Did you just say all that to get me into bed? Was it all just bullshit?"

Kyle runs his fingers through his hair. "Of course it wasn't. I'm just not ready yet, okay? I need more time. Is that too much to ask?"

I sigh, turning back toward the mirror before sitting down in front of it. "No, it's not. But when someone you love and trust tells you three years, you don't expect almost another three to pass you by with still nothing."

Kyle suddenly growls. "I'm sick of repeatedly having this same fucking argument. Why can't you just accept the fact I'm not ready? The more you push this, the more I don't want to have any fucking kids." I open my mouth, but he cuts me off. "Fuck this. I'm sleeping on the couch. Looks like I *am* one of those suckers at work after all."

Kyle storms out, leaving me in tears. I knew he could be cruel, but that really hit me hard, and I'm sure he knew it. He's the type who always wants to win an argument and, as long as he gets his point across, doesn't care just how much his words sting.

Trying to push that aside, I think back to Sarah and Ethan's house tonight. We had just finished our meal. Yes, wine was involved, but even in my woozy state, I knew I wanted to do this for them. I didn't understand what I felt inside, but I knew I was doing the right thing. Why? Well, I haven't figured that out yet, but I know, in my heart, this is meant to be.

"Sarah and I accept the fact we cannot get pregnant naturally. We still want a baby, so we're exploring other avenues, aren't we?" Staring at Sarah, Ethan places a loving hand over hers.

I was always a little jealous of the way he looked at her. It makes me wish I had that in my marriage. Mine isn't falling apart, by any means, but Kyle can be a little aloof with me at times. It's almost like he's in lust with me, rather than love. From the moment he gets home from work at night until the moment he's ready to leave the next morning, he constantly wants sex. In the beginning, it was exciting. Now, it's become a replacement for love and companionship. It's as if I'm only his crutch. I want the sex, but I also want to be cherished. I don't think that's too much to ask.

"What other avenues are you looking into?" I ask, briefly looking across at Kyle, who gives me a stern look. The look that tells me not to go there. He always tenses up whenever anyone talks about babies. It pisses me off sometimes.

Sarah pushes her golden locks from her shoulder and smiles, which seems a little off tonight. It makes me wonder if she's given up hope. I pray that isn't the case because they would make a beautiful baby together.

Sarah is as stunning now as she was when we first met. We've known each other since secondary school. Despite us being polar opposites...she has blonde hair, I have dark; she has dark blue eyes, I have light brown; she's five-four and petite, I'm five-eight with curves...we've always gotten along.

Come to think of it, Kyle and Ethan are opposite, too. Kyle, having thick blond hair, is not much taller than I am, whereas Ethan has short dark hair and towers over me. He's also more toned than Kyle, working out at the gym down the road from my job. He lives a healthy lifestyle, hoping it would produce a healthy baby. I know he is going to be a fantastic father.

"We're thinking of surrogacy."

Ethan's voice halted my thoughts. "Surrogacy? I ask."

Ethan smiles brightly, but Sarah's is still off. "Yes. We realise now that IVF won't work, so we've been talking about a surrogate mother. Someone who could carry our baby."

I frown, looking at Sarah. "You mean one who will carry the egg from you?" I look at Ethan. "And the sperm from you?"

"Not me." I snap my head to Sarah. "My infertility runs a little *more complicated than that. Not only do I have endometriosis, my eggs are of poor quality. The best solution is for another woman to carry Ethan's baby."*

Ethan grabs Sarah's hand and looks at her. "Our baby."

The sadness in Sarah's face makes my heart ache. "It's no use, though. The chance of us finding someone who is willing to carry our baby is virtually nil."

Just then, something comes over me. It's almost like clarity has formed in my head. It feels as though I know why I have been put on this earth. Like, for the first time in my life, I have a purpose.

Before thinking about the implications, I blurt out, "I can be your surrogate."

Tears fall as my husband's cruel words whirl around my head. He could have been a little more understanding, even interested as to why I want to do this. Yes, I am curious to know what it feels like to have another life growing inside me—even knowing I won't be a mother to the baby. I have been friends with Sarah for eighteen years. We grew up together, met our husbands together, laughed together, and cried together. We are almost like sisters. I wouldn't think twice about doing this for my sister, so Sarah's definitely no different.

Despite my husband's obvious disgust at the thought, I need to go ahead with this. Something inside me still says it's the right thing to do.

But I guess convincing Kyle is going to be harder than I imagined.

COMING SOON - TAILSPIN

Devon Jackson is a smug, arrogant prick. He's also CEO at Worldwide Airways, and I'm the lucky one who lands a job as his PA—a job I soon learn to regret taking.

I do absolutely everything for him, from organising his appointments to picking up condoms for him every Friday afternoon.

Why do I put up with it?

Because, despite it all, I am obsessed with him and have been since I was fifteen. He treats me like dirt, yet I still come back for more.

To him, I'm untouchable. And not only to him, but every other man on the planet. The fact he's my brother's best friend has seen to that. They're both possessive jerks.

And I put up with it...for a while.

Once I put my foot down, the dynamic changes. And it is at that moment I find out how he *really* feels.

In fact, I find out so much more than I bargain for. Not only is Devon host to some serious demons, but he also holds a very big, dark secret. A secret that could destroy our relationship before it gets a chance to begin.

EXCERPT-SIREN
OUT NOW - PROLOGUE

I stand over my father's grave, wiping the tears that threaten to fall onto the soil beneath my feet. I'm wearing a black dress, which is cut just above the knee, and on my feet is a pair of brand new, black and red Louboutin high heels. I scream *class*, but I am also the perfect image of a daughter in deep distress over her father's untimely death.

And what an untimely death it was.

I clutch my chest, heaving sobs of grief as I bend down to lay new flowers at his grave. I have been coming here every single day, bringing new flowers to replace the old ones. I pick up yesterday's flowers and toss them aside as I trace the line of my father's name on his headstone.

Here lies Richard Valentine, loving father to two daughters. Born 26th January 1970, Died 15th July 2016.

That was three weeks ago. His body was found buried in Virginia Water in Surrey—only nineteen miles or so from where I live. He was buried deep, but a storm sixteen days ago unearthed his decaying body. He had a stab wound in his back which was determined to be the cause of his death. It was murder, of course, and it is only now that the police are investigating.

At first, they thought he had run away—possibly met a girl, got swept off his feet, and was living by the beach, sipping cocktails with a buxom blonde. My sister kept on the case, though. She tried to tell them that it wasn't like him to just disappear without at least keeping in touch. I vouched for her to the police, but I also reminded her of that time when he disappeared for a year without a trace and came back just as suddenly as he had left. I knew the real reason why, but I didn't divulge it to my sister or to the police. That little secret was between Daddy and me alone. The two police officers gave each other that look... The one that says, "Yeah, there's no foul play here." They just thought he had found the girl of his dreams and was busy acting the part of the doting boyfriend to his new plaything.

As I think on this, I stroke his grave tenderly and sweep away the leaves that have fallen from the nearby trees. I need to make sure that it is clean and tidy before kneeling down at his grave and throwing my arms over the gravestone. With my arms shielding me from anyone who may be watching, I take in a long, deep breath. A smirk rises on my face as I utter the words, "You always loved it when I threw my arms around you, didn't you?" I sigh, scooting up to get closer to his headstone before spitting on his grave.

"I hope you're enjoying your time in Hell, Daddy."

EXCERPT-SCARS

No amount of physical or emotional scars left behind could ever actually reveal true heartache. The evil from which they were formed cuts so deeply into your bones that it seeps into your bloodstream and pumps through your veins until it's ringing in your ears. The scars never **truly** show themselves... Never reveal the brunt of their true force. While they are a symbol of survival, they are also reminders of things we would much rather forget—of pain that cannot be shed.

I have become an orphan ... left to pick up the pieces of a broken heart which can never be fixed. I am incurably and irreparably hopeless.

Time stood still the day my family was ripped away from me. I lost myself—my very identity. I was chosen to live. I was chosen to carry with me the burden of being the one who survived. I was left with the question which haunts me endlessly:

Why me?

Why me?

Why me?

And now, I lie in a small room. Four walls are what welcome

me day after day. No sharp objects, no ropes... Not a thing I could use if I wanted to end it all. He took me. That's why I'm here. He will never let me decide my own fate. He will never let me choose my own destiny.

He will never let me go.

It was he who chose me. It was he who had been stalking me for the last nine months. And it was he who pulled me from the car on that fateful day—two, maybe three weeks ago. He won't leave me in peace... He will never leave me in peace.

He is forever waiting in the wings, watching me. I am his, he tells me. As long as I have breath in my lungs, I will always be his. He rules my head, my body, and my heart. But the most frightening thought of all is that ... pretty soon ... he will rule my soul as well.

With that last thought, I clutch the duvet to my chest.

I would have expected to be alone with my family gone, but he's certainly made sure that my situation could have been worse.

Far worse.

I get fed three times a day, provided with refreshments on a regular basis, and a little later, I get treated to hearing his voice over a speaker in the corner of my room. He talks to me. He wants me to tell him about my life, my fears, my longings, and my dreams.

He has not once entered my room, but now, I long for it. I long for the contact so much that my insides burn. I am relieved to hear his voice, but now his voice alone is not enough.

I want more.

I need to see him. Need to be with him... I need to touch him. I crave the contact. To feel skin on skin.

He has started to invade my dreams so much that I cry out during the night. He knows they're about him; he tells me so. I talk in my sleep, apparently, and he likes that. He also tells me that he likes the sound of my voice. For some reason, that makes me smile. I have no idea why.

He abducted me and is holding me prisoner against my will. I didn't ask for this. He forced me. So, why do I long for him the way that I do? Why do I seek out his company? It wouldn't make any sense to a normal person... I guess that means I'm not normal.

Despite it all, I still feel that frisson of excitement every time I hear his voice. I still smile the minute I hear the thumping of the speaker. And my heart still beats a million miles an hour every time I hear the sound of his velvety voice.

Six days ago, I began asking him to come visit me, and I've repeated my request every day thereafter. All I hear from him is the same response: "It isn't time yet."

"Why isn't it time yet?" I would ask.

"For now, I can't say. I just need you to trust me... To realize that this is for your own good."

His response both frustrates and angers me. It's been that way for days, but today things suddenly changed. I have become desperate for his contact, so I altered my request.

"I want you to come to my room... I need you to come to my room... I'm desperate for you to touch me... To hold me like you did that night in the little house... Please make it happen, J. Please?" All has been silent from that moment on. I have been sitting here, feeling my heart beating erratically for the last hour—ever since I pleaded with him.

My heart aches.

My body quivers.

My mind races.

My pulse speeds up more when I hear a noise coming from my door. Maybe he is just coming to feed me, but I know from the patterns to which I've grown accustomed that it's too early for that. He has taken my watch from me, so I have no concept of actual time, but I have gotten used to relying upon my internal clock. And my clock is telling me that it is too early to be fed, so what could it be?

I gasp when I hear the tapping. That sound—the sound of footsteps—taunts me.

I clutch the sheets even more tightly to me once I realize the noise is getting louder. There is nothing I can do but sit and wait to see what will happen next.

Silence falls, and I watch the door like a hawk. I stare at the handle, which, for now, remains still. I swear that it, too, is taunting me. I swear it knows of my trepidation and is deliberately staying still just to tease me.

I hold my breath—biding my time—as I sit here, rigidly clutching the bedclothes. It feels like hours, but it's only been mere seconds since the total silence began.

And then, it's happening. I gasp again, clutching the sheets more tightly still as the handle on the door moves down, and the door pushes forward. For a fraction of a second, nothing happens. Total silence fills the room again as the creaking door comes to a stop. My heart starts hammering in my chest, and my body trembles as anxiety ripples through my insides and prickles my skin.

Nothing is there apart from the door—which is now ajar—and the slight shadow of his body as the light shines on the bedroom wall.

I remain seated, waiting in earnest to see what will happen next. Involuntarily, a sharp intake of breath floods my lungs and pains my chest when I see the shadow of one foot moving forward ... then two. My eyes widen as I tighten my grip with both hands this time. My breath escapes in little wisps as the shadow increases its density. I gasp as I see a foot ... followed by a hand.

And then...

He emerges.

BOOKS BY JAIMIE ROBERTS

Take a Breath, and Take it Deep – Both have been pulled from Amazon for rewriting and editing. Release dates for both to come.

Until I Met You – Released 1st June 2014

DEVIANT – Released 31st October 2014

Redemption – Released 3rd April 2015

CHAINED – Released 17th July 2015

A Step Too Close – Released 17th September in 2015

Luca (You Will Be Mine) – Released 15th January 2016

Luca (Because You're Mine) – Released 26th February 2016

Scars – Released 23rd June 2016

Siren – Released 6th September 2016

Possession – Released 10th March 2017

A Surrogate Love Affair – Release date in April 2017

Tailspin – Release date to come

Tethered – Release date to come

Her Guardian Trilogy – Release date to come

AUTHOR BIO

Jaimie Roberts was born in London, but moved to Gibraltar in 2001. She is married with two sons, and in her spare time, she writes.

In June 2013, Jaimie published her first book, Take a Breath, with the second released in November 2013. With the reviews, Jaimie took time out to read and learn how to become a better writer. She gets tremendous enjoyment out of writing, and even more so from the feedback she receives.

If you would like to send Jaimie a message, please do so by visiting her Facebook page:

https://www.facebook.com/AuthorJaimieRoberts.

Printed in Great Britain
by Amazon